The MUSE

JEWEL E. ANN

USA Today & Wall Street Journal
BESTSELLING AUTHOR

The Muse

The Chain of Lakes Series

Jewel E. Ann

Cover Design: Boja99designs

Photo: © Anna Shields Photography

Formatting: Jenn Beach

To Carter, my favorite troublemaker

Playlist

"Wi$h Li$t" - Taylor Swift

"Complicated" - (Triple J Like a Version) | GRAACE

"Iris" - Live Sessions - Josh Ross

"Cello Suite No. 1 in G Major Prélude" - Johann Sebastian Bach, Yo-Yo Ma

Serenade" - Franz Schubert, HAUSER, Robert Ziegler, London Symphony Orchestra

"Dangerous Woman" - Power-Haus, Tom Evans, Future Cello

"Nothing Else Matters" - Cello Version -Jodok Cello

"Moon River" - 2CELLOS

"Tired" - Sarah Proctor

"Hellos On The Loose" - Bo Staloch

"Everywhere, Everything" (With Gracie Abrams) Noah Kahan

Maybe the journey isn't about becoming anything. Maybe it's about unbecoming everything that isn't really you, so that you can be who you were meant to be in the first place.

—Paulo Coelho

Chapter ONE

Flynn

"My wife doesn't like sex, so keep it in your trousers. I'd hate for you to embarrass yourself."

Dude ...

What's happening?

First: Nothing about my "it" is embarrassing.

Second: What does it say about him if his wife "doesn't like sex?"

Third: Who calls jeans *trousers?*

I force a tight smile and nod because, this morning, I took Rupert Rawlings' cypress green Chevelle convertible for a joyride after giving it the platinum mobile detail service. He said he was golfing. I thought that meant four hours at a golf course, not thirty minutes with a simulator in the basement of his old mansion overlooking a lake just outside of downtown Minneapolis—a hub for outdoor enthusiasts, owners of designer dogs, and anyone who shops at Whole Foods.

I've been sitting in this same spot for forty minutes while he's dicked around on his computer and stepped out of his office, twice, to make calls. At least he's finally explaining the job he's offering me *in lieu* of going to jail for grand theft auto—which it was not.

I inhale the scent of lemon furniture polish and musty old books. "What exactly are you hiring me to do besides keeping it in my *trousers?*" I ask, sprawled out on the cool, tufted brown leather sofa in Rupert's office. The value of this single room exceeds that of any place I've ever lived. The arched doorway and floor-to-ceiling windows open to a view of the lake beyond the trees. Custom walnut cabinetry and shiny brass fixtures. Must be nice having money to burn on stupid shit.

"Do you know who you remind me of?" he asks, reclining in his cushy desk chair, hands laced behind his full head of black and gray hair.

"Yup, because I read minds." I tear my gaze away from the wood-paneled ceiling to observe his reaction.

Rupert smirks. "You remind me of myself at your age."

"Are you implying you were awesome or I'm destined to be a gazillionaire?"

"You're the mind reader, so you tell me."

I roll my eyes and sit up, running my hands through my hair. Maybe a ride in a police cruiser is the better option. "If your wife has to get herself off," I say, "then *awesome* is off the table. Guess that means I'm gonna be a rich fucker." I twist my lips. "They say money can't buy happiness, but everyone I know thinks that's bullshit. Personally, I hate rich people. They're so out of touch with reality."

This *rich guy* clears his throat, lifting an eyebrow at me.

I shrug. "Prove me wrong. I don't think money buys

happiness. I think it's a burden. Money makes it too easy to become an entitled asshole."

"Like me?"

"Dunno yet. I'll let you know." I scratch my chin. "But blackmailing me isn't helping your case."

He eyes me for a second before gripping the arms of his chair to stand. "I don't need a case, because I have nothing to prove to anyone. I believe it's called FU money. And no, it doesn't buy happiness. Happiness is a fleeting emotion—at best." The top of his crystal decanter clinks on the marble counter before he pours half a glass. Just one. This guy could work on his hospitality.

"Are you a shrink or something?" I ask. "Sounds like something a shrink would say."

Rupert chuckles, facing me while leaning his backside against the edge of his desk. He sips the alcohol, dark eyes trained on me. I'm not afraid of much, but this guy could turn a simple joyride into a grand theft auto charge.

What must his life be like? I bet he has a dozen other suits just as fancy and expensive as the one he's wearing. A person to shine his shoes before they get a single scuff. Maybe he's a lawyer, and that's how he knows he could put me in jail. I'd guess he's in his fifties, but his hands are devoid of calluses. It's unnatural. Not a speck of dirt under his trimmed nails. Does he get manicures with his wife?

I glance down at my grease-stained hands folded between my spread legs. Thick callouses. Two knuckles larger than the others from jamming them.

Pins and plates hold me together. I have so many scars from stitches that my friends call me Frankenstein's monster.

"This is generational money," Rupert says, sweeping his gaze around the office as if he's not seen it a million times.

"My wife's family. Her father and her grandfather were inventors. They've held over three hundred patents for surgical instruments and other medical devices. She's an only child, and her father died before he could disown her for marrying me." Rupert squints out the window before grinning, taking another sip of his drink. "My dad worked in the automotive industry, and he drank. A lot." He holds out his glass and stares at the remaining ounce before swirling it. "Then one day, he crossed three lanes of interstate, killing my mother, younger brother, and four others in a head-on collision with a passenger van. He lived only to die years later in prison from a heart attack. It was the best day of my life."

I shake my head. "You know nothing about me, but thanks for that heartwarming story."

"Flynn, do you think I'd bring you into my home and offer you a job without doing my homework? Flynn Oren Morley. Twenty-five. No high school diploma. In foster care from age three. Eighteen months in juvie. One year in jail for felony grand theft. Two years for assault. You have thirty-seven dollars in a bank account. No credit cards. You've worked at the same detail shop for the past three years, and your boss (whom I've known and respected for years) thinks highly of you despite your taking a customer's car for a joyride on more than one occasion. In his words, 'You've found Jesus.' Did I miss anything?"

"Blood type?" I ask.

"B positive." He sets his empty glass aside and crosses his arms. After a beat he grins.

"O negative." I give him the middle finger.

Rupert shrugs. "It was short notice. Give me another day

or so and I'll know how many times you've sold sperm and plasma to pay for food and tobacco."

"I don't use tobacco. It's not, *what Jesus would do*," I say, but I make a mental note to check into selling my sperm. If I can get paid to jerk off, what's the point of ever looking for another job?

"Good to know, Flynn. But I reserve the right to drug test you whenever I see fit," he says.

"Whatever, dude. What's the deal with your wife?"

He scratches his clean-shaven jaw. "She needs a muse."

After a beat, I nod slowly.

"Do you know what a muse is?" he asks.

"Of course, I do."

Nope. Not a clue.

"Great. You'll hang out with her."

"You know I already have a job. Right? And I have an interview next week for a mechanic at Smith's."

"You did. But now you have me and only one job option."

"What? No. Dude, I've been waiting forever. And I finally have a shot at this job with Smith's. Sorry I made your weak heart skip a few beats by taking your car for a little joyride, but you don't own me."

"Very well. We'll let the police handle it." He grabs his phone from the desk, taps the screen several times, then brings it to his ear.

Goddammit!

"Stop," I say, rubbing my forehead before blowing out a hard breath. "What does this muse thing pay?"

He pushes off the desk, then slides his phone into the inside pocket of his jacket. "Flynn, as long as you do your job for me, I will take care of everything you need. If you don't do your job for me, then you still won't need money because you'll be in jail. Questions before I introduce you to my wife?"

"How long do I have to work for you?"

"Until my wife finds inspiration."

"Inspiration for what?"

He heads toward the door. "To live."

Chapter TWO

Flynn

"Ya ever thought about renovating this place?" I ask as we climb the split staircase to the second floor. This house looks like it should have velvet ropes and plaques that explain its dull history. Everything is hand-carved wood, stone, and decorative moldings. No carpet, just huge Oriental rugs and marble steps that echo every time his polished shoes hit them.

I slow my pace, neck stretched toward the stained-glass dome skylight high above the stairs.

"This was one of the first houses built in—" Rupert begins the history lesson.

"Modern society?" I ask, cutting him off.

The artwork on the walls feels like fifty different variations of the *Mona Lisa*. Perhaps his rich wife is a descendant of Mona, and these are photos of their bloodline.

He glances over his shoulder just as we reach the second

floor. "One of the first houses built in this area. Most owners have extensively remodeled their homes. Some have torn them down and replaced them with new construction." He continues down the wide hallway lined with more paintings and a few narrow tables holding vases and sculptures of naked people with no heads.

Where's the television? Foosball table? A treadmill? It's hard to imagine something as modern as a golf simulator in the basement.

"Originally, I wanted the house next door. But the son of a bitch stole it from me when my father died. Even in death, my dear old dad screwed me over. Anyway, I bought this house just to fuck with my neighbor. My wife has allowed very few renovations."

I hang back several steps when he grips the ornate brass knob on the paneled door of the room at the end of the hall-way. The chances of me liking this guy are slim, but it doesn't stop me from feeling a little respect for his buying this place just to fuck with his neighbor.

"Sweetheart, I have someone I want you to meet," he says, cracking open the door and poking his head inside the room before nodding for me to follow him.

There's nothing cozy about this museum. Who sleeps in a four-poster bed with claw feet? And why is there a wood fireplace in a bedroom? There's also an antique looking desk, a light blue velvet bench at the end of the bed, a turntable, and a high-back cream chair (that resembles a throne) by one of the four grand windows. Sure, it's impressive, but it's not homey. It's cold and lifeless.

The twiggy woman eyes me from her throne as she slides a bookmark into her novel, then rests it on her lap. She removes her gold-framed reading glasses, blue-eyed gaze lifting, offering me a tiny smile as she combs her pointy finger-nails through her silvery blond hair sharply angled at her jaw. I once had a math teacher who looked like her. She sent me to the nurse's office because I wouldn't stop scratching my head. Lice.

Mrs. Rawlings is pretty, just like my math teacher. If she doesn't like sex, Rupert must not know what he's doing.

"Callie, this is Flynn. He needed a job, so I hired him to be your muse. Also, the gallery called, and your painting is done. Flynn will drive you to pick it up," Rupert says with his back to her, gazing out the window.

Callie blinks at me several times. Then she wets her lips and stares at her hands, fiddling with her rings.

"Questions?" He turns away from the window, hands in his pockets.

I focus on her. Surely, he's not asking *me*. Of course, I have questions. At least a hundred.

They have a stare-off which ends in her rolling her eyes toward the ceiling and releasing an exasperated huff.

"Great. I'll let you two sort out the details and decide when you want to leave." He adjusts his loose tie, like he either never committed to wearing it or he abandoned the urge to remove it. Then he rests his hand on my shoulder, giving it a firm squeeze before leaving me with his wife.

She eyes me up and down, letting her gaze linger on my feet. I wiggle my toes. Both socks have holes and are white in name only. Grungy jeans with torn knees. And an orange Howard's Mobile Detail shirt with mink oil stains. I look like a guy most people would remove from their home by force.

Callie stands and adjusts her white, loose-fitting tank top over her long, flowing skirt; gold necklaces dangle with pendants from her slender neck. Again, she eyes my attire and smirks while stepping past me toward a dresser with doors, where she pulls out a gray cardigan and slips it on.

I clear my throat. "This is my first muse job, so feel free to give me pointers."

Rolling the long cuffs of her cardigan, she laughs and mumbles, "Men."

I'm a man, so how do I respond?

"I told that big oaf he's uninspiring, so he hires me *a muse* who needs pointers. Where did he find you?"

"I detailed his car."

She glances up. "So you have a job and he stole you?"

"I took his car for a joyride, then he offered me a job."

Callie squints for a few seconds, then she relaxes. "You're working for him so he doesn't have you arrested."

"Something like that."

"Good grief." She jerks her head toward the bedroom door while walking to the bathroom. "Go home."

Is it that easy? He hires me. She fires me. All is forgiven?

I doubt it.

"What if I take you to the gallery, and you wait to fire me? Maybe I'm a natural at this muse gig."

Click.

The door closes behind her.

Great. Is she slitting her wrists? Downing a bottle of pills? Who gives someone like me the job of keeping their wife alive? He must want her dead. And when it happens, he'll blame me.

I glance around the room, coming close to sitting on the edge of her bed before rethinking what's on the backside of my jeans and how it might rub off onto her white bedding. Instead, I sit on a padded footstool beside the bathroom door, which might be too small to hold my six-foot-two self. But now that my butt has landed on it, knees hugged to my chest, I feel committed to the stupid idea and stay in this cramped position.

There are angels and clouds painted on the ceiling. I knew they must be related to the dude who painted Mona. I chuckle and shake my head.

As the door clicks open, I wipe the smile from my face. Callie steps past me and jerks her head toward the hallway. I jump up and fall in line behind her.

"Maybe you should put a leash on me," I say.

She halts, then turns. The top of her head reaches my shoulders, and she tips her chin to look at me. How does she make me feel this small with one look? Oh, that's right. She's so rich that no matter how tall I am, it will always seem like she's looking down on me.

But then, she snorts, eyes sparkling with amusement before her lips purse and she shrugs like the leash is a possibility. I instinctively stroke my neck as if I can feel the collar tightening like a noose, which makes her grin swell a little more before she pivots and heads downstairs. Like an obedient dog, I follow with my tail between my legs.

She leads me through a formal living room, a library, and a laundry room with dark cabinets, a brass chandelier, and an arched stained-glass window. *So weird.* Who puts a chandelier in a laundry room?

They have a six-car garage with carriage-style doors and iron hinges, shiny epoxy floors, and four vehicles: the infamous joyride car, an older, burgundy red Porsche, a white Bentley, and a black Tesla—which is the one she leads me to.

"A Tesla because it's self-driving?" I ask, opening the driver's door.

"It's quiet," she says. "The world has enough noise."

I close the door and glance right while reaching for the seat belt. "Is it locked?" I holler, looking for the locks while she stands at the door. Then I step out of the car and peer at her over the roof.

"Manners matter, Flynn."

Shit.

I jog around the car and open the door for her.

She smirks, sliding into the seat. After I return to the driver's side, she studies me while fastening her seat belt.

"Sorry," I mumble.

We pull out of the garage and take a right onto the one-way street as she types the address onto the screen. It's an address in the North Loop, the Warehouse District, which is a hub for entertainment, dining, and shopping.

"Do you have kids?" I ask.

She doesn't reply. Maybe she didn't hear me.

"Do you have—"

"A son," she says.

I nod several times. "Does he live at home?"

"Not anymore." She stares out the window.

"What does he do?"

Before answering, she takes a deep breath. "Whatever he wants."

Spoiled rich kid.

"Well, that must be nice," I say without trying to sound too sarcastic.

"Nice?" she whispers like an echo. "I suppose it is."

"How old is he?"

Her lips twist for a second. "Twenty-eight. Do you have siblings, Flynn?"

"Not that I know of."

"Interesting answer. Tell me about your parents," she says.

"Can't. Well, my mom had long, black hair."

"Your mom died? Or she no longer has black hair?"

I shrug. "She disappeared when I was three."

"I'm sorry."

"Me too. I guess. But if she left me, how great of a mom was she?"

"Who raised you?"

"I did."

Callie turns toward me, but I don't look at her. Pity is my least favorite emotion.

"I mean, there were others. People who were supposed to be responsible for me, but I think they just wanted the money. Ya know, those who think fostering kids is a good side gig?"

"Sorry to hear that. I know plenty of good people who have fostered children, and the stipends don't cover everything, but they don't expect it to."

"Yeah, well, I haven't experienced that."

"What?"

"Good foster parents."

She doesn't respond, but after a few miles pass, she touches my wrist with her freakishly icy hand. At first, it startles me, but then I realize she's trying to still my hand—my fidgety drumming of it on the steering wheel.

"Sorry," I say.

"I need a calm muse."

I need to search up the meaning of muse. But calm? No. I've never been calm. What does that feel like? I'm not even a calm sleeper. My roommate says I talk in my sleep.

I park along the street on the opposite side of the old

brick building with residential lofts on the second floor above the gallery. Then, I hop out and cross the street. When I turn, Callie waves from the car, fingers fluttering.

"Crap," I mumble, looking both ways before jogging back across the street and opening her door.

"Manners matter, Flynn." She smirks, stepping out of the car.

I have many scars on my body as reminders to have good manners. If all she gives me is a sarcastic grin, I'll take it.

"Sorry," I mumble, for the millionth time.

She hooks her purse over her shoulder, saunters to the stoplight, and presses the button to cross. There are no cars coming from either direction. Does she ever break the rules?

The walk light illuminates, and she looks both ways (twice) before crossing the street. When we reach the gallery, I open the door for her like a gentleman. She grins, and I try not to, but then she playfully pokes my stomach, and it tickles, so I can't help myself.

"Mrs. Rawlings, how nice to see you," a woman with short, wiry blond hair says while walking toward us. She's dressed in a one-piece outfit which looks like a tuxedo, but with shorts. And her shiny black heels are so pointy she could use them as ice picks.

"Good afternoon, Savvy. You look beautiful."

Savvy runs her hands down her outfit. "Aw, thank you."

"This is Flynn. He's a gift from Rupert. My muse."

I pull my shoulders back like a dumbass who's proud of being a muse for some rich woman, even though I have no clue what it means. I'm a triple D, and it's biting me in the butt.

Dyslexic.

Delinquent.

Dropout.

"That's quite the gift. I'm Savvy." The woman chuckles while introducing herself, hand offered to me.

I shake it. "Flynn."

"Can I get either of you something to drink? Wine?" She focuses on Callie.

"Wine would be lovely."

"I'm good," I say when Savvy shifts her attention to me.

Callie elbows me, and I squint at her without saying *what the fuck*, but I think it.

"I don't like wine." I shrug. "And I'm not thirsty."

Callie touches her fingers to her chin and then moves her hand forward and downward. What is she doing?

I sigh and blow a kiss back to her because I don't know if she's roleplaying in front of Savvy, pretending we're lovers, or what. But I don't want to go to jail, so I sit, shake, roll over, and *blow kisses*. Whatever these entitled weirdos need, I'll do it.

Savvy giggles, cupping a hand over her mouth to regain her composure. "That's sign language for 'thank you,'" she says.

Shit ...

"You're welcome." I say with a shrug. But I don't know why she's thanking me.

Callie clears her throat and points at Savvy, who presses her lips together to hide her grin. I'm glad they're so amused by me. I fucking hate rich people.

"I'll get your wine," Savvy says, turning on her heel.

Callie clasps her hands behind her and stares at me. "What?"

"When someone offers you something, whether you

accept it or not, you say *thank you. Yes, thank you.* Or *no, thank you.* But always, *thank you.*"

I frown. "Sorry."

She brings her fingers to her lips. This time she actually kisses them and dramatically blows in my direction.

Fuck you sits on the tip of my tongue, but I swallow it back down because she delivers her kiss with a smirk, and surely people who smirk aren't suicidal. And that's my job, right? To make sure she doesn't off herself.

"Here you go." Savvy returns, handing Mrs. Rawlings a glass of white wine.

Is it free? Is this what happens when you're wealthy? Water coolers with tiny paper glasses turn into wine in stemware?

"Sam will bring your piece out in a few minutes, and then we'll get it wrapped up for you," Savvy says.

"Thank you." Mrs. Rawlings sips her wine and inspects the art on display.

The front door chimes, and a young woman steps inside, removing her bike helmet. Her long, dark hair hangs over one shoulder in a messy braid. She lights up when she sees Savvy.

"Hey, June." Savvy perches on the stool behind the counter. "Restroom break?"

"Yep," she says as her gaze snags on me, but I immediately look away while standing a little straighter and running a hand through my thick hair, which could use a trim.

"How many do you have?" Savvy asks.

"Uh, six," June says, setting her helmet on the counter. On the back of her shirt is a tire logo with *Billy's Bike Tours.*

I sneak a glance at her, and she quickly looks away.

When she disappears around the corner, Savvy eyes me for a second with a grin.

June returns and puts on her helmet. "Thanks," she says, shifting her attention to me so quickly I can't avert my gaze before she catches me ogling her. And then it just sticks. She doesn't look away, and neither do I.

I'm not sure what's happening. I can actually feel my heart in my chest. She makes me sweat.

"Didn't know Minneapolis had bike tours," I say as if I need to take one.

This girl's smile is so damn sexy. I definitely need a bike tour.

"Well, now you do," she says, before biting her bottom lip.

Mr. and Mrs. Rawlings have me by the balls. I'm not the guy who says stupid shit and blows kisses to women old enough to be my mom. And I'm not this awkward with women. But I'm out of my element, standing among expensive, ugly art while having my composure rattled even more by a random girl in biking shorts, wearing a mischievous smile as if I'm the butt of a joke. Don't ask me why I find it so sexy. I just do.

Her unwavering, brown-eyed gaze bleeds confidence one minute, but then she glances away like she's blushing. All I know is she's mesmerizing. It's unfair to those of us who didn't win the gene pool lottery. Even the tiny scar above her lip adds to her mysteriousness. It makes her look like she's been through something. And the way she unhurriedly floats from one side of the room to the other has me in a stupid trance. I once stayed with a family who fostered a sixteen-year-old girl. She always looked calm and unbothered no matter the circumstances, just like June.

As if June knows she's too cool for me, she fastens her helmet and eyes Savvy. "Thank you, Savvy."

"Wait!" The word spews from my mouth like someone punched me in the gut.

June leans her back against the door to nudge it open, gaze on me.

This girl is so beautiful. My mouth dries up, and I feel Savvy and Callie staring at me as though I'm on the verge of saying something important. Every second of silence feels like ten. Yeah, I'm actually sweating through my shirt.

"Cat got your tongue?" June says.

No. A cat has never had my tongue. I'm the guy who has the first and last word with everything, even if it lands me in trouble.

With her, the words are slow, but they're coming. Almost there—

June laughs. "Time's up. Gotta go." She turns and waves to a group of people climbing onto their e-bikes across the street.

"That was brutal," Savvy says, wrinkling her nose while Callie cocks her head, studying me.

"Here it is." A young dude with his hair in a ponytail and round wire glasses holds up a framed painting of the back of a little boy sitting on a park bench feeding ducks.

"That shade of gold frame makes the sun's reflection on the water pop," Savvy says.

Callie nods and wipes a tear from her eye. I can't imagine what kind of painting would make me cry. Does money make people irrationally emotional about stupid stuff?

Ponytail dude sets it on the table behind the counter and slides foam over the glass, then cardboard corner protectors onto the frame. He shrink-wraps it and places it in a box with more padding before handing it to me as Callie taps her credit card. My eyes bug out at the number of zeros. Am I in charge of carrying a painting worth more money than I make in a year?

"Thank you, Mrs. Rawlings. I hope you enjoy it," Savvy says. "It was nice meeting you, Flynn."

"Thank you," I say louder than necessary to make sure I get points for good manners.

Callie returns the hint of a smile, then leads the way out the door.

"When's the last time someone took you shopping?" she asks as I set the painting in the back of the car.

"Legally?"

She rolls her eyes. "Yes. Legally."

"Can't remember. Maybe never."

"Follow me." She takes off in the opposite direction. Her short legs move pretty fast for her age.

Is she okay leaving her painting in the back of her car where someone could steal it? I know a few people who would have that out of there in no time. Not so long ago, I was one of those people.

Chapter
THREE

Flynn

Mrs. Rawlings leads me to a high-end clothing store. I'm not a shopper, but I'm sure the inside of this place is much nicer than the inside of a jail cell. So I open the door and glance down the street as she steps inside.

"I'll be right back," I mumble, eyeing the end of the block, where June is taking a photo of her tour group in front of a sculpture. "I promise," I add without waiting for Callie's permission before I sprint down the sidewalk and cross the street, holding out my hand to give an apologetic wave to the man in the BMW who has to slam on his brakes so he doesn't hit me.

"Let me take it," I say to June as she holds up her phone to take pictures of the group posing with their bikes.

She squints at me.

"Then you can be in the photo too," I say, taking her phone and nodding for her to get in the picture.

"I don't need to be in—" she starts to say.

"Just say thank you and get over there." I grin with way more confidence than I had at the gallery.

She slides into the middle, and I take several shots. Then one of the tourists asks her about a nearby restaurant, so I quickly add myself to her contacts, including a goofy selfie, then I set a reminder on her phone for eight o'clock tonight: *Call Flynn, the sexy guy from the gallery.*

"Thanks," she says with a laugh when I hand her phone back to her. "I was going to take a selfie with them in the background. It's the customary tour photo. You ruined that."

I shrug. "This one will be more memorable."

"Why is that?" She slides her phone into her crossbody bag.

"Because you'll always remember who took it."

"Is that so?"

I glance toward the clothing store and mumble, "Yeah. Listen, I'm Flynn, by the way. And I have to go, but I'm sure I'll see you around."

"Don't count on it. The Twin Cities have close to four million people."

I jog across the street before looking back at her. "Oh, I'm counting on it."

June bites her lower lip and grins. *I'm back!* The temporary glitch in my brain from the gallery has vanished.

Callie is nowhere in sight when I step into the store filled with boring music, a pungent cologne stench, and displays of men's clothes that look entirely too layered. Who wears two shirts and a jacket at the same time with shorts and leather loafers?

"Can I help you?" A bald guy with a measuring tape

draped around his neck eyes me over his reading glasses low on his bulbous nose.

"I'm looking for a woman about this tall." I gesture with my hand at my shoulder. "Blondish-gray hair, and—oh, there she is. Never mind," I say, stepping past him toward Callie, who's next to a display with her arms full of clothes.

She eyes me with an unasked question. I'm getting really good at reading her, and this is only my first day.

"The girl with the bike helmet, the one at the gallery? She needed me to take a picture of her and the tourists."

"Welcome. Can I get a dressing room started for you?" A young woman, who looks like Barbie, asks while taking the men's clothes from Callie.

"Thank you," she says to the woman.

"Is Mr. Rawlings meeting us here? Because those clothes are not my style."

"Flynn," Callie says, "I don't think you have a style, but we'll find one for you."

"Jeans, a T-shirt, and black boots are a style. Probably the most classic style," I say.

She ignores me while browsing more racks of clothing.

I obey. *Ruff. Ruff.* Try on clothes. She picks the winners, and we leave with bags of shit I'm calling uniforms because I have no desire to wear them around my friends. They'd probably steal them right off my back and sell them.

"Dude, did you rob a store?" Monroe asks after I open the apartment door and toss the bags of clothes onto the sofa, which doubles as my bed.

This place always smells of fabric softener. Naomi, his

girlfriend, thinks all of Monroe's clothes reek of gas and grime. He's a diesel mechanic, so that tracks. Personally, I'd rather smell gas than fabric softener or overpowering perfume.

"No," I say, grabbing a beer from the fridge while Monroe washes the dishes because we don't have a dishwasher, and Naomi gets pissed if this place isn't clean. "I took a customer's car for a joyride and got caught. So now he owns my ass unless I want to be charged with grand theft auto, which is not what happened. But who's going to believe me?"

Monroe pauses his scrubbing. "So he took you on a shopping spree?"

"No. His wife did."

"Are you banging his wife?"

I smirk behind the can at my lips. "No. She supposedly doesn't like sex. I think it's an issue isolated to wealthy people. Maybe when you have the money of a king, it's more satisfying than sex." I take a long pull of my beer before shrugging. "Poor folks like us have to fuck. It's really the only form of pleasure we can afford."

Monroe snickers "One hundred percent. So, are they adopting you or what's the deal? Why do they care what you wear?"

"Mmm, that reminds me." I set my beer on the counter, pull my phone from my pocket, and search up *muse.* I don't think my job has anything to do with Zeus and Mnemosyne, so I look at the second definition. *The source of inspiration for a creative person.* "I'm the muse for this rich dude's wife," I say. "They live in an old mansion overlooking the lake. Huge garage. Fancy cars. And supposedly he thinks she's going to kill herself, and

I've been hired to inspire her to ... I don't know. Not kill herself? So she bought me clothes to wear. Ridiculous clothes."

I empty the bags onto the coffee table littered with weird things like fake plants in a vase atop a stack of books and some sort of stone statue of a chubby dude. Buddha or some shit like that. It's all Naomi's. "This shirt was over five hundred bucks," I say, holding up a lime green bowling shirt with weird-ass designs on it. They might be seahorses. "It's printed silk. Ever heard of that?"

"It's butt ugly," Monroe says.

"I know. And linen pants." I hold up the light gray pants that I will never wear when I'm not *inspiring* Callie. "Isn't linen something you sleep on or use to wipe your mouth?"

He laughs, drying his hands with a towel while shaking his head. "Don't know, man. I've never had linen money."

"Italian leather loafers." I pull the shoes from the box. "The lady at the store said to wear them without socks. Can you see me wearing leather shoes without socks?" I toss them onto the sofa and sigh while parking my hands on my hips and inspecting the rest of the preppy wardrobe. I wonder how much I can sell it for when this gig is over?

"What do you do to inspire this rich woman?" he asks.

"Good question. Today I drove her to a gallery to pick up a painting she had framed. Then we shopped for these clothes. After that, I returned the van to the shop, got chewed out by my boss for the joyriding incident. But then he hugged me, which was uncomfortable, and said Mr. Rawlings would be good for me." I collapse onto the sofa covered in clothes.

"How long do you have to work for them?"

"Dunno."

"How much does this muse job pay?" Monroe opens a bag of Doritos.

"No clue. I didn't exactly have a choice in the matter. He said my needs will be taken care of. Whatever that means."

Monroe slowly chews on a chip, gaze pointed toward the floor.

"What?" I ask, because I know that look. He's not telling me something.

"I'm surprised they don't have you live with them."

"Why would I live with them?" I shove the clothes back into the bags and kick them under the coffee table so Naomi doesn't do her annoying throat-clearing thing while scowling at me until I read her mind.

"I mean," Monroe shrugs, "if they offered you a room, you'd never be late to work, and you'd have an actual bed. Probably your own bathroom. Rent free."

"It would feel like a prison—someone always scrutinizing me."

"Like Naomi?"

I frown. "Let me guess. She wants me out even though she doesn't want to admit she's living here, and you secretly don't want her living here. I'm your last defense. The buffer zone. If I move out, she'll replace your furniture and buy plants which need to be watered. Amazon will deliver packages with her name on them. And you'll be banned from taking a shit in your own apartment while she's here. Oh, wait. That's already happened."

"That's not entirely true," he mumbles after shoving a chip into his mouth.

"Stop lying. You know I'm right. Last week, you ran down the street to take a dump at the gas station because she was soaking in the bathtub, and you're too damn weak around her to just perch and drop a load on the goddamn throne you pay for every month. The Rawlings have a toilet in their garage. That will be you someday."

"Says the guy who has never had a girlfriend."

"I get laid," I say, lacing my fingers behind my head.

"Yeah, well, I don't have to wear a condom." Monroe puts a chip clip on the bag and returns it to the top of the fridge. "And I don't have to go out every night like a caveman hunting for food. No pickup lines. No wondering if a boyfriend or husband is going to find my dick in his girl and beat the crap out of me while I'm fully exposed." He eyes me, knowing that's a low blow. "So," he continues, "if I have to run down the street every now and then to take a shit, it's still better than your situation."

"I'll have you know, I met someone today. She could be the one."

He laughs, plopping his skinny ass into the worn brown leather recliner. "I doubt it, but spill."

"Why do you doubt it?"

"Because you have a terrible habit of oversharing way too early. Did you tell her you grew up in foster care?"

"No."

"Does she know how many broken bones you've had? The number of scars on your chest and back? All that shit?"

"No."

"Well, that's amazing. What did you talk about?"

"We didn't talk about much. She's a bike tour guide or something like that. And she had her group waiting for her, and I had Mrs. Rawlings with me. But she has my number, and I bet she calls me tonight. Probably a little after eight if I had to take a guess."

"A little after eight?" He eyes me with a single raised eyebrow.

"It's just a guess." I grin.

"Is she hot?"

"Hot is not the right word for her. She's beautiful in an effortless way. Not all made up. Nothing fake about her. She has this cute little scar above her lip."

"A scar above her lip?"

I nod.

"Like someone hit her?"

I shrug. "Or like she face-planted on her bike."

He winces. "Ouch."

I chuckle. "It's a scar, not a recent cut. It's not like it happened today."

"Maybe it's from correction of cleft lip or cleft palate."

"Huh? What is that, and how do you know anything about it?"

"Because I graduated high school. And I can read."

"Fuck you. I can read."

"Yeah, at a third-grade level."

"Well, I'm a better mechanic than you, and I've never had formal training."

He shrugs. "Maybe. But I'm an actual mechanic, and you're a muse. I bet you didn't even know what a muse was when that rich guy hired you."

I flip him the bird, but not without grinning.

Monroe laughs because he knows me too well. "I gotta wash my sheets," he says, standing and stretching his arms over his head. "Clean sheets gets my girl horny." He smirks while passing the sofa.

After I spend the next hour mindlessly clicking YouTube videos on rebuilding engines, I throw a frozen burrito in the microwave and fetch another beer. Naomi waltzes through the door, eyeing me while removing her heels and curling her wavy blond hair behind one ear.

"Oh, hi," she murmurs.

The "oh" is an obvious *oh, you're still living here?*

"Oh, hi," I parrot like, *oh, you're still sleeping here?*

I want to like Monroe's girlfriend because he's my friend, but she's so judgmental. Her way of doing everything is always the right way, like bath towels must be folded vertically. I disagree—they don't have to be folded at all. And when she speaks, she uses this tone, like she's talking down to everyone else. Except with Monroe she ends every sentence with an exaggerated fish-lipped kiss while pinching his chin like an angry mother.

"Aren't you tired of living on a sofa? You eat, sleep, and drink on that thing," she says, opening the fridge.

"Thanks for your concern. This sofa feels like the only stable thing in my life. I can't imagine ever leaving it or this apartment for that matter," I say, just to get her worked up.

She lifts her head out of the fridge and wrinkles her nose. "Do you know how pathetic that sounds?"

"You mean heartbreaking? All I have are an old sofa and the world's best friend. I would never survive without either of them. Did you know Monroe and I shared a foster home when we were thirteen? And then we ran into each other at a gas station several years ago. I was living out of my car. He took me in. That's the kind of friendship that lasts a lifetime." I take a bite of my burrito and chew slowly while she scowls at me.

"Where is he?" she asks, slamming the fridge door and marching toward the bedroom.

I laugh just as my phone dings with a text: ***I feel violated***

It's two minutes after eight. It has to be her. So I call the number.

"When someone texts you, you don't call them. That's not cool. The whole point of texting is so you don't have to call people," she says in a tone which sounds like a song even if she's trying to sound exasperated with me. She's no match for Naomi.

I put her on speaker just long enough to add her to my contacts. "Where are you?"

"You think the solution to my feeling violated by your adding yourself to my contacts and setting a reminder in my phone to call you is to ask my whereabouts? My parents taught me better than that."

"Lucky you. I didn't have parents or anyone to teach me shit. So that's probably why I didn't hesitate to violate you."

"That's just sad," she says.

"I don't want you to be sad or feel bad for me. I'm just stating facts."

She laughs. "Okay. You got my attention. Now what are you going to do with it?"

"Dunno," I say, trapping my phone between my shoulder and my ear while carrying my plate and empty beer can to the kitchen. "I still can't believe you called. I have never caught a falling star—until today."

"*I'm* the falling star?"

"June, you're the whole damn galaxy on a cloudless night, a hundred miles out of the city."

"That's ..." She pauses, leaving me hanging. "That's actually really sweet."

I grin, feeling most excellent because I have no clue what

I'm doing, but I know *sweet* is good—and something I've never been.

"But," she says. "For the record, I didn't. I texted."

"But you didn't have to. So let's do this. What's your last name, June?"

"Malone."

"June Malone." I like the way her name rolls off my tongue, almost as much as I like the way she grinned while biting her lip after I took the group picture.

"What's your last name, Flynn?" There's a hint of humor to her question.

Does she find me amusing in an irresistible way? I hope so.

"Morley."

"Age?"

She likes me.

"Twenty-five. You?"

"Twenty-six."

"Aw man ... I've always had a thing for older women."

She giggles as I collapse onto the sofa and stare at the water-stained ceiling. "So were you at the gallery with your girlfriend?"

"Huh?"

"You said you have a thing for older women. And you said you don't have parents. So who was the woman at the gallery with you?"

"Who said the woman at the gallery was with me? Maybe we were just there at the same time."

"Oh? In that case, what did you buy at the gallery?"

"Nothing. I was there with that woman."

June's laughter makes me feel warm everywhere, like a third beer filling my veins.

"She's my boss. Or my boss's wife. I'm not sure who's in charge. It's a new job."

"What's the job?"

"I'm a muse."

"A what?"

"A muse. It's—"

"I know what a muse is. But I didn't know it's a job."

Fantastic. June is not only pretty; she's smart, too.

"Rich people," I grumble. "They can't do anything themselves. I don't know if she's depressed or suicidal or what, but I'm supposed to inspire her to live. That should be her husband's job. A friend's. A sibling's. Literally anyone but some strange guy who she's never met."

"Wow. That's so sad. Sounds like she needs a therapist."

"I hope that's not what they mean by a muse," I say. "My form of therapy would be to tell her to get over whatever she thinks is so awful. Must be real rough living in a mansion. Never having to worry about money. Spending every day reading books and shopping for art. Touch some grass, lady. There are people who have real problems, and your husband hired you a muse. Fucking ridiculous."

"Okay, then. Tell me how you really feel," June says.

"Do you disagree?"

"I don't know them, so I can't judge them based on their wealth," she says.

"You can. It will stay between us."

"So if you were wealthy, would it be fair for people to judge you because of it?" she asks.

"Absolutely, because I'd probably be an entitled dick."

She giggles. "As opposed to ..."

"Hey, you don't even know me, *yet*."

"True."

"Where are you? We should hang out," I say.

"It's late, Flynn."

"Damn. Is twenty-six the new forty? Late? It's a little after eight."

"I'm trying to be polite."

"Polite? Because you don't want to hang out with me? Then why did you call—text. Why did you text?"

"I thought I'd give you a chance to sweep me off my feet."

"Are you suggesting I've failed at doing that?"

"Well, how would you rate yourself?"

"You haven't ended the call, so I'd say I'm killing it."

"I should go, Flynn."

A surge of panic hits me like it did when she walked out of the gallery and I froze. "You're beautiful."

She doesn't reply right away. Why did I say that? I'm sure she knows she's beautiful. How could she not? I close my eyes and press the heel of my hand to my forehead.

"I'm listening," she says.

I open my eyes and mentally scramble for something else. What's the follow-up to telling her she's beautiful?

"I'm listening too. You should say *thank you* or compliment me back." Words fly out of my mouth before getting proper permission from my brain. If she doesn't appreciate sarcasm, I'm fucked.

"You're tall," she says.

"Thank you. I try my best."

June chuckles, and I sit up *tall*.

"You have a great smile," I say.

"Thank you. You take good group photos," she replies.

I can't help the shit-eating grin on my face. "We're

hitting it off. I think we should take this conversation to dinner."

"I already ate."

"But did you have dessert?"

After a few seconds, she says, "I did not."

"Let's meet at Sebastian Joe's in twenty minutes."

"I don't know ..." The hesitation in her voice stirs the panic in my chest. Why does she have this effect on me?

"Well, I don't know either, June." I stand and kick around the shopping bags, looking for something to impress her. "That's why we should have ice cream and find out."

"Find out what?" She laughs.

"Whatever it is you need to know. Meet me and I promise you'll have your answer before ten." I pull a shirt out of the bag and smell it out of habit.

New shirts smell pretty damn good.

"Nothing weird?" she asks.

"I'll get Oreo or peanut butter. Nothing weird like cinnamon or mocha."

"That's not what I meant."

"I know it's not. Just walk out the door. Don't overthink it." I pull the phone away from my ear and shrug off my shirt.

"Fine," she says.

Again, that unavoidable grin steals my face.

Chapter
FOUR

June

"Where are you going?" my roommate, Ally, asks as I slide into the bathroom while she shaves her legs on the edge of the bathtub.

"Going for ice cream."

She glances up from her leg as I apply lip gloss. "You have a date?"

"No." I rub my lips together, eyeing her reflection in the mirror. "It's just ice cream."

"With a guy?"

I grin.

"Juju, you can't drop that on me and then leave. Who is he? How did you meet? Is he cute? Duh. Of course, he's cute. Is he sexy? Rich? A basketball player?"

I giggle, capping my lip gloss. "I met him at the gallery when I stopped on the tour to use the restroom."

"Oh, so he's into art. That means he's rich." She flips her

sandy blond hair over her shoulder and bats her fake eyelashes at me.

"No. He's definitely not rich. He was there with his boss."

"So what's his job?"

"I'm not sure," I say, combing my fingers through my hair that's wavy from being in a braid all day. Ally will ask too many questions about a "muse." And explaining something I don't understand yet, will cause me to run late.

"Be safe. I want all the details when you get home. Unless you stay the night at his place." She rinses her razor.

"I'll be home by ten thirty. And if I'm not, call the police."

"Do you have pepper spray?"

"Of course," I holler as I grab my bag from my room and head to the door. "Byeeee."

My flip-flops slap the concrete stairs to the exit next to the salon on the ground level below our apartment. When my ride pulls up to the curb, I push open the secured door, then anxiously hop into the back of the vehicle.

Ten minutes later, I arrive at Sebastian Joe's. Flynn's outside, hands in the pockets of his dark blue jeans which look brand-new compared to the ripped, stained jeans he had on earlier. His dark wavy hair slides into his eyes when he glances up as my driver stops. He pushes it out of his eyes with a smooth swipe of his hand. Flynn is sexy in a mysterious way that both intrigues me and feels like a red flag at the same time.

"You didn't chicken out," he says when I step out of the car.

"Funny. I was just getting ready to say the same thing to

you." I slip my phone into my crossbody bag, then adjust my black, fitted crop top.

Flynn gives me a slow, appreciative appraisal that makes me blush when his gaze finally settles on my face.

"I only brought enough money for single scoops," he says, opening the door.

"I can pay." I giggle at his comment and the way I have to wedge past him to get inside, like it's his goal to make me brush up against him.

"That would make me a prick," he says.

"Would it, though?" I turn and playfully squint at him.

He adjusts the collar of his short-sleeved shirt. I reach for the back of it, finding a tag attached with a gold safety pin, the way nicer stores tag their clothes.

"Leave it," he says, tucking it into the shirt. "My boss took me shopping after I saw you. But if I get fired, I'm returning the clothes. They're worth at least three months' rent."

My smile falters for a second as I realize he's not joking.

Not about the shirt.

Not about one scoop of ice cream.

"What can I get you?" The teenage girl behind the counter asks.

Flynn gestures for me to order first.

"I'll have a single scoop of the salty caramel in a cup, please."

"A scoop of peanut butter," Flynn says. "In a cone."

I smile at him, and he smiles back for a second before quickly blurting out, "Please!"

I suppress my laughter as he digs money from his pocket. It's crumpled and faded like it's been through the laundry.

She gives him change and scoops our ice cream.

"Thank you," I say when he holds open the door again so we can sit at a café table outside.

"You're welcome." He licks his ice cream.

"Do you live nearby?" I ask.

Flynn shakes his head before taking another lick. "It's too early to say. I don't know if I can trust you yet. Ask me again before you head home."

He's ...

Funny.

Handsome.

And I think unintentionally charming.

Definitely quick-witted.

"Do you have a lot of experience as a muse?"

His eyebrows lift. "Why? Do you need one?"

I shrug, dropping my chin to stare at my ice cream as I sink my spoon into it. "Who doesn't need a little inspiration?"

"Me."

"No?" I slant my head to the side.

"I'm not suicidal."

"I don't think inspiration is reserved for suicidal people. Artists need inspiration."

"I don't think the painting my boss picked up at the gallery was her painting."

"Well"— June shrugs—"maybe not. Still, sometimes people feel like they're losing their way, and inspiration can be a roadmap to get back on track. Maybe she feels like she's lost her way."

"She's worth a gazillion dollars. I'm not saying it buys happiness, but what does she possibly have to feel lost about?"

"You know," I tap my spoon on my lip several times, "money doesn't solve all the world's problems."

"One hundred percent agree," he says. "But I think the people who hoard most of the money in the world think it solves the world's problems. Why else would they hoard it?"

"Security, I suppose." I shrug. "But it doesn't cure all diseases."

He bobs his head. "But money buys medical care."

"Loneliness."

Another headshake. "Everyone wants to have rich friends. No reason to be lonely."

"Love."

He laughs. "Have you seen how many old rich dudes have young, hot girlfriends and wives?"

"That's not love."

"I bet the women *love* the money, and the old dudes love getting ..." He clears his throat. "Well, let's just say they love getting attention in the bedroom."

"That's not love. That's lust. People lust after things in the bedroom. They lust after money. Gratification is not the same as your heart aching in your chest when you miss the ones you love."

"Does this feel like too deep of conversation for a first date?" he asks.

"Oh?" I widen my eyes. "You think this is a date?" I mumble over the bite of ice cream hitting my sensitive teeth.

"Were you in an accident or a fight?" he asks, pointing to his lip in the same place as I have a scar on mine.

"Neither. I was born with a cleft lip, and that's the scar from the surgery to repair it."

"Wow. Monroe was right." He bites into his cone.

"Who's Monroe?"

"My roommate."

"You told your roommate about me?"

"Maybe." He glances away, but I don't miss his tiny grin.

"Maybe I should tell people it's from a fight. That's cooler, right?" I say, just to see his reaction.

"I mean ..." he shrugs. "It's your scar. You can say whatever you want. I have my own stories."

"About scars?"

Flynn shoves the rest of the cone into his mouth and lifts his shirt, exposing his chest riddled with scars of different sizes and shapes. "I was treated like shit in foster care," he mumbles while chewing. "But I tell people I was in the military, and their pity turns into gratitude for my service. Way cooler."

I can't peel my gaze from his chest until he lowers his shirt. There are *so* many scars.

"See. You're giving me that pity look," he says.

"I don't pity you. I mean, it sucks that you feel the need to lie about it." I lift my gaze to his. "But I said yes to meeting you for ice cream. You have no idea how special that makes you."

His grin swells. It's a beautiful, genuine smile. And I like the way his eyes shine when he looks at me.

"But"—I glance at my watch, feeling vulnerable, like he can see my attraction to him—"I should go." There's nowhere I need to be, but I think playing hard to get, at first, is a good idea.

"We just got here," he says.

I show him my empty bowl. "We had ice cream. Now it's gone." I stand.

"Let me give you a ride home so you don't have to pay for one."

"We haven't established that level of trust yet." I toss my cup and spoon into the garbage by the corner of the brick building.

"We? I'd let you give me a ride home," he says, shoving the unused napkins into his pocket.

I follow his hand before looking at his sly grin.

"They'll throw them away. I'll use them at home," he says.

This guy ...

"I'll get a ride this time. But thank you for the ice cream." I slide my phone from my bag.

"*This time* means there will be other times."

Shit.

I said that.

I press my lips together while my thumbs move across my phone's screen. Then I look up at Flynn and shrug. "We'll see."

He has the sexiest grin. "So, should I kiss you now or wait until your ride gets here?"

"Whoa there, bud. I don't kiss on a first date."

His face sours as he crosses his arms over his chest. "Then what do you do on a first date?"

"On this first date, I eat ice cream. What do you do on a first date?"

"Dunno. I don't date. I'm just making this up as I go."

"You've never dated?"

He studies me for a second. It's a weird pause in conversation. *Gah!* I wish I could read his mind.

"I have not," he says with confidence. "Does that make you feel special?"

"You're twenty-five, and you've *never* dated? Never had

a girlfriend? Never ..." I stop myself from digging, sounding too desperate to know him.

His head jerks backward. "Never what? I'm not a virgin, if that's what you're wondering."

"I wasn't." I nod to my ride in the approaching black SUV.

Flynn hooks up with girls, and he's probably a walking STD. Good to know.

"Not even a kiss on the cheek?" he asks.

I chuckle and shake my head, stepping closer to the curb. "Sorry."

"What about tomorrow? Is it too early for a second date?"

"I think one is enough." I risk a quick glance at him.

"What? No. What did I do wrong? Is it because I asked about your scar? I don't give a shit. If anything, it makes you look more beautiful. Special. Not like every other boring girl who never passes up an opportunity to stare at her own reflection and thinks she's perfect."

My ride stops at the curb, and I step toward it, turning just before opening the door. "If you don't date, then why me?"

He narrows his eyes as if he doesn't understand the question.

"Flynn, you have to be quicker than that," I say, opening the door.

"Is it really my fault that you leave me speechless?"

I stop and listen, but I don't look at him.

"Do you think I like feeling weak and fumbling my words? Do you think I want to lose sleep tonight, thinking about you? Do you think a guy who doesn't date, wants to learn the rules to a game I clearly have never wanted to play?"

"You haven't answered my question." I climb into the back seat and shut the door.

Smack!

I jump when Flynn's palm slaps the window. "It's just a feeling," he says, his words muffled on the other side of the window. "And that says a lot coming from me because I shut off my feelings years ago."

"Want me to wait?" my driver asks.

I stare at Flynn, and my lips twitch, fighting a grin. "No," I say. Pressing my hand over my heart, I close my eyes. If he's not the boy my father warned me about my whole life, he might just be the reason I moved to Minneapolis. A fresh start. Endless possibilities.

Chapter FIVE

Flynn

"Last night you said you had to be at work by six this morning," Naomi says, turning on the kitchen light because she's pure evil.

I lift my head and squint, reaching for my phone. It's dead, so I pull on the cord, but it's not plugged in. "What time is it?" I mumble.

"Six fifteen."

"Shit! Motherfucker!" I throw the blanket onto the floor and bolt off the sofa, snagging one of the shopping bags of clothes on my way to the bathroom. I'm royally screwed and probably going to jail.

Less than a minute later, I throw open the door, grab my phone and charging cord from the coffee table, and hightail it out of the apartment with the echo of Naomi's annoying cackle and the aroma of her vanilla coffee behind me.

My piece of shit brown Ford Taurus gives me fits when I

try to start it, but after banging the palm of my hand against the steering wheel and the dash, it rattles to life. The AC doesn't work, so I crack the windows.

The Rawlings are twenty minutes from my apartment, and that's with no traffic. I'm hitting rush hour.

Thirty minutes later, I jog toward the house from my crappy parking job across the street; I tuck in my shirt and run my hands through my hair. There's a slight minty taste left in my mouth from the toothpaste I squirted into it while taking the world's fastest piss earlier.

"Please be in a good mood. Please ..." I mutter while ringing the doorbell.

The solid wood raised-panel door opens slowly. Rupert eyes me with a blank expression as he tightens the sash of his maroon robe over his navy pajamas.

I open my mouth to spew my excuse, and he slams the door shut.

Gulp.

"I'm an idiot," I say, scrubbing my hands over my face. I *desperately* don't want to go back to jail.

The door clicks open again, and I quickly drop my hands and compose myself.

"Make it swift, honest, and good if you don't want me to call the police," Rupert says.

Swift, honest, and good?

"Uh ..."

He closes his eyes and shakes his head half a dozen times. "Your reason for being late," he says impatiently.

"My phone is my alarm, and it was dead because I thought the cord was plugged into the wall. It wasn't. I'm sorry."

"Are you drunk?"

"What? No." I blow in my hand and smell my breath. Why does he think I'm drunk?

"High?"

"No."

"Were you with a woman last night?"

"No. Why? Want some tips?" As soon as those words leave my mouth, I internally cringe. As if I'm not on thin ice already, why did I say that?

"Is that all you offer? Just the tip?" he asks.

"It's usually all they can accommodate," I say because I'm incapable of not saying stupid stuff.

Rupert lifts his chin and scratches his neck, and he does so with a grin. "You're an arrogant little shit."

"Why are you so certain my dick is small?" I step inside without waiting for a formal invitation. "Yesterday, you suggested I keep it in my 'trousers' so I don't embarrass myself. I'm not embarrassed. And I've received nothing but compliments. If you know what I mean?"

He closes the door and slides his hands into his robe pockets. "What do you have going on here?" He nods at me, eyes focused on my clothes.

I glance down. "Uh ..." I smooth my hand along the button-down shirt. "Mrs. Rawlings bought these for me."

Rupert steps closer, trapping the jeans tag between his fingers and giving it a yank.

"Stop!" I say a half second too late.

He raises an eyebrow at me.

"I can't take it back without a tag."

"You're wearing it. Why would you take it back?"

"To pay rent if this job doesn't pan out."

He slips the tag into his pocket. "I thought we discussed

this. If this job doesn't *pan out,* you won't be renting anything."

"I'm keeping your wife *inspired.*" I offer a toothy grin as if he'll pat me on the back for knowing what "muse" means. "So I don't think you'll be sending me to jail." I roll the waist of the jeans to remove the safety pin and string that remains from the tag. The safety pin is bent open, ready to jab me in the side. Maybe I should let it. Then I can sue him.

Rupert grunts and turns, heading up the stairs. "So far, she's not impressed. Do better. Start with coffee. She likes it in the form of herbal tea with a slice of lemon and a few drips of honey."

Coffee. Herbal tea. Lemon. Honey. Got it.

I rummage through the kitchen. Thankfully, there's already a pot of hot coffee. I pour it into a mug and deposit a bag of organic herbal tea into it. Then I cut a lemon and squeeze half into the coffee with some honey. I'm not sure how many "drips" because honey runs more than it drips. Feeling confident and successful with my first task of the day, I carry the coffee to Callie's bedroom and knock on the door.

When she doesn't answer, I ease open the door and poke my head inside. She's on the floor by the window, legs criss-crossed, hands on her knees.

"I have your coffee."

She opens one eye.

"Well, it's tea, too."

She squints that one eye.

"Herbal tea. Honey and lemon." I grin triumphantly.

When she crooks her finger at me, I step in front of her.

"Where's the belt?" she asks.

My grin fades. "The belt?"

She nods.

"Oh." I glance down at my jeans, minus the belt. "I was in a rush this morning. It wasn't in the bag I took into the bathroom. I'll wear it tomorrow." I set the mug on the table beside her throne-looking chair.

Callie points to the coaster, so I move it onto the pink and white marble coaster. She stands with ease, not like an old lady lumbering to stand, instead, graceful in everything she does. Bending forward with her arms crossed, she inspects the drink before wrinkling her nose.

"What?" I ask.

"It's black."

"That's the coffee," I say.

"I don't like coffee."

"Mr. Rawlings said you like your coffee as herbal tea with lemon and honey."

She looks at me, and after a few seconds, the corner of her mouth bends into a tiny grin. "You steeped my tea in coffee?"

"Well,"—my gaze ping-pongs between her and the mug—"yeah."

Her shoulders bounce with a little chuckle. "What he meant is I don't drink coffee. He calls everything coffee. I like tea instead, not *too*." Her eyes narrow as she picks up the mug and reads the tea tag.

"It was the first box I found that said 'herbal.'"

She hands me the mug. "Smooth Move tea has senna. Do you know what senna does?"

"No." I take the mug.

Callie returns a tight-lipped smile, and I wait. But that's all she offers, so I guess I'll look it up.

"Want me to get another tea? Not steeped in coffee?"

She slowly nods.

With a controlled sigh, I turn and head downstairs.

"How'd you do, son?" Rupert says, now dressed in black joggers and a crisp white tee, drinking a glass of something green while staring at his phone, back against the fridge. It smells like Pop-Tarts.

"I steeped senna tea in coffee and added honey and lemon."

He snickers while I pour the concoction into the sink. "There's a glass electric kettle in the pantry," he says. "Use it to heat the water. On the shelf above the kettle, there's a copper-colored tin with peppermint tea bags. Senna is an herbal laxative."

"Shit. You know, you could have told me all of this earlier." I open the pantry door that matches the cabinets. It's basically a second kitchen with another fridge, a counter, stove, sink, and a floor-to-ceiling wine rack behind a glass door. *Fucking rich people.* I wonder if they ever lose sleep thinking about people living on the street with cardboard for a bed and a sandwich from a dumpster that will serve as their only meal for the day.

"I didn't tell you earlier," he says, "because I wanted to see how savvy you were."

"And?" I call from the pantry.

"And what? I think we know the answer. Do you really want me to say it?"

Something clicks to my left. It's the toaster ... and Pop-Tarts.

After I fill the kettle and plug it in, I return to the kitchen, pulling my phone and charging cord from my back pocket to charge it on the counter. "Say what? That you think I'm an idiot?"

"Do *you* think you're an idiot?"

"Nope." I pluck a new spoon from the drawer for the honey. "I think you've set me up to fail at this job, and there's nothing I can do about it."

"The only way you can fail is by not trying."

"Try what? I don't understand this job." I head back into the pantry to fill the mug with water and grab a tea bag.

"You'll figure it out," he says when I come out of the pantry.

"Why can't you be her muse? What's wrong with you?" I ask. "Besides the obvious."

"What's the obvious?" He eyes me with distrust before drinking the rest of his green beverage.

"Your age and you wear pajamas with a robe and slippers. You're not horribly out of shape. You're acting healthy by drinking that green crap, but you have Pop-Tarts waiting for you in the toaster." I bob the tea bag in the water. "Maybe things down below aren't working like they used to. I don't know, and I don't care. Maybe you should *try* a little harder. And don't people like you have servants or something to make tea?"

"Servants?" He laughs, passing me to retrieve his Pop-Tarts. "I don't believe that's a common term anymore."

"You know what I mean."

"We have employees, like yourself, who do things for us. A housekeeper. Someone who washes windows. But that's about it. We cook our own food. Launder our own clothes. Now, my neighbor? The asshole who bought the house I wanted? He hired a homemaker. That was her title. She wore 1950s housedresses and heels. She gardened. Baked me a pie for my birthday, and did God only knows what else." He returns, holding his Pop-Tarts by the edges.

"Yeah." I toss the tea bag into the trash. "That's weird shit. Unlike hiring a *muse*."

"Touché, Flynn." Rupert sets the Pop-Tarts on a plate, then rinses out his glass. "But I didn't actively look for you. You sort of stumbled into this job."

"Well, my life has been an endless series of stumbling into shitty situations."

"Then stop stumbling. Keep your head up. Walk taller and with purpose."

I roll my eyes. "You act like luck has nothing to do with it."

"Luck matters." He spreads butter on his Pop-Tarts. "As luck would have it, I showed you mercy. This could be life-changing for you."

"Doubt it," I mumble, stealing one of his Pop-Tarts on my way out of the kitchen.

I knock twice before opening Callie's door.

She meets me in the middle of the room and takes the tea from me. After a slow sip, she smiles. "Much better."

I wipe my face for any crumbs while focusing on the wall filled with framed photos. Real people photos. Not Mona Lisa-style paintings.

There's a photo of Callie at a beach with a young boy. There are other pictures of the boy, but older. I glance over my shoulder at her.

"Your son?"

She nods before easing into her chair.

"Oh, he's married?" I point to the wedding photo.

"Was," she says as I continue to study the photos. There's one with her son and a little boy.

"You have a grandson?"

She stares out the window. A tiny smile touches her lips as she nods and blots the corners of her eyes.

Shit. I'm making her cry. There must be a family rift. What do rich people fight about?

"I grew up in the system since age three. So if I have kids, they won't have grandparents. I hope your son knows how lucky his kid is."

She fiddles with her wedding band, gazing past me to the wall of photos.

"People say children who suffer abuse often abuse their own kids," I say.

Callie's gaze shoots to me.

I shake my head. "But that's bullshit. I'll never lay a hand on my kids. Just the opposite. I'll probably end up in prison for killing anyone who tries to lay a hand on them or says one negative word about them."

"You'll make a good father."

I sit on the bench at the end of her bed and blow out a deep sigh. "You know that girl from the gallery? The bike tour girl?"

Callie nods.

"I had ice cream with her last night."

"Oh yeah?"

"It didn't go well. I mean, I thought it was going great. I wore some of the new clothes you bought me. I paid for the ice cream. We discussed the scar on her lip, which, as my roommate suspected, is from a cleft lip. But I said nothing bad about it. It's unique. I mean, I know no one wants to have a birth defect, but she's basically the prettiest woman I've ever seen. Perfect, really. Which means the scar is kind of perfect too. Anyway, things were good. I offered to drive her home. She wasn't comfortable with that, so I suggested another date, and then she asked me why I wanted to date her. That's where it all went to shit." I bow my head and run my fingers through my hair.

"She doesn't even know I've done time," I say. "That'll probably be a real deal-breaker, anyway. I just fumble my words around her, and I can't think. Not quickly. And when I couldn't give her an immediate answer, she left."

"You've been in prison?" Callie squints.

How does Rupert not tell his wife that he's hired an ex-convict?

"Uh ... yeah. I stole something for someone, and I should not have. And I assaulted someone, but it wasn't really my fault. But it happened after my first time in prison, so no one believed me. But I know just the word *prison* is pretty alarming. Just look at how you reacted."

She slowly shakes her head. "I'm not really reacting. It was just a question. But I understand why it's not an easy thing to tell people, especially if you're trying to impress someone. You'll figure it out. Now ..." She stands. "Let's take a bike tour today."

Is she serious?

"I'm wearing jeans and leather *loafers* without socks."

"Follow me." She breezily saunters past me, out the door, and down the long hallway to the other side of the house.

"Oh, Jesus ..." I cringe as we pass through a bathroom where Mr. Rawlings is buck naked in the shower, his backside to us so he doesn't notice the intrusion. He's whistling a tune, and it smells like vanilla. Is that a loofah in his hand?

In his closet, she picks out biking shorts and a shirt one would wear in the Tour de France. Then she plucks short white socks from a drawer and slides a pair of white tennis shoes from a shelf.

No. I'm not wearing this old guy's clothes.

"We're not the same size," I say instead.

She frowns and shoves everything into my chest, forcing me to take them, then she leaves the closet, shutting the door behind her with me still inside it.

"Jail would be better than this," I grumble, changing into the ridiculous costume because that's what it is. It's Halloween bullshit. No one wears this on a city bike tour. The padded shorts are too big for me. The only thing that fits is the shoes. June will take one look at me and know her decision not to grant me a second date was correct.

The door opens.

Nooo!

Full-frontal Rupert stares at me. I try not to look, but his dick size clearly isn't the issue with his marriage.

"It's genetics, young man. I'm sure you do the best you can with what God gave you."

I lift my gaze to his stupid smirk.

"Want to tell me why you're in here, wearing my clothes?" He steps into the closet, and I retreat to keep a safe distance.

"Your car was just a decoy," I say. "My goal all along was to get into your closet to steal your Tour de France gear."

He barks a laugh while pulling on his boxer shorts. "I like your sense of humor. But seriously, where is Callie taking you?"

"City bike tour," I say, quickly gathering my clothes and sidestepping him to get to the door.

Pulling on his dress pants, he squints at me. "That's unexpected. Did she say why?"

I'm more comfortable talking to Callie about my

personal life. Maybe it's because she doesn't give me shit. She feels safer to me.

"Well?" he prods, buttoning his dress shirt.

"When we were at the gallery yesterday, the tour guide stopped by to use the restroom."

"And she invited you and Callie on a tour?"

"Sure."

"Christ, kid. Out with it." He sighs, tucking in his shirt.

"The tour guide has a thing for me."

He opens a drawer and picks out a neatly rolled tie. "Hmm, she has a thing for you or you have a thing for her, but she's out of your league, so my wife is playing matchmaker?"

"Didn't you marry out of your league?"

"Yes." He chuckles. "But I don't think you're as charming as I was at your age. It's your generation."

"Well, I don't think girls in my generation are looking for charming guys."

"No?" He faces the full-length mirror and ties his tie. "What are they looking for? Thieves?"

I want to wipe that smirk off his face, but that wouldn't end well for me.

"Big dicks?"

I don't have a good comeback because I'm too busy wondering what girls are looking for in guys. If I take sex out of the equation, I've got nothing. And June wouldn't even kiss me, so I'm sure sex is off the table for now.

"Be yourself," he says. "It leaves less to live up to."

Myself. Who would that be? Sounds like some spiritual shit. Soul-searching. Whatever. Maybe I should stick to easy hookups.

"Should I start with my criminal record?" I ask.

"I might wait a bit before unloading your résumé. You want her to listen with an open mind because she's gotten to know you. What's her name?"

I shrug.

He turns, eyeing me in a way that makes me squirm. I hate how good he is at doing that to me.

"June. Her name is June."

He sits on a dark gray padded bench at the end of his dresser and pulls on black socks. Then, he slips his feet into shiny black shoes. "You've met a woman named June in June. Feels like a sign. You should tell her that. Women like it when guys feel things like fate."

"Sounds cheesy as fuck to me."

"It would. You're twenty-five. Basically, you're a dick with a job. You like cars, booze, and pussy."

Nope. Not gonna talk pussy with a guy who's old enough to be my father.

"But any girl worthy of chasing will not be impressed by those pastimes."

"Okay." I press my lips together and give him a sharp nod while backing my way out of the room. "Thanks for the talk. I'll give all your *expert advice* careful consideration."

"Yeah, I'm sure you will." He steps into the bathroom and fixes his hair in the mirror.

I find Callie downstairs in a biking getup that matches the one I'm wearing.

Seriously, kill me now.

People will either think I'm dating a cougar, or they'll think I'm taking a tour with my mom—in matching outfits.

An orange jumpsuit is looking better and better to me.

Chapter SIX

Flynn

CALLIE PURCHASES our tour tickets at the counter. A family of four is being fitted with their bikes and helmets. I don't see June anywhere. Even though she's the reason for today's Adventures of the Muse and Minneapolis's Richest Woman, I will wholeheartedly believe there is a God if June is not working today.

"Flynn?"

Too late.

June steps into the rundown shop, pulling her hair over her shoulder to braid it. She makes a slow inspection of my attire. There's a limit to everyone's confidence. This is mine.

"Nice digs. Are you buying a bike?" she asks.

"My boss wanted to take a bike tour."

She shifts her gaze to Callie at the front desk. "Oh, that's ... interesting. Well, let's get you fitted for a bike and helmet."

I adjust my shorts. They hide nothing in the front and

make me look like I'm wearing a soggy diaper in the back because they're too big.

"Thanks, Tim," June says to the guy helping the family of four. "I'll take it from here. Sorry I'm a little late. My roommate lost her car keys and was crashing out."

I tear my gaze from her as Callie hands me a tablet to sign away my life for the bike tour. After I give it back to her, June nods for me to step closer, giving me a helmet. I put it on, and her fingers graze my neck as she adjusts the strap. My dick had better not get any ideas about an erection in these goddamn bike shorts. Just in case, I rest my folded hands over my junk and think of Rupert's naked backside covered in hair and a ridiculous number of moles. Anything to discourage my boner.

"How's the muse job going today?" she asks. Her brown eyes flit from the strap to my face. Her voice is soft, like she's intentionally trying to keep everyone else from hearing her.

"Look at me. Who wouldn't be inspired by this?" I mumble.

She giggles. "How does that feel?"

I know she's talking about the helmet and the strap, but all I feel is warmth and a shit-eating-grin level of happiness just being close to her. "Fine," I say in a raspy voice before clearing my throat.

"Have you been on an e-bike before?"

"No."

"Okay. Then go stand over there by those two kids, and I'll walk you through it after I get your boss fitted with her helmet."

"You really take bike tours seriously, huh?" the adolescent boy says to me.

I bite back the *fuck you* and opt for a screw-you smile instead. His older sister elbows him, as she should.

"Nice to see you again. We didn't get to formally meet at the gallery. I'm June." She shakes Callie's hand.

"It's my pleasure. I'm Callie."

As my shitty luck would have it, Callie has been on an e-bike, so it's just me and the two kids getting trained. After we pass the quick test, June leads the group across the street to the bike lane. The family stays in front with June, followed by Callie and me bringing up the rear. What's the point of this?

We stop at various buildings, parks, and monuments for June to rattle off her prepared speeches on things like the history of mining and logging, a mill explosion, and the story of a bridge collapsing. At some point she mentions Paul Bunyan and an ox. She teaches me more history than I learned in school. Everything she says fascinates me because she's the one saying it.

"This is my favorite stop for spotting wildlife," she says when we take a break along the trail in the middle of a park. "Last week, I saw an American woodcock doing its mating dance over there and a beaver by the water."

I snort.

Everyone shifts their attention to me, so I clear my throat. "Sorry. I think a bug flew into my mouth."

Callie nods as if I'm telling the truth, and the family just as quickly returns their attention to our trusted tour guide. But June keeps looking at me through narrowed eyes. Come on, woodcock is funny. And the fact that it does a mating dance is even funnier. Right?

"Let's take a fifteen-minute break. Now's a great time to

use the restrooms over there if anyone needs to," June announces, wiping the sweat from her brow.

It was only supposed to get into the 80s today, but it feels much hotter.

Callie and the family of four remove their helmets and head to the restrooms. June takes a drink, then plucks a protein bar from her crossbody bag.

"You and Callie look cute today in your matching outfits," she says before biting into her bar.

I rarely calculate my responses to things. That's probably one reason I've spent time in prison. But I like this girl so much, it's hard not to carefully weigh my words, hoping they're the right ones to impress her.

"It was my idea," I say with a shrug.

June covers her mouth while she laughs mid-chew. Is sarcasm her love language? God, I hope so.

"But this tour was her idea?" she asks.

I nod, removing my helmet and running my fingers through my sweaty hair. "Sure was."

June eyes me with skepticism.

"It's true. Just ask her."

"Does she know we had ice cream last night?"

"Yeah, but she doesn't know what flavors. I'm not one to kiss and tell."

Again, June can't hide her grin, but I can tell she's trying to while staring at her protein bar before taking another bite. Making her smile is quickly becoming my new obsession. My past is filled with memories of people scolding me with my three least favorite words: that's not funny.

I can smell the blueberries from here as June scans the park, looking anywhere but at me. My attention remains glued to her.

"Stop staring at me," she says.

"Can't."

"Why?"

"Because you're so beautiful, it's a little unfair to everyone else."

I think she's blushing, but it's hard to tell in this heat. "Stop," she whispers, risking a glance at me.

"Not even a woodcock doing its mating dance could distract me from looking at you. A beaver is another story." I shrug. "But the American woodcock is no match for you. So you'll just have to deal with my staring."

June makes a sad attempt at rolling her eyes before looking at me. She wrinkles her nose. Is she trying to look tough or serious? That's not the way to do it. It only makes her look more irresistible.

"I meant what I said last night. No second date," she says.

"I know. But do you still mean it today?"

She studies me in silence.

I look like an idiot. Hell, I am an idiot. But I'm also hopeful because I see the indecision on her face. Her brain is telling her one thing, but another part of her body is telling her the opposite.

"Fine," she says begrudgingly.

I grow an inch taller, chest inflated with confidence. As the others return to ruin the moment, slowly putting their helmets on, I worm my bike to the front of the pack, right behind June.

"Teacher's pet?" she asks, wiping her mouth with the back of her hand.

She has no idea what a terrible student I was, but I'm eager to learn whatever she's teaching.

After the tour, the family of four thank June and hand her a cash tip. I can't tell for sure, but it looks like fifty bucks. Callie hangs her helmet on the handlebar of her bike and retrieves a crisp hundred-dollar bill from her wallet.

When June turns, Callie hands her the money and offers a kind smile. "Thank you for the lovely tour. You're a delight."

I'm sure that hundred bucks covers a tip from me as well, but I'm not the one handing it to her, so it doesn't feel like it's from me. God, I hate this feeling. There's a crumpled-up five-dollar bill in my wallet, but it's in Callie's belt pack since these stupid biking shorts don't have pockets. But what am I supposed to do? Ask for my wallet in front of June? Then pull out a measly five bucks?

"Wow, that's very generous of you," June says to Callie. "Thank you so much."

"You're most welcome. Flynn, I'm going to use the restroom before we leave." She points toward the sign to the right of the counter.

June's attention settles on me as she pulls the tie from her braid and combs her fingers through her hair. It's pure torture.

"I don't have my wallet on me. I'll tip you on our date if it goes well."

Her nose crinkles. "Okay, because that won't feel weird." She laughs.

"Now that I think about it; I don't really want to date you. Feels like a lot of pressure."

She deflates. "Oh. Well, then—"

"I just want to be with you."

After a few blinks, she smiles at her feet. "Be with me?"

"Yeah." I shrug.

"Well," she chuckles, "you're with me now."

"Mmm ..." I hum and grin. "Don't I know it."

She bites her bottom lip for a second. "Okay, so when do you want to *be with me* again?"

I look over her shoulder as Callie comes out of the bathroom. "Like ... now. Later. Always. If I could tuck you into my pocket and take you with me, I would. But"—I pat my legs—"no pockets."

June studies me before I'm rewarded with a slow grin. "That's the weirdest thing anyone has ever said to me."

Callie peruses the bikes for sale as if she's in the market for one, but I know she's giving me time with June.

Time to say stupid shit.

Time to make June not want to see me again.

It's possible the most common pickup line isn't *I want to tuck you into my pocket.* But my insecurities have always stayed in my head, no need to let them out now. Yet I step closer to June, bypass my fears, and pretend I have the slightest clue what I'm doing.

"But in a good way, right?" I bite my lip like she did and peer down at her, waiting for a response.

Please say yes.

And there it is. That smile. The drug of all drugs.

"Yeah," she whispers with a tiny nod.

Down, boy. That's enough. Leave her wanting more.

After the pocket suggestion, what more could she possibly want? Regardless, I turn and nod at Callie, who's probably had one eye on us the whole time.

"Thanks. We appreciate your business," June says.

Callie flutters her fingers like the wave she gave me at the gallery when I forgot to open her car door.

I don't wave at June. I wink. For the record, I have never winked at anyone in my life. It feels so wrong, but June's grin is the grandest reward, so I add winking to the list of weird shit I now do because I met a girl.

Scratch that. I met *the* girl.

The moment we get into the car, Callie stares at me. Occasionally, I return a quick sideways glance as I drive us back to her house.

"Just say it. You're obviously dying to say something."

That's all it takes to make her look away. I feel instant regret because, despite Callie's wealth, I might like her. People reveal themselves even when they're silent. It's the tiny facial expressions. The feeling that you have their undivided attention. She makes me feel seen and heard. It's a whole vibe with her that's hard to explain.

"Nothing," she murmurs. "I'm just happy for you."

Happy for me? Does that mean she's not happy for herself?

"You know, there's nothing you could tell me I couldn't handle," I say. "Believe it or not, I'm good at keeping secrets." I grunt a laugh. "I've had some really disgusting people insist I keep their secrets. Not because I wanted to. I usually kept them because I was trying to protect someone else. It might make it easier for me to do this muse job if I knew what has you down."

She keeps her attention on the road ahead of us. After a few blocks, she reaches across the console and squeezes my hand.

It's a nice touch. I haven't had a lot of those.

Chapter SEVEN

June

It's been a week. A WEEK!

For a guy who seemed to want to go out with me again, he's made no effort to contact me.

"Will you hand me the remote?" Ally asks as we eat takeout on the sofa.

I don't remember the last time I saw her eat without her laptop next to her along with several open books. She's in her last year of law school, and I commend her dedication.

"Hey!" She gasps when the remote lands in her lo mein.

I cringe, pausing my chopsticks at my mouth. "Oops. Sorry."

"What's up with you?" She fishes the remote out of the white carton and wipes it with a napkin. "You've been mopey and distracted. Constantly staring at your phone."

"Flynn hasn't called or texted."

"I'm sure he will. How long has it been?" she asks, but I

know she's only half engaged in our conversation as she turns on the news.

Every night. The world news.

People our age don't get their news from television, except Ally. She listens, eats, studies, and still manages to ask me about my moping.

"It's been a week since he took my bike tour."

"What's he do? Maybe his job has been hectic."

"He's a muse."

She stops everything and slowly glances up at me while turning down the TV volume. "A what?"

"A muse."

"Is that your way of telling me he poses for nude paintings?"

I laugh. "No. Well, at least not that I know of. The husband hired him to inspire his wife to live." I wrinkle my nose.

"Huh?" She mirrors my expression.

I shrug. "I know. It's a little odd."

"A little? Is this person suicidal?"

"Maybe. I don't know. She seemed fine on the bike tour, but that doesn't mean anything."

"So your guy's job is to keep her alive?"

"I'm not sure. I'd ask him more about it if he'd call me."

"After your ice cream date, you said you weren't too sure about him. And now you're itching for him to text you?" She shoves lo mein into her mouth.

I tap my chopsticks against my lips. "He's ..."

"Hot?" she asks.

"Well, yes. But that's not it."

"Rich?"

"I already told you, I don't think he's rich. But I don't need a rich man."

"Says no one. Marry rich. It's one less thing you'll have to fight about."

"Flynn feels messy."

"Messy?" Ally laughs. "I don't know anyone in their right mind who actively pursues *messy*."

"He says he's never dated," I say.

"He's a liar. You're right. That's messy. And it's a red flag. Let me save you the heartache and just tell you now—you can do better."

I set my half-eaten carton of fried rice on the coffee table. "Well, if he's not a liar, then he's unlike any guy I've ever met. He's handsome. Confident, but not arrogant. His smile makes me feel giddy. But I swear it's his humor that I can't get enough of. It's kind of a dry humor, but I get it."

"I still don't have a good feeling about him, but if you insist on learning everything the hard way, then just text him. That's allowed, you know?"

I pick up my phone next to my Chinese food. After staring at it for several seconds, as if I can will him to call me, I sigh and stand. "You're right. It's not like texting him makes me look desperate. I'm not desperate. I'm just going to call him so I know if he's blowing me off or just dead."

"Just dead?" Ally chuckles.

I start to text Flynn but change my mind and call him instead as I head to my bedroom.

"Hey, June," he answers.

"So you do remember me," I say.

"Of course. I was going to call you, but—"

"Save it. I've heard all the excuses." I close the bedroom door and hop on my walking pad by the window because I think better when I'm moving. "In fact, I'm only calling to tell you not to worry about calling me."

"Oh. Uh ... so let me get this straight. You just called to tell me not to call?"

"Exactly."

"I see. Well, since you called, then I don't have to. We can just make plans now."

"No plans. I think you're bad for me."

"Trust me. You're much worse for me than I am for you," he says.

"Wait. What?" I increase the speed on my walking pad to compensate for the extra energy his words give me. "How can I possibly be bad for you?"

"I've slept like shit for the past week because I've been thinking about you."

I can't stop the thrill that runs through me even though I don't want to feel this. Not yet. He hasn't earned it. "Seems like a line of BS since all you had to do was call me."

"I couldn't ask you out again until I got paid. Now that I've been paid from my last week at my previous job, I can take you to dinner or whatever you want to do."

It's whiplash. The thrill dies, and I have to slow my pace. This is a first—a guy who's had to wait for a paycheck just to take me out. Flynn doesn't have to tell me this. He could make up an excuse.

He's been busy.

His dog died.

He caught the flu.

"I could have paid for us to go out," I say.

"Oh, sure. You're right. I should have called and asked you to take me to dinner. What was I thinking?"

I open my mouth to tell him to swallow his pride, but I think he already did in order to tell me the truth.

"You still there?" he asks.

"Uh, yeah. Sorry. I was just thinking."

"What were you thinking?"

I don't know why I'm trying to hide my grin. He can't see me. I love this feeling. Butterflies. Intrigue. Euphoria.

"I was thinking we should take a walk," I say.

"A walk?"

"Yeah. A walk around the lake."

"Then what?"

"I don't know. We'll figure it out."

"Well, I work tomorrow. But they usually run out of things for me to do by three."

"Perfect. My last tour ends at three, so let's meet at four."

"I could pick you up," he says.

"Of course, you could. I'm pretty light."

"Ha. Ha. You know what I mean."

My face hurts from grinning. Is Flynn Morley the version of "normal" I've been searching for?

Chapter EIGHT

Flynn

I DON'T HATE my job. I just don't understand it.

One day, I'm mowing the lawn and trimming the hedges. The next, I'm taking Callie to see a movie—with goddamn subtitles. A dyslexic's nightmare.

She doesn't seem depressed or suicidal. Of course, I don't know what that would look like. If anyone had a reason to feel that way, it would be me. There's no way she's been through anything like I've experienced. I've wanted to hurt people, maybe even kill a few. But through all the pain and feelings of abandonment, I've never once thought about ending things.

"I've always wanted a cat," Callie says on the way to the car after the movie.

I have the rest of her popcorn that she didn't eat, as well as half a bag of M&Ms which I dump into my mouth before they melt.

"A white cat, like the one in the movie," she says.

"Then get a white cat," I mumble over the chocolate while opening her door.

"Rupert doesn't like cats. He's a dog person. Sally, our dog, died last year. He was heartbroken."

"Explains the dog wash in the garage," I say before closing her door.

After I get into the driver's side, I stow the bag of popcorn on the floor behind her seat. "Who came up with the name Sally," I ask.

"Rupert's mom's favorite song was 'Mustang Sally.'"

Guess I won't be making fun of the dog's name, since his mom died.

"I should get him another dog. It's been long enough," Callie says.

"I bet he'd want you to get a cat. He seems concerned about you." I pull out of the parking lot.

"I don't think you understand how much he hates cats."

"I'm sure he loves you more than he hates cats."

She looks out her window and sighs, but doesn't say anymore. So I do what any good muse would do, I drive to a feline rescue shelter.

"Flynn." Callie eyes me, frowning when I pull into the parking lot.

"We're just going to look. What's the harm in looking?"

Lucky for Rupert, there are no white cats when we peruse the ones available for adoption. Unfortunately, there's a small gray kitten with a white face, belly, and paws that look like socks. His name is Loki, and Callie has hearts in her eyes.

I smirk at her.

"Don't give me that look, young man. I'm just holding him." She kisses his head as he purrs nonstop.

I bite my lips together to hide my grin.

"Loki is a cuddler," the stocky guy with long, brown hair says as Callie pets Loki. "He likes a place with lots of windows where he can watch what's going on outside. And he's great with a litter box. His previous owner had to let him go because she was moving to a place that didn't allow pets. He's only six months old."

"Well, we're just visiting," Callie says, handing the kitten back to the guy. "I'm not in the market for a ..." She wrinkles her nose. "Why isn't he purring for you?"

He shrugs. "He must like you better."

"I don't think that's it." She takes Loki back as if to prove a point. He instantly starts purring.

"Oh ..." Her expression melts.

An hour later, we pull into the garage with the newest member of the Rawlings family and bags of cat supplies. She carries Loki into the house, and I follow with the bags.

Just as she heads upstairs, Rupert appears at the top, eyes squinted. They have a silent stare-off.

"You're fired," he says to me.

"No, he's not," Callie says, continuing up the stairs. "Flynn said you surely love me more than you hate cats. Is he right?"

Why did she have to say that?

"His name is Loki and he only purrs for me." She holds him up to Rupert's face.

He flinches, rearing his head back, and she laughs while continuing toward her bedroom.

"A word in my office," Rupert says to me.

"Follow me, Flynn. I have a project for you. My husband will just have to wait for his *word*."

With a tight smile, I shrug and squeeze past Rupert as he glares at me.

An hour and a half later, I'm still sorting through Callie's boxes *and boxes* of stationery on her bedroom floor, organizing the cards into groups—birthday, anniversary, thank-you, and sympathy.

She clears her throat. When I look up at her petting Loki, she wrinkles her nose. "Slow down. You're bending the envelope. What's your hurry?"

I sigh, straightening the corner of the bent envelope in my hand. "I have a date with June at four."

Mrs. Rawlings checks the time on her gold watch. It's three fifty. "Why didn't you tell me?" She makes it sound so simple, like her husband didn't hire me as an alternative to my going to jail.

"It's no big deal," I lie. "I just haven't been given official hours with this job, so when we made plans, I assumed I'd be done by now because I've been for the past week."

"Well, go!" She makes a shooing motion with her hand.

I shake my head. "No. I'll finish this."

"Flynn. Go! That's an order."

Is she mad?

"Seriously. I'm fine. I want to do this for you. I need this job."

She kneels on the floor across from me, setting Loki free to roam around. "I needed this day. The movie. Loki. And now I need this," she says, taking the cards from me.

"Need what?"

She pauses, looking up at me. "I need you to see where it goes. The nervous boy feigning confidence. The smitten girl playing hard to get." Pulling in a long breath through her nose, she smiles. "It's familiar. And I ..." she closes her eyes for a second. "I just *need* it," she whispers.

"Well"—I check my phone—"I don't know if she'll wait for me. But I'll try."

"Run."

I laugh while standing. "I didn't wear running shoes, but I'll do my best."

"Flynn?" Mrs. Rawlings calls after I'm several feet down the hallway.

I turn.

"Manners. I promise no matter what happens, if you have manners, she'll want another date. And you'll know when it's the right time to tell her about your past. Because you *do* have to tell her."

"Manners," I repeat with a quick nod. "Past. Got it."

It's a big lake. I should have specified where we'd meet, so I text her.

Flynn: U here?

June: I was. But u were late. A girl has to have standards

"Shit." I drop my head back and stare at the cloudy sky before closing my eyes. "I'm such a fuck-up," I grumble.

"Words matter."

I whip around in a half circle as June saunters toward me in denim shorts, a tight, black tank top, and white sneakers. Of course, I stare at her legs so long she calls me out with a knowing grin. But it's not just her legs. The smile and the mischievous sparkle in her eyes is enough to render me speechless. I feel like the best version of myself when she looks at me. A version of myself that I've never seen, but often imagined.

"There are no two words more powerful than *I am*. So remember, what you say after those two words matters." She slides her hands into her pockets and starts walking along the path.

I guess we're not holding hands.

"In that case," I say, catching up to her. "*I am* sorry for getting here late. This new job of mine has unpredictable hours."

"Ah, yes. I'm sure there is nothing predictable about the muse business. After all, inspiration is unpredictable."

"I feel like you're making fun of me or my job. Which is it? And are we going to walk around this whole lake?"

"This whole lake?" She giggles. "You mean like two? Three miles?"

"Listen. I've been thinking about it. And I should have texted you before I got paid. Even like a: *Hey, what's up. You look beautiful today.*"

June playfully nudges my arm. "How would you have known if I looked beautiful via text?"

"It's just a fact. Like water is wet and ten thousand miles between oil changes is risky business."

"Flynn ... Flynn ... Flynn ... you are so unexpected."

"In a good way?"

"Yes." She sidesteps a pile of dog shit. "In a very good way."

"Cool. Listen, we should eat. I have money now."

"We could have gone to eat a week ago. I had money then," she says.

"Then you should have invited me to dinner."

"Perhaps." She tucks her chin. "But I was waiting to be swept off my feet."

I laugh as a man jogs past us with his two golden retrievers. "Sorry. I didn't know asking a girl to buy me dinner was the new way to sweep her off her feet." When I look over at her, she keeps her chin down, grin partially hidden.

"You know what I mean," she mumbles.

"You forget I don't date. So, I don't know what you mean. Is this what you mean?" I wrap one arm around her back and my other under her legs and pick her up.

"Flynn!" She twists her torso to hook an arm around my neck as if she's worried I might drop her.

Never.

I can smell her perfume. It's sweet, just like her. It feels soft where her warm skin touches my neck. This almost counts as a hug, and now I don't want to let her go.

"Let's go to dinner." I step off the trail and head up the small hill toward my car. "I'm buying."

"Put me down before you drop me."

"Why would I drop you?" I try to keep my attention in front of me, because looking at her face this close to mine only makes me want to kiss her lips, which are *right there* for the taking.

"People are staring at us," she says with less urgency.

"Excellent. They're probably thinking *that guy just swept*

her off her feet. PAY ATTENTION, EVERYONE!" I yell as June gasps, covering her mouth, eyes wide. "THIS IS HOW YOU SWEEP A WOMAN RIGHT OFF HER FEET!"

"Oh my gosh! I can't believe you did that."

"Well, this is the second time you've mentioned being swept off your feet." I grin, stealing a quick look at her face just as I stop at my car.

She's so beautiful. What am I doing? This girl is out of my league. I ease her to her feet, but she doesn't let go of my neck. Facing me, she runs her hands along my skin, toying with my hair. It makes my heart pound in a new way. I wet my lips and swallow hard, gazing over her head for a second to hide my nerves.

"Kiss me," she whispers.

The end.

I'm over. Done for. Eviscerated. A tall tree ready to fall to the ground with a big *thunk!*

"Nah," I say so cooly I don't recognize the idiot's voice as my own. "I don't think it's proper to sweep you off your feet *and* kiss you on the same date."

Stupid. Fucking. Idiot!

What is happening? Has some evil spirit or alien hijacked my brain? Of course, I want to kiss her. I want to kiss the life out of her, take a breath, and do it all over again.

Fingers tangled in her hair.

Tongue down her throat.

My body pinning hers to the side of my car.

But now I can't.

As she deflates, arms flopping to her sides, I swipe my fingers over my mouth to hide my grin. I have no clue what I'm doing.

She stares at my chest and scrapes her teeth along her bottom lip several times. "Well, that's a first."

Of course, it's a first. No heterosexual man in his right mind would refuse to kiss her. I should just tell her I'm kidding and seal my lips to hers until we're both blue in the face.

"Well, I was hoping I'd be your first," I say instead. That's it. I don't know who or what's in charge of my thoughts and bodily functions. What's next? Will I piss myself in front of her?

"Get in," I say before jogging around the car to the driver's side.

Screech!

The wheels in my head grind to a halt, and all I see is Mrs. Rawlings eyeing me with unspoken words. So I quickly turn back around and wink at June, who's giving me a dead stare.

"Just kidding," I say with easy confidence while I show off my manners by reaching for the door handle.

"Maybe I should meet you there," she says, without stepping aside to let me open it.

"Because I drive a piece of shit?"

Her nose wrinkles. "No."

"You don't have a car."

She adjusts her crossbody bag and straightens her shoulders. "I'll get a ride?"

"Get in. I'll let you pay me to drive you to dinner."

"What?" She laughs. "You won't let me pay for dinner, but you'll let me pay you to drive me to dinner?"

As a car approaches, I step to her side, putting myself between her and the oncoming car just in case they're not paying close attention to the road. After it passes, I look down at her. Her back is against the door as she watches the car, then she looks up with those deep brown eyes. It's impossible to pull my gaze away from her mouth. God, I want to kiss her.

I slowly dip my head. Her lips part and eyes disappear for a second behind a blink that's just as heavy as her breath. I slide my hand along her cheek, and she leans into my touch.

Her delicate, silky skin.

That dizzying sweet perfume.

The tug of my shirt as she grips it.

My pounding heart drowns out the rustling leaves, distant cars, and hum of a lawnmower up the hill beyond my car. I close my eyes and, at the last second, turn my head so my cheek brushes hers while my lips settle next to her ear. And I whisper, "Put ten dollars on the dash. Tip is optional."

June doesn't move for a few seconds. Then, as I take a step back, she shakes her head several times, like she's knocking out the cobwebs. Her expression shifts. I'd say it's a little evil.

Before she grows horns and bares her pointy teeth, I open the door, forcing her to step aside.

"My damn," I say.

That hint of evil vanishes, replaced with a snort and the biggest grin she's given me yet. "Madam," she says with a giggle.

"That's what I said," I say with a straight face.

She slides into the seat. "Sure. Sure. But really it should be *Miss*."

My composure holds strong as I close her door. But when I make it to the back of the car, I smack my hand against my forehead. "You're an idiot!"

After I get in the driver's side, this POS starts on the third attempt. June clears her throat.

I squint at her, daring her to say anything about my cheap-ass car, the pungent smell of pot (not mine), and other nasty smells (also not mine) mixed with pine air freshener. The air freshener *is* mine, hanging from the rearview mirror.

"Seat belt," she says.

"Oh ... yeah." I rein in my scowl and tug at the seat belt. It's tangled on the floor beside my seat because it no longer retracts into its casing. This car is older than I am. A freebie I snagged at the junkyard before someone compacted it into a pile of scrap metal. I had it running in less than two days.

"Stupid thing," I mumble, trying to work the knot out of the seat belt. When I finally get it fastened, I look at June.

She has the goofiest expression on her face from attempting to hide her amusement.

"At least I have a car," I say like I would to a buddy giving me shit, not the girl I'm trying (unsuccessfully) to impress while simultaneously playing hard to get. I'm not sure what my game plan is. It's like a skunk playing hard to get with a white, floppy-eared bunny rabbit.

She curls her lips between her teeth and slowly nods while humming a soft, "Mm-hmm."

"What do you like to eat?" I ask, pulling away from the curb with some extra gas before it dies on me.

"Food."

"Ha. Ha."

"Good food."

"So like chicken fingers and fries?"

"Careful, Flynn. I don't know if you're allowed to sweep me off my feet twice in one day."

I shoot her a quick sidelong glance.

"You look more like a salad girl. I don't know where to get good salads. I don't eat a lot of 'em."

"Why do I look like a salad girl?"

"Cuz you're skinny."

"So are you," she says.

"So chicken fingers and fries?"

June laughs. "Yeah. Chicken fingers and fries."

Chapter
NINE

June

I DON'T LIKE chicken fingers. The smell of Flynn's car makes me gag with bile. When I step out of it at the restaurant, I hide my cringe because something sticky on the car seat makes a gooey sound as I peel my butt from it.

His brow furrows when I wrinkle my nose. "Shit. Was there something on the seat?"

I try not to laugh. The seat is black, but I'm pretty sure the original fabric color was beige. Yeah, there's a lot of *some-things* caked on the seat.

"It's fine," I say. Wiping my backside.

He twists his torso, inspecting my butt.

"Are you staring at my ass?" I keep my hand over the sticky spot because I don't want to make him feel bad.

"I'm inspecting your shorts. I'll get that seat cleaned tomorrow." He closes my door, and we head into the restaurant. "And you have a nice ass," he says. "In case there's a poll about it or something like that. Ten out of ten."

I playfully nudge him, any excuse to touch him because I'm *dying* for him to kiss me. Grab my hand. *My ass.* Whatever. Just touch me!

He keeps his gaze ahead of us, but he still grins and nudges me back.

While he orders at the counter, I pick out a table. This is my first fast-food date. I'm about to eat food I don't like while trying not to think about the mystery sticky substance on my shorts. Yet my head continues to spin from him literally sweeping me off my feet, the near kiss, and the way he instinctively put himself between me and the car driving down the street.

If he were my muse, I'd write love songs about all the things I never knew I wanted—until him. Songs about falling. Butterflies. Goosebumps. And of course, being swept off my feet.

It's too soon. Too fast. Too everything.

It's also undeniable, and if I'm being honest, it feels uncontrollable.

Flynn carries the tray of food to the drink station, fills our cups, and grabs napkins and packets of ketchup. When he spots me, he grins. I've seen a lot in my life, things other people would only dream of, but this man smiling at me might be the vision that hits me hardest in the chest. He's just ... I don't even know the right words. Definitely unexpected in the best possible way.

"I didn't know if you wanted coop sauce or just ketchup, so I got both. You deserve options," he says, sitting across from me.

"I don't know what coop sauce is, but I'll try it."

"I know this isn't fancy—"

"It's perfect," I say, interrupting him. "Like really *really* perfect."

He eyes me while taking a drink of his soda, grinning around the straw.

"I'm serious." I laugh, opening a packet of ketchup.

"I'm not a fancy person." Flynn opens his ketchup with his teeth.

"I hadn't noticed." I dip my chicken into the special sauce.

"It's weird seeing the stupid shit that matters to rich people."

"Define stupid shit," I say.

"A big house. The Rawlings' mansion is ridiculously big for two people. They don't even sleep in the same bedroom, and it's still too big. They have one child and a dining room table that seats twelve."

"Maybe they like getting good sleep. Maybe they like having dinner parties." I shrug before taking another bite of chicken. It's better than I expected. Just one more *unexpected* moment with Flynn Morley.

He dips at least five fries at the same time into his pile of ketchup. "If I had a wife, I wouldn't sleep on the other side of the house. Ya never know what could happen. If she couldn't sleep with me in bed with her, I'd just sleep on the floor."

I slow my chewing.

"What?" he says.

"You'd sleep on the floor?"

"Of course. The man of the house should protect what's important. What's more important than family?" He shrugs a shoulder, but then he chuckles. "But what do I know? I've never had a family. Maybe that's why I think I'd do whatever it took to protect one if I had the chance."

I now believe Flynn has never dated, because if he had, he'd be married. Some woman would have snatched him up. I don't know if I'm ready to snatch anyone up, but I'm definitely putting Flynn on my wish list. Clicking the heart icon. And I know I'll think about him long after our date ends.

"But seriously," he says. "Can you imagine that life? A big house. Never thinking twice about what something costs? Steak for dinner? Fresh produce. Eating a whole avocado with your breakfast?"

I chuckle. "I think that *is* the life to imagine. I fear the life you had growing up is what's unimaginable."

"Don't do that." He shakes his head. "Don't feel sorry for me."

"Flynn, you're eating dinner with Minneapolis' best tour guide. No one can feel sorry for you." I give him my best flirty grin. Playing hard to get is overrated. Or maybe it's not. I think he's been playing *me* for the past week, and he's still doing it.

He chews slowly, studying me. "You did that on our first date too."

"Did what?" I narrow my eyes.

"You jokingly suggested that I should feel lucky to be with you."

"Oh, no. I mean. Yeah. I'm totally joking." I hope he knows I'm kidding. I'm just nervous.

He uses his middle two fingers to slowly wipe his mouth. "Well, you should be serious because I'm *seriously* feeling lucky to be with you."

I'm sure my face is every shade of red, unable to hide my

attraction to him. "Thank you," I whisper before clearing my throat. "I feel lucky to be with you too."

"Liar." He chuckles, leaning back in his chair.

"I'm not lying." I reach across the table and hold out my hand.

He stares at it for a minute, like he doesn't trust me. But as he lifts his gaze to my face, he rests his hand on mine. My fingers tease his wrist, and he does the same to mine.

The chills are real. And those butterflies flutter out of control.

"When are you going to kiss me?" I ask.

My mom said she didn't play it cool with my dad when they met. I knew I would be different. And I tried to be cool and make Flynn chase me, but I'm failing.

"I don't know." He gives me a sexy smirk. "I feel like we missed our first-kiss moment. This attraction now feels worthy of more than a kiss."

I giggle, sitting back in my chair while grabbing my drink. "We're not going to walk before we crawl."

His eyebrows slide up his forehead. "June, are you implying that you want to get on your knees?"

"Oh, my gosh! No."

Flynn eats up my embarrassment like a second helping of chicken fingers. "Are you done?" He points to my leftover food.

I nod. "It was good, but I'm full."

"Well, can't let it go to waste." He shoves the rest of my fries into his mouth, chews a few times before swallowing, and inhales the rest of my chicken.

It's hard to keep my smile from faltering. Does he go without food when he runs out of money between paychecks?

"Wanna get out of here?" he asks after downing the rest of his drink and mine.

"Sure."

When we pull out of the parking lot, I don't ask him where we're going. He's pretty good at surprising me, so I let him take the lead. We end up near the lake. A different lake. He turns onto a street that heads up a steep hill.

"That's the Rawlings' mansion." He points to the right.

"It's beautiful."

"Ya think?"

"Of course," I say. "It has an old charm to it."

"Yeah, but would you want to live there?"

I shrug. "I mean, I would. It's just a house."

"Just a house? Are you blind?"

"No," I mumble, staring at the house. "I'm not blind. I see everything that's special and heartbreaking."

"Heartbreaking?"

I nod. "It's heartbreaking because the people who live here have hired someone to inspire *life*." I touch my palm to the window as if the view before me is a picture in a frame. "But it could just as easily house kids, a dog, maybe a bird or two. Laughter could bounce off the walls and echo in the rafters. But either way, it's just four walls and a roof."

"June, that place has a lot more than four walls."

I face him and grin. "You know what I mean."

He bobs his head. "Yes and no. You're much smarter than me."

I want to lean forward and kiss him, but I fear he'll deny me again.

"No kids. No bird," he says. "But there's a cat. After the matinee (with those ridiculous subtitles), Mrs. Rawlings mentioned wanting a cat, so I took her to a shelter. Of course, her grumpy husband doesn't like cats, but she ended up adopting one anyway."

"You went to a matinee today?"

He sighs with a frown. "Unfortunately. This job is so random. I'm sure Mr. Rawlings loves that he no longer has to take her to movies with subtitles."

"And then you took her to adopt a cat?"

He nods. "Why are you grinning like that? I know, it's a stupid job. Rich people are stupid. Well, they're probably not actually stupid, but they do stupid things. Too much money makes you—"

"Stupid?" I laugh.

"Exactly."

"Let's go knock on their door," I say.

"What?" Flynn's face sours.

I open my door. "Let's go say hi."

"You don't stop and say hi to your boss." He turns off the car and jumps out when I close the door, making my way to the sidewalk. "June, I just saw them a little over an hour ago. This is weird and a terrible idea." I grab her wrist, and she turns toward me.

"They're just people, Flynn."

"Rich people."

"Sad people," I say.

He rolls his eyes. "I'm off the clock. It's not my job to inspire anyone at the moment."

"Kindness isn't a job. You don't have to inspire anyone. We'll just say hi." I pull out of his hold and continue toward their front door.

"Jesus. This is crazy. What am I supposed to say when Mr. Rawlings answers the door? They might not even be here. Maybe they've gone to dinner at some fancy schmancy place."

"Maybe," I say before ringing the doorbell. "If that's the case, then we'll leave."

"I think we should break up," he says with the grumpiest expression.

I giggle until I feel it in my belly, until the front door opens.

The man at the door resembles George Clooney. It's striking, really. He eyes Flynn with confusion before softening his gaze for me. "Hi," he says.

"Hi. I'm June, Flynn's friend. We just happened to be in the neighborhood, so Flynn showed me your house. And I suggested we pop in and say hi."

He studies us for a few seconds. "Rupert," he says.

"Rupert, mind if we come in?" I ask. "I'd like to say hi to Callie again. Unless we're interrupting dinner?"

"No such luck," he says with a grumble.

"Or we could leave you alone. And I'll just see you tomorrow," Flynn says.

"Nonsense." I grab Flynn's hand, excited to have an excuse to do so. Then I pull him inside without waiting for the official invitation from Rupert. I love how small my hand feels in his.

"She's pretty, Flynn," he says.

"Thank you," I say as we slip off our shoes. "You have a lovely home."

"It's not as nice as my neighbor's, but I won't bore you with that story or how his wife hired him a homemaker. Alice, she made me a pie, but I didn't eat it because I figured it was poisoned."

Oh my gosh. I love his grumpiness because he's not that good at it.

"Hello," Callie says, at the top of the stairs, holding the gray and white kitten. "This is a surprise." She floats down the marble steps in a satin kimono robe and fuzzy white socks.

"He was here an hour ago. I wouldn't call it a surprise," Rupert says. "Well, June is a surprise. Not as surprising as a *cat*, but still unexpected."

Callie rolls her eyes.

Rupert returns a grin that's flirty and confident. Oh, this is fun. I might be a little envious of Flynn's job. On one hand, I wasn't sure what to expect with Rupert. Yet he's also exactly how I imagined.

"What are you two lovebirds up to?" Callie asks.

Heat fills my cheeks when I look at Flynn to see his reaction to "lovebirds."

"June wanted to stop and say hi," Flynn says. "Although I'm not sure why."

Callie reaches the bottom of the stairs and hands her kitten to Flynn, then she puts her arm around my waist. "Because she's a lovely young lady. Come. Do you like tea?" She leads me past the foyer to the kitchen. "Rupert, why don't you offer Flynn a drink?"

"Because I didn't hire him to drink with me, and he's holding that stupid cat."

"Well, he's off the clock, so he's not your employee. And *Loki* is our new baby." Callie releases me when we enter the kitchen. "I hope you weren't too upset by Flynn being late. We didn't know you had plans. He was organizing cards for me. And before that, he suggested I get a cat, which led to bringing Loki home, much to my husband's displeasure."

"He's a cute kitten. And what's up with the cards?" I ask as she opens the cabinet door and disappears into the pantry.

"Greeting cards. I used to make my own. I went through a phase of making my own paper, and that led to cards with pressed flowers and seeds. You know, the kind you can plant to grow flowers or a tree?"

"That's cool. I bet they're beautiful." I run my fingertips along the cream marble countertop with gray veins. It's much thicker than newer granite tops.

"They're fine. It was just a phase I went through. I've been through a lot of phases. If you speak with my husband for more than five minutes, he'll work my *pastimes* into the conversation."

I want to ask her about her current phase and why she needs a muse.

Callie emerges from the pantry with two cups of tea. "Follow me," she says. "When I'm not in my bedroom, I enjoy time in either my morning room or the covered balcony." She nods for me to sit at a glass-top café table by the window. "Of course, it's lovelier in the morning with the sun." She sets our teacups on the table and sits across from me.

"Thank you." I bob the tea bag a few times.

"You look so familiar," she says. "I thought it the day I saw you in the gallery and again when we met for the bike tour."

"Oh?" I glance up at her. "How so?"

Her pale blue eyes narrow. "I'm not sure. Menopause has scrambled my thoughts. I feel like I have holes in my memory, broken connections, and a two-second recall. Have you lived in this area your whole life?"

"He's asleep," Flynn says, sauntering into the room with the kitten. "Dozing off in his desk chair. He had his *word* with me about the cat, and while I was trying to explain the movie and why I suggested a kitten, he just … dozed off." Flynn strokes the kitten's head while meandering around the room, looking at the art on the walls and a few family photos on a coffee table beside a gold, crushed velvet sofa.

"Did you make sure he's still alive?" Callie asks.

Flynn whips his head in her direction. "Should I?"

She chuckles, pulling her tea bag from the cup and setting it on a ceramic leaf-shaped plate between us. "No. If it's his time, it's his time."

"Don't let me interrupt you," Flynn says, sitting on the sofa and kissing the kitten's head.

Finding a guy who likes cats wasn't on my list, but here we are, and I'm not mad about it.

"Sorry," I say. "What did you ask me?"

"Have you lived in Minnesota your whole life?" Callie asks.

"I'm from India. My parents adopted me when I was three. I grew up in California."

"What an interesting coincidence. Did Flynn tell you he was three when he went into foster care?" She eyes Flynn.

I shake my head, glancing at him over my shoulder.

He doesn't look at us, focusing on Loki.

"What brought you to Minnesota?" She returns her attention to me.

"It's not California."

Callie laughs. "Very true. How long have you been here? Clearly long enough to learn the history of this area well enough to be a bike tour guide."

"I've been here three years. When I first moved here, I worked as a barista, and I still do that in the winter. I have a knack for latte art." My gaze flits to Flynn, and I half expect him to be looking at his phone, but he's not.

He eyes me with an expression of wonder. I get that giddy feeling again.

"On a whim," I say, "I took a bike tour, and that's when I decided it might be the best job ever."

Callie laughs. "Oh, I love that about you. It's so genuine and innocent. There's nothing pretentious about it. Just pure joy for something." She sighs. "I miss those days."

Her response evokes so many questions, but I don't know her well enough to ask them.

"How old are you, if I may ask?" Callie sips her tea.

"Twenty-six."

"What did you do in California after high school? Did you go to college?"

Flynn laughs softly, and Callie glances at him. "What's so funny?"

He shrugs. "Well, who goes to college to be a bike tour guide or a barista?"

"A lot of people have degrees they don't use," Callie says.

"That's why I didn't finish high school," he says. "I knew I didn't need a degree."

I roll my lips together to keep from grinning while Callie studies him. It's surprising that she doesn't correct him. College is not the same as high school. But after several seconds, she nods. "Perhaps you're smarter than my husband gives you credit for, Flynn."

"Will you tell him that?" he asks.

Callie returns a sincere smile. "I will."

"Did you go to college?" I ask Callie.

She turns back to me. "Yes." Her gaze clings to the cup in her hands.

I wait for her to elaborate, but she doesn't. It feels like an invisible line I shouldn't cross.

"What's your degree?" Flynn asks, unaware of the invisible line.

Callie's forehead tightens, and she dismissively waves her hand. "I have several degrees. Nothing important."

"Sounds like a waste of money," Flynn says. Then he puckers his lips for a second. "Wealthy people don't care about wasted money, huh?"

"Well"—she nervously laughs, lifting her teacup to her mouth—"I can't speak for all wealthy people, but my father and grandfather were frugal with their money. They reinvested almost everything. My grandma used to say they were rich because they lived as though they were poor. When my father died, though, my mother spent her money more freely. She had the mentality that life is too short to save it all for death. But I'm an only child, so yes, college wasn't a financial burden. And at the time, it didn't feel like a waste of money."

Flynn looks at me with an indecipherable expression.

"June, do you have siblings?" she asks.

"No. I'm an only child too."

"I had all kinds of siblings," Flynn says. "If you'd call them that. Just other kids in foster care."

I know he doesn't want pity, but I can't help my sad smile.

"You have a lot in common with my husband," Callie says to Flynn.

He squints. "Mr. Rawlings was in foster care?"

Callie sips her tea before nodding.

"He told me about his mom and brother, and then about his father, but I just assumed he was an adult by then and just ..." Flynn shrugs. "Moved on."

"He was twelve when his mother and brother died. His dad went to prison. Rupert lived with his grandparents—his mom's parents—but they weren't financially able to take care of him, and his grandfather had cancer. His dad's parents were divorced and had basically disowned his father years earlier, so Rupert ended up in foster care. Then he ran away and got into trouble, so he spent time in a detention center. When he turned eighteen, he enlisted with a recommendation from his detention officer."

"It's late," Flynn says while standing. "You'd better put your husband to bed."

I'm caught off guard by his abruptness, as if he's not interested in anything Callie has to say about Rupert. Perhaps it stirs up bad memories from his own past.

Callie grins. "He's a big boy. If he doesn't make it to bed on his own, that's his problem."

I scoot back in my chair, following Flynn's cue to leave. "Thank you so much for the tea."

Callie looks at me and nods. "It was my pleasure. Please feel free to come by anytime. It's ... nice," she says with a somberness to her voice.

"I guess I'll see ya in the morning," he says when we step into the kitchen where I put my cup in the sink.

Callie rests her hands on his cheeks, and his body stiffens. "Take good care of her," she says. "Manners and respect. Okay?"

I tuck my chin to hide my smile. Flynn doesn't know it, but he officially has a mom.

"Sure," he says, handing her the kitten. When he turns his back to her, he gives me a little eye roll like Callie is crazy. I'm not sure Flynn knows how to let people genuinely care for him.

That's kind of heartbreaking.

Chapter TEN

Flynn

"That was odd," I say, starting my car on the second try.

"What was?" June asks.

"Callie got pretty tight-lipped when I asked about her degree. Was she a stripper or something?"

June snorts. "I don't think that requires *several* degrees. Everyone has secrets for different reasons."

"I know. It just seems like a weird secret." As we drive down the hill, I glance at June. "What's your secret?"

"What's yours?" Her eyebrows jump up her forehead.

"I asked you first."

"Well"—she looks ahead—"if I tell you, then it won't be a secret."

"I don't think we should have secrets," I say, and I mean it, but I don't know if I can walk the walk. Not yet.

"That's a big step. No secrets, huh?"

I pull over along the side of the road. "We have a problem."

"Your car is broken?"

"I don't know where we're going. Am I taking you home? If so, you have to tell me where you live. Are you coming back to my place? If so, then I have to be *honest* with you about my living situation."

Her lips part with a slow breath. "Are you living in your car?" she whispers.

I chuckle, but she doesn't.

Shit.

She's serious.

"Not anymore," I say. "I told you I have a roommate. Do you think he's waiting at some bar for me to finish my date so he can get back in this"—I circle my finger around—"our house?"

Her eye twitches. I know she's trying not to be shocked by me, my past, and my whole messed-up present situation. Monroe was right. I give too much too soon. But I don't want to be with someone who can't handle it. Maybe that's why I'm alone, residing on a sofa. I should slow down before I lose her.

"Do you want to order a ride? I'll wait here with you, and when they pick you up, I promise not to follow you."

This time, she can't hide her flinch. "Flynn," she whispers.

"It's fine." I run my hands through my hair. "I wouldn't trust me either."

Her hand rests on my leg, and I stare at it, wanting nothing more than to hold it. Kiss it. Pull her into my arms. When I picked her up at the park and carried her to my car, it was the first time in ... forever, that I remember feeling someone else's body so close to mine without it being a forgettable hookup.

"The gallery," June says, pulling her hand away from my leg.

"The gallery?"

She nods. "I live in an apartment across from the gallery, above the salon."

"So why did you use the bathroom at the gallery instead of running up to your apartment?"

"Because I was …" she swallows hard. "I was taken."

"Taken? What does that mean?"

June stares at her folded hands for a few seconds before lifting her head and offering a shaky smile. "On my twenty-first birthday, I went out with friends. Got my first legal martini. Danced. Laughed. Gossiped. Then I snuck off to the restroom because I was feeling sick. And I …" She pulls in a shaky breath. "I don't remember what happened next. Everything was dark. There was a humming noise. And I felt this vibration. That's when I realized I was in the trunk of a car."

Fuck me …

She swallows hard, wringing her hands. "It was only three days. And then it was over. I wasn't injured or abused. And despite years of therapy, there are just some things that make me nervous."

"Strangers and telling people where you live?"

I'm not good at this stuff—knowing the right thing to say when other people are hurting. All I know is a lifetime of suppressing every single emotion until I no longer feel anything.

"You're safe with me," I say, hoping it's a good start.

"Yeah?" she whispers before biting her lower lip.

I put the car into *Drive.* "Yeah. There's really nothing I wouldn't do to keep you safe."

"Thanks," she says timidly.

I stop at the light, stealing a quick glance at her as she picks at her pink fingernail polish. "You're beginning to have that effect on me."

"What effect?"

"I don't know if there's a name for it." I scratch my neck just as the light turns green. "When I was fifteen and in my last foster home, there was a ten-year-old girl who they took in, but the husband treated her like a dog. One day, I'd had enough, and I took a baseball bat to him. So I guess this protective feeling is something like ... touch her and I'll kill you."

Through the corner of my eye, I see June's mouth open, then quickly clamp shut. Did I go too far?

"For the record, I didn't actually kill him. He was just hospitalized for a while, and I spent time in juvie."

She doesn't speak for the rest of the drive to her apartment, so I bite my tongue. Anything I say might only make it worse. When we arrive, I park on the street and hop out to open her door. This manners thing is growing on me. Callie will be so proud.

Just the thought that I give a shit about anyone being proud of me is an unfamiliar feeling. I don't know if I like it—caring what other people think.

June steps out of the car and adjusts her bag over her chest, keys ready in her hand. But she doesn't look at me. "Thanks for the ride," she murmurs before heading straight to the building.

"I'll walk you up to your apartment," I say, following her.

"I've got it."

"Are you mad?"

"No."

"Then why won't you look at me?"

She pauses her hand with the key in the lock, keeping her back to me. "I think we're moving too quickly."

"Too quickly? You asked me to kiss you, and I did not. I'm still not going to kiss you. I just want to make sure you make it to your apartment safely."

"It's just up a flight of stairs. This door automatically locks behind me. I'll be fine." She pulls open the door and removes her key.

"So this is it? This is what I get for being honest with you? You told me about someone kidnapping you. That doesn't change how I feel about you. So why does the fact that I now feel even more protective of you change things between us? Because I beat up a fucking awful human ten years ago? Because I spent time in juvie?"

"Is that it?" She turns, holding the door open with her shoulder. "Have you only hurt bad people? Never good people? Have you ever gotten in trouble for doing something wrong that wasn't an act of protecting an innocent person?"

Did Callie tell her I took Rupert's car for a joyride? I didn't hurt anyone, not even the car. Maybe I'll just tell her everything. If she can't handle it, then clearly, she's not worth my time.

I inhale a long breath, readying the words, but I choke on the truth.

"Ya know what, June? Fuck it," I say. So much for telling her everything. Why give her any more of myself when I know she can't handle the truth. "This is why I don't date," I continue. "One minute, things are great. Some girl is batting her eyelashes at you begging for a kiss. The next, she's either giving you the cold shoulder or sending your ass down the street to take a shit at a convenience store." I head toward the car. "Hope you enjoyed your chicken dinner and fancy tea. Nice knowing ya." I climb in my car and slam the door. Thankfully, fate's on my side because it starts on the first try. So I shove it into gear and floor it, leaving a little tire rubber on the street.

When I have to slam on the brakes at the red light, do I look in the rearview mirror to make sure she gets inside the building safely? Of course, because I like her, even though I now hate *how much* I like her.

For the rest of the evening, I sit on my sofa with a beer in my hand and two more in line on the coffee table while Monroe and Naomi screw each other's brains out in the bedroom. It's loud and annoying, but by the end of my third beer, I slump to the side, pull a blanket over part of my body, and pass out for the night.

"I'm only waking you up because you're Monroe's friend, and he likes it when I'm nice to you," Naomi says, smacking my cheek several times.

I bat her hand away and slowly sit up. One of the empty beer cans falls off my lap and onto the floor.

"You're not going to keep your job if you don't start setting an alarm," she says, opening the fridge to retrieve the creamer.

"What time is it?" I rub my temples.

"Five fifteen."

I lumber to my feet and drag my ass to the bathroom.

"You're welcome," Naomi calls.

I don't reply with a thank-you, but I also don't give her the middle finger. My restraint is equivalent to a thank-you.

By six, I'm showered, dressed in rich people's clothes, and knocking on the Rawlings' front door. I don't know why anyone needs inspiration at six in the morning. If she's depressed, just keep sleeping. In my experience, the world is more tolerable at nine in the morning than it is at six.

"I left you a message," Mr. Rawlings says after opening the door in his usual burgundy robe and old man pajamas.

I pull my phone out of my pocket. It's dead. "What was the message?"

He frowns as I tuck my phone back into my pocket. "Callie is not feeling well today."

"She's sick?"

He shakes his head. "Some days she doesn't get out of bed for ... reasons. Today is one of those days. So your services won't be needed today."

"Dude, I'm awake. My head is splitting. She was fine last night. She got a cat for god's sake." I invite myself inside.

"Well, she's not today." He holds out his hand to stop me as I kick off my shoes and step toward the stairs.

"What's wrong with her?"

He scowls. "That's not your concern. Now, I said we don't need you today. So, I suggest you turn back around and leave. Go charge your phone so you don't miss my messages."

I turn around to put my shoes back on. "Ya know"—I pivot toward him—"she's been fine. And I haven't been able to figure out what I'm doing here. A muse? Her inspiration? For what? But on the day she won't get out of bed, you don't need me? That's bullshit, man." I shoulder past him.

He grabs my arm, and I pull away.

"Do you want me to call the police?" he asks.

I stop halfway up the stairs. "Fuck it. Call the police. I'm just going to tell your wife goodbye before I go to jail."

"Goddammit," he grumbles, following me.

I stay a good ten paces ahead of him. When I get to Callie's room, I don't knock. Instead, I slip inside and shut the door behind me. It's dark because the sun's not up to filter through the cracks in the pulled drapes.

"Rupert, I told you to leave me alone," she says in a raspy voice beneath the pile of blankets on the bed.

"June is scared of me. I blew it," I say, collapsing into her high-back chair; its wooden legs releasing a screech in protest. "And I didn't even tell her the worst part."

"Flynn?" Her dark silhouette takes form as she sits up in bed.

"She begged me to kiss her at the park. But no. I was a gentleman. Manners. All that good shit. Opening doors. God, you would have been so proud of me. Then I made the mistake of being honest with her about something in my past, and she couldn't handle it." I plant my elbows on my knees and drop my head, running my fingers through my hair. "Hell, she could barely look at me."

"Flynn," Callie rasps. "This isn't a good day for me."

"Well, join the club. I was so angry last night I drank one too many beers, forgot to set my alarm, and had to be woken up by Naomi, my roommate's girlfriend. She technically doesn't live with us. Yet, lately, I've been feeling pressure to move out. Gotta room you want to rent me?"

Her silhouette disappears. "We'll talk tomorrow," she says, muffled like she's back under the covers, but I can't tell for sure because my eyes haven't adjusted to the darkness.

"Come on. I'm doing my best to inspire you. Isn't that why your husband hired me? I can't have you slitting your wrists or downing a fucking bottle of pills—forgive my language. But that will look terrible on my résumé ... once I get out of jail. Oh, did I mention the police are on their way? I guess what I'm trying to say is, you don't have any reason to be depressed. You're rich. Your husband obviously cares about you. I bet you've never been to jail. You *have* the option to stay in bed all day."

Silence.

That's it? She has nothing to say?

"What did you tell her about your past?"

I sit up in the chair and clear my throat just as Loki rubs up against my leg. "I told her I beat a man with a baseball bat for treating a young girl like a dog."

More silence.

I drum my hand on my thigh.

She sighs. "Hold still."

I freeze.

"That's a lot to put on someone who doesn't know you very well."

"He was a terrible man," I say.

"Does June know this man?"

"No."

"Was she the girl you were protecting?"

"No."

"Does she know the girl you were protecting?"

"No."

"Then it's too much. If she doesn't feel invested in you, the man, or the girl, then it's too much."

"He put a fucking prong collar on her!" My fingers grip the arms of the chair.

Callie slowly sits up, swinging her legs over the side of the bed. Then she turns on the lamp.

We squint against the light for a few seconds as our eyes adjust.

"Vigilantes are complex. Sure, their intentions can be honorable. But to people who aren't vigilantes, such extreme actions can seem appalling. Have you ever seen the show *Dexter*?"

I shake my head.

"Well, it's about a serial killer who only kills other serial killers."

"An eye for an eye," I say.

"Yes. But not everyone lives by that mantra. All I'm saying is you need to give people a chance to know you before you give them everything. If people on dating apps only listed their bad or questionable traits, no one would swipe left or right or whatever direction you're supposed to swipe."

I deflate, closing my eyes briefly. "She asked me to kiss her. I thought ... I don't know. I thought we were there. So now what?"

"I don't know, Flynn," she rubs her temples. "You have to tell her everything, or she'll feel lied to. But you could lose her." She shakes her head. "I can't make this decision for you. But it's never a bad idea to show her your softer side. Flowers. Write her a poem. Bake her something."

"I don't have a softer side. No money for flowers. I've never written a poem, so there's no need to start now. And I don't know how to bake. What else do ya got?"

Callie rubs her hands over her face before sliding her fingers into her hair. Her weary expression triggers my guilt. I like her. Even if I don't understand why she needs a muse, I like her. She's kind, and I haven't had a lot of that.

"I have a garden." Her tired eyes find me, and she smiles, but it's forced.

"You want me to pull weeds?"

"No." When her feet hit the floor, she rests her hands on her hips to stretch her back. "I want you to go into my garden and find the prettiest flowers in full bloom and cut them at a forty-five-degree angle, leaving about four inches of stem, and tie them into a bouquet."

"How many?"

Her hands flop to her sides, and she gives me a blank expression before shrugging. "That's for you to figure out."

"What do I tie them with?"

She pads her feet toward the bathroom. "Figure it out."

The door clicks shut before I can ask another question, like what I should do if Rupert has me arrested before I can gather the flowers? *Figuring it out* on my own, I tiptoe down the hallway, listening for sirens or chatter from the main floor. All I can hear as I descend the stairs is the thrumming of my pulse in my ears.

"You're an arrogant little shit with no respect for authority."

I jump at Rupert's voice behind me. Where was he hiding?

With a slow gulp, I gather as much false confidence as I can. "Maybe. But you knew that when you hired me." I stop at the landing and he nods for me to keep going as he catches up to me.

A suit has replaced his robe and pajamas.

"Sit," he says when I reach the last step.

I do as I'm told.

"No. Sit on the floor."

This feels eerily similar to the man who put a prong collar on the girl I defended.

"Are you trying to belittle me?" I ask.

He narrows his eyes, pausing several steps above me. "Have you been belittled?"

After a beat, I slowly nod.

His lips twist as he navigates the last few stairs, sidestepping me. When he turns to face me, he crosses his legs and lowers his butt onto the marble floor in front of me.

I laugh a little to hide what feels like a fist to my gut. "What are you doing?" I shake my head, but I can't look at his stupid face because he's not grinning. He's being nice. I don't like *nice* because I don't know what to do with it. I'd rather he punch me.

"I wanted you to obey for one goddamn moment. That's all. I never want you to feel beneath me or anyone for that matter. And I don't want you to feel the need to be an asshole to prove that you're tough or worthy of respect. It's exhausting, demoralizing, and unsustainable. Trust me."

"Get up," I say.

"Why?"

"Because this is stupid. Just get up." I hold out my hand.

He studies me, gaze locked to mine while he takes my hand. When he's on his feet, he squeezes my shoulder. "Good talk."

"Was it?" I squint.

He releases my hand and heads back up the stairs. "Did Callie fire you?"

"No."

"Then I guess you earned your paycheck today."

"Think I'll ever see an actual paycheck?"

He stops and turns. "How much money do you need?"

Is he serious? This has to be a trick question.

"Pay me what you think I'm worth," I say as if he asked me if I want the money in his right or left pocket.

His lips twitch like he's holding back a grin, then he slowly nods.

I grab my shoes, but I stop him before he reaches the top of the stairs. "Just so you know, my rent is seven fifty."

Mr. Rawlings doesn't respond, continuing up the stairs.

Chapter ELEVEN

June

I FINISH DRYING my hair and open the door. "Oh! Jeez, you scared me," I say to Ally, who's right on the other side of it. She shoves me back into the bathroom.

"There's a tall and very hot guy who just ran back down to his car to grab tools from his trunk to fix our leaky sink drain."

"What?" I squint. "Doesn't sound like Kevin, the handyman. He's short and not so hot. A new guy?"

She rolls her eyes. "It's Flynn. He showed up with a bouquet while I was emptying the bucket under the sink. The next thing I knew, he was mumbling something about running back down to his car to get tools to fix it."

I bite my lower lip.

"What's that look about? I thought you liked him?"

I nod several times, and then I shake my head. "He's

been through it, if you know what I mean. And I don't think I need that right now."

"Been through it?"

I nod.

"You mean he's had a rough life?"

Again, I nod.

"Well, that explains the dirty shoelace tied around the flowers."

I scrunch my nose.

"What do you want me to do? I have to get to class. And honestly, if he can fix the leak, I say we let him do it before you kick him out."

I roll my eyes. "Ugh! Whatever. I'll take care of him. Just give me a minute."

"Well"—she looks at her watch—"I don't have a minute. I have to go. So hopefully he doesn't rob us before you do whatever it is you need to do."

I bristle.

"You're the one who said he's been *through it*. Oh!" Her eyes widen. "He's back," she whispers.

Ally closes the bathroom door behind her, and I check myself in the mirror again, opting for some lip gloss—*not* because I care what he thinks. My lips are just a little dry. I straighten the high waist of my floral linen pants and adjust my white crop top before opening the door.

"'Toodle-oo," she says, smiling at me before leaving.

Ally was right. Flynn looks good in his dark jeans and black graphic T-shirt with a bird and "Shindig revival" on it.

He's clasping a freshly cut bouquet in one hand and a wrench in his other hand while standing by the sink. "Hi," he says.

"Hey," I say in a weak voice because I regret how I acted last night.

And he brought flowers ... and a wrench.

Flynn holds out the bouquet. "I picked them myself. And I cleaned the sticky stuff off the car seat."

I grin at the obvious. "They're lovely. Thank you."

He nods to the sink. "I'm going to fix this leak for you, then I'm going to suggest we start over. So just think about it. You know where I'll be." He lies on his back, the top of him under the sink.

I smell the flowers.

"I said too much yesterday," he says. "You don't know me well enough to understand I'm not a serial killer."

"Excuse me?" I laugh nervously while untying the shoelace.

"I-I mean ... shit, this is coming out wrong again. I'm not a serial killer. Not. A. Serial. Killer. Uh, can you hand me a towel?"

I stare at his abs peeking out from where his shirt has ridden up a few inches.

"June?"

"Huh?"

"A towel?"

"Oh yeah. Here." I hand him the one hanging over the oven handle.

"Thanks. I'm gonna have to get some silicone caulk. I tightened it, but it needs to be recaulked." He slides out from under the sink and stands.

I give him a nervous smile before filling a glass with water and putting the flowers into it.

"Listen"—he wipes his hands—"I'm not a bad person. That's what I mean. I would never hurt you. If the Rawlings can trust me, can you give me another chance? I promise not to say stupid shit that's scary."

I set the shoelace on the counter next to the vase. "Stupid shit like not being a serial killer?"

He cringes, sliding his hands into his pockets. "Yeah. Callie put too much stuff in my head, and I'm not saying the right things in the right order or at the right time."

"Oh? You talked to Callie about us?"

"Yeah. She was having a bad morning. Rupert told me to go home, but I ignored him."

"I'm sure he appreciated that."

Flynn rolls his eyes.

"Did Callie suggest the flowers?"

He twists his lips. "Maybe. But I swear to God, I cut and tied them."

I return a half dozen nods.

He holds out his hand. "I'm Flynn Morley, a full-time muse and part-time idiot who really likes you."

I can't think past my emotions. Every hint of uneasiness is quickly erased with moments like this. So I slide my hand into his. "Don't forget part-time plumber. And I'm June Malone. Part-time tour guide. Lover of historical romance. Naps. And men with tools in their cars."

His grin swells as he slowly shakes my hand. "The pleasure is all mine."

I disagree. The warmth of his big, calloused hand engulfing mine feels quite pleasurable. His gaze drops a few inches, and he wets his lips, which is even more torturous. I glance down for a beat, my hand still holding his. You can see my nipples through my bra and tight shirt. He has that effect on me, and I don't know if I should turn and fix the situation or pray he feels powerless and relinquishes a kiss.

When his eyes shift, meeting my gaze again, he quickly releases my hand and takes a step backward. "So"—he swallows—"are we good? You know, to start over?"

"I'm sorry," I say. "I overreacted last night. It was—"

"Too much," he says.

"No." I cover my face for a few seconds and sigh. "I just had certain *feelings* for you. So I rushed things. And what you told me felt like a reality check. I needed to learn more about you before taking the next step. Really, I scared myself more than you scared me. I just took it out on you, and I'm sorry."

A tiny line forms between his eyebrows, and he offers a slow nod.

"So we take it slow," I say, more to convince myself.

"Slow," he echoes.

I'm dying. He must be bad for me because I've never felt this anxious and unhinged. "But ..." I shrug. "It seems a little silly to start completely over. Maybe we can pick up where we left off and forget about that minor hiccup last night."

"Where did we leave off?" Flynn asks, and I don't know if he seriously doesn't remember all the close moments or if he's messing with me.

"Well, we held hands at the Rawlings' house. So we can check that off the list." I use my index finger to make a checkmark. "So I suppose next might be ..." Clasping my hands behind me, I rock onto the balls of my feet and back down again as nervous energy threads through me.

"Next might be?"

I shrug.

"Sex?" he asks.

My face flushes faster than I can gasp my next breath.

Flynn smirks. "Joking. Listen, I'm perfectly content just being in the same room."

"I'm perfectly content having sex." I grin and let him decipher my level of sincerity. *I* don't even know if I'm serious.

Flynn returns a nervous laugh, casting his gaze over my head for a second. "June, if and when we have sex, I promise *content* will not be a strong enough word for how you'll feel."

As if burning me to the ground with that statement isn't enough, he takes a second gander at my nipples. I need thicker padding in my bra, new underwear, and a tall glass of water—maybe a cold plunge. My jaw slackens, but nothing except my labored breaths escapes.

"Cat got your tongue?" He throws my words back at me.

"Kiss. Me." My restraint vanishes. Standards? What standards? Self-respect? That's overrated.

"June, if I kiss you, it won't stop there, and I think we both know it. And I'm working pretty hard at this manners thing."

"Fine then. Say please, and when it's over, say thank you."

Poof!

There goes the last shred of my dignity.

The grin on Flynn's face explodes. God, he has the sexiest smile.

"Actually, I should go. I don't know if I am dismissed for the day," he says, jabbing his thumb over his shoulder.

"Yeah, I have a lot on my agenda today, too. So ..." A lie. I have the day off and no plans. I love lazy days. Organize a few drawers. Read for a while. Take a walk. Grab lunch. Even squeeze in a short nap.

"Your roommate seemed nice," he says.

"Ally is the best."

"Have you been friends for a long time?"

"Only since I moved here. I met her through an app that matches roommates. She's going to law school."

Flynn nods, and I get the sense that he's stalling. I hope it's because he doesn't want to leave me and not just that he doesn't want to get back to work. In case it is for me, I take a step closer to give him options.

"Thanks for the flowers. And fixing the leak." I take another step, sliding my hand around his wrist while lifting onto my toes so my lips reach his cheek. Before I kiss it, I pause, giving him the chance to turn toward me so our mouths fuse.

He doesn't, so I kiss his cheek and linger a few seconds before dropping to my heels.

"You're welcome," he whispers, blinking several times before ducking his head, lips brushing my cheek before kissing it. "And the leak isn't fixed yet, but I'll get it done."

Plumbing has never sounded so sexy. This is torture.

It's hot in here, so I swallow hard and pull my hair over one shoulder. His gaze follows my hands, and suddenly it's not only hot in here, it's really quiet. I still when he reaches for my hair, sliding a few locks between his fingers while dipping his head again. This time, he teases his lips along my neck while his other hand skates to my waist and the bare skin between my crop top and pants.

My jaw slackens as I fight the unsteadiness in my knees.

Flynn kisses my neck from my shoulder to my ear, and I feel his grin when I shiver. How is it possible to shiver while on fire?

I tease his nape with my fingernails, and his grip on my waist tightens as his other hand cups the back of my head, angling it so our mouths line up. I lean in for a kiss, but he pulls back a fraction and grins.

I might kill him.

"Fuck you," I whisper. That word rarely comes out of my mouth, but he's pushed me to my limit.

His grin swells for a second before he comes back in and kisses me. A real kiss. How will I explain this kiss to Ally, my mom, or my grandkids one day? Sure, to everyone else, it would seem like *just* a kiss. It's not. It might be better than sex, chocolate, and cocaine—all combined.

My only fear? It's going to end. And Flynn has somehow made himself the gatekeeper of kisses. How long before I get another one?

Another hit.

Another high.

My free hand grips his arm to steady myself as he walks me backward a few steps until my back hits the wall. My lips part a little more to let him taste the inside of my mouth. A low moan vibrates between us, and I'm not sure if it's me or him.

He ghosts his fingers along my ribs, thumb brushing the bottom of my breast over my shirt. Then he slides it a fraction more, and his thumb barely moves, almost like a twitch, but it does so along my nipple.

I might orgasm just from that.

And then ... nothing.

He stands straight, hands at his sides while rubbing his lips together. I touch my lips as if I need proof that the kiss happened. In doing so, I grin.

Flynn's shoulders pull back an extra inch. "It's shaping up to be a pretty damn good day," he says.

Why does his declaration make me blush even more? I chuckle and nod slowly. "Agree."

"I'll call you tomorrow," he says.

I continue to bob my head as if it's on a spring. He opens the door beside me, and I snap to attention as he steps into the hallway and turns.

"Thanks for letting me kiss you and touch your boob," he says with the most matter-of-fact expression.

I roll my lips between my teeth and nod several times. He's so ... everything!

Confident.

Sexy.

Yet, vulnerable and funny.

In the next breath, he's halfway down the stairs. I close the door and lean my back against it.

Don't do it.

I can't help myself. He's gone, but I still feel his hands on me. I cup my breast over my shirt, grazing my nipple like he did, and my other hand slides down the front of my linen pants.

Chapter TWELVE

Rupert

"HE'S A TERRIBLE MUSE," I say to my wife from the doorway to the second-floor balcony overlooking the gardens on the opposite side of the house as the lake. It's a muggy day. Even the air smells like warm earth, the inside of a compost bin.

Callie doesn't turn to look at me. After a long inhale and equally slow exhale, she nods. "I called you uninspiring, so you found a man who is the younger version of you, and you thought he'd be better?"

I sit on the edge of the lounger beside hers, hands folded between my legs. "You liked the younger version of me."

She grunts a laugh, leaning her head back and closing her eyes. "I liked our life when it was innocent."

I stare at her bare leg, poking through the opening in her robe. She's as beautiful as ever. I miss our playfulness, the passion, our unlikely love story. I miss *her* even though she's right here. We live like strangers in this big house. Acquaintances on a good day.

"I was far from innocent," I say.

She cracks open one eye and surprises me with a smirk. "Neither is Flynn."

"Yeah, but I like the kid."

"He's not our son."

I track a hummingbird making its way to the feeder hanging from a hook off the edge of the railing. "I know. However, you were going to stay in bed today, until he barged into your room. Now, here you are."

"He's not our son," she repeats.

"Yet, *here you are*," I say.

"I think you just wanted to make up a weird job like when Hunter Morrison hired a *homemaker*. Bragging rights. What's next? Are you and Hunter going to see who can hire a knocker-upper first?"

I cough a laugh, pressing a fist to my mouth. "If I want someone knocked up, I'm still plenty virile to do it myself."

She rubs her temples. "My father is dead, but I know he just lifted his lifeless hand and smacked it against his forehead because his daughter married an idiot. A knocker-upper was a human alarm clock during the Industrial Revolution. Don't you remember in *Great Expectations*, Mr. Wopsle gets knocked up? They used a long stick to tap on the window."

Thirty-three years of marriage, and she still amazes me. I married the prettiest, kindest, smartest woman in the world. And I don't even have to say it anymore. She knows this look I'm giving her, and it still makes her blush and smile even if it's not enough to bring her out of her dark place when she goes there.

"Flynn's friend, June, looks so familiar. Don't you think?" she asks, quickly changing the subject because she doesn't take compliments well, not even the silent kind.

"Not really. But she seems nice. I'm not sure how he got her attention."

Callie rolls her head to the side and gives me a look with one eyebrow peaked. "How did you get my attention?"

I sit straight, hands on the edge of the lounger. "My charm."

"Pfft ..." She rolls her eyes.

"My good looks?"

"Try again."

I frown. "I don't like the version of this story where you claim to have only given me a second glance because you knew I was the kind of guy your father hated."

"Well, Mr. Rawlings, that's the only version there is of the story."

"Not true," I say, reclining in the lounger. "There's two sides to every story. And your father passed away many years ago, yet here I am. You haven't rehomed me yet."

Her sigh sounds like a grumble. "I'm just too exhausted to train another."

I don't tell her she's training Flynn. Reminding me twice he's not our son is enough for one day.

"Hey, guys. I let myself inside."

Speaking of Flynn.

"As long as you haven't stolen anything," I say to him.

"No offense," he says, shoving my feet off the side of the lounger so he can sit on the end. "But aside from your car—"

"Which you already tried to steal."

"*Borrow*," he says.

Callie snorts.

"There's not much around here that's my taste."

"No offense taken," Callie says.

"What does taste have to do with anything?" I ask. "Thieves don't steal things they want. They take what's valuable to sell."

"Oh, thanks for the tip, Mr. Rawlings. Mind sharing the combination to your safe while we're on the topic?" Flynn says.

Again, Callie snorts.

Flynn unknowingly does his job so well.

"How did June like the flowers?" Callie asks.

"Well, you were right. Girls still dig that sh—stuff." He gives me a tight grin.

"Flowers are timeless," she says. "A little cliché on Valentine's Day, Mother's Day, birthdays ... but they are always the best first step after an argument. A proverbial white flag."

The word *proverbial* goes right over his head. I can only imagine how he'd respond to *knocker-upper*.

"What's next for the day?" Flynn drums his hand on his leg, the same leg that's bouncing. He's incapable of sitting still.

Callie sees it too.

"Aren't you golfing?" she asks me.

I lumber to my feet. "As a matter of fact, I am. I'll see you later." I bend down and kiss the top of her head.

"Lie back," she says to Flynn as I head toward the door.

"For what?" he asks.

"Your job for the rest of the day is to sit with me."

"And do what?"

"Nothing. Just be."

I snicker to myself.

Chapter
THIRTEEN

Flynn

"How was your day, darling?" Monroe says in a high-pitched voice when I step into our apartment after work.

I give him the bird, and he laughs, standing by the toaster oven, waiting for his pizza to cook. He eats a pepperoni Totino's pizza every day after work as a snack before the poop sheriff arrives and feeds him a meal with perfectly balanced macros.

"I got paid," I say.

"Thought you got paid the other day."

"That was my last paycheck from the detail shop. This is from the Rawlings." I hold it an inch from his face.

He rears back, eyes bulging. "Fuck me."

"Right?" I stare at it.

"You *have* to be screwing his wife. Or him. Dude, are you sucking his dick? No judgment. I might suck dick for that paycheck."

"Nope." Again, I hold it in his face. "This is a sexless paycheck. Although, Mrs. Rawlings made me sit in a lounge chair beside her for *three goddamn hours!*"

He pulls his pizza from the toaster oven. "And?"

"What do you mean, *and*? That's just it. There was no *and*." I steal a hot pepperoni and pop it into my mouth.

Monroe elbows me.

"Every time I so much as moved, she told me to sit still. If I started to talk, she shooshed me. No music. No using my phone. It was the worst kind of torture, and I was ready to quit, go to jail ... whatever. But then I found an envelope with this check in it, shoved into my shoe by the door when I went to leave."

After he cuts his pizza, he pulls his phone from his pocket. "Is that for one week?"

"I think so."

"Eight-hour days?"

I shake my head. "Closer to ten."

"Do you get paid during your lunch hour?"

I shrug. "Lunch hour? I don't take lunch. We eat lunch, but I eat with her. There is no time clock. I don't know who's tracking my hours. I'm just following orders so I don't go to jail."

"Well, fuck you, Flynn. You steal some rich dude's car, and he hires you to take a nap beside his wife to the sum of a hundred bucks an hour. *That's* what you're getting paid to be a dumb-ass muse! You're moving out."

"Because I lucked out?" I laugh.

"Because you're making six figures."

I collapse onto the sofa and stare at the check. "This is not six figures. It's four."

"It will be six if you work for them for like ... six months.

Probably less. And my weekly paycheck is three figures. And I'm paying sixty percent of the rent. You're only paying forty." He sits in the recliner with his pizza.

"You get the bedroom and closet. I have the sofa and an old chest. That's why I'm paying forty."

"Flynn," he mumbles, carefully chewing the hot pizza, "you're holding a check for five grand. You can afford your own apartment. You can afford your own fucking house."

I twist my lips, nodding slowly. "True. But I don't have job security. Hell, for all I know, this is my first and last check from them."

"You gotta go. Naomi is itching for a ring. It's time."

"Yeah," I mumble. "Give me a bit to figure something else out. I floated the idea of living with them, but Mrs. Rawlings ignored me. Granted, she wasn't having the best morning, but ..."

"I don't think they're going to pay you this kind of money *and* let you live with them. That check isn't a living wage, it's a thriving wage. Hell, in our corner of the world, it's rent plus a little FU money."

I internally laugh at his FU money reference after hearing Rupert's speech.

"I'm talking two-ply toilet paper and fancy coffee drinks every morning," Monroe continues. "You can have literally any streaming service your heart desires. NFL ticket? Don't even give it a second thought. Boom! It's yours."

I shake my head and chuckle. "I might even start taking my own bags to the grocery store."

"Put money in the red bucket at Christmas," he says.

"Tell people to keep the change." I lace my fingers behind my head. Sure, we joke. But I really don't know what this check means or if I'll see another. In fact, having this money is already making me uneasy. I hate how it's giving me an unexpected high, which feels like the first step to being out of touch with the morals I swore I'd never compromise.

The next morning, I sleep in until my roommates wake me with their extracurricular activities. It's Saturday, my day off, so I don't have to rush my shower. In fact, I use some of Naomi's fancy bath gel to shave my face to match the rest of my cool, rich man's vibe. Then I head straight to the bank to cash the check before Rupert changes his mind. I still don't want to be wealthy, but I'm okay with not being dirt poor for a few seconds.

With two fancy coffees stacked on top of each other, I ring the buzzer to June's building.

"Yeah?" her roommate answers.

"It's Flynn," I say.

"Juju's at work. Sorry."

My momentum for the day dies, even though the "Juju" part makes me smile. "When will she be back?"

"I'm not sure. She had a few errands to run after work, so it depends on how long it takes to get a ride."

"K," I mumble before heading back to my car, realizing what must be done. Time to shop.

After four stops, a few negotiations that turn into arguments, and a little frustration, I get what I need. Then I head back to June's apartment and hit the buzzer. No one answers this time, so I wait on the bench across the street in front of the gallery.

I wait over two hours.

Could I text her? Of course. But I want this to be a total surprise.

When she steps out of the black SUV and heads to her door with her arms full of grocery bags, I jog across the street.

"Hey, don't I know you?" I say.

June bobbles her keys, and they clink on the ground as she twists her neck to look at me. "Hi!"

I eat up her grin, that look that says she's happy to see me. It's not a look I see very often. I pick up her keys.

"It's the dark gold one," she says, nodding to the keys.

I unlock her door and then take the grocery bags from her.

"How long have you been here? Why didn't you text me?" She leads the way up the stairs.

"I wanted to surprise you."

"Oh?" She giggles. "Why is that?"

"Obviously because I have a surprise for you."

She unlocks the apartment door and holds it open for me. "I assumed *you* were the surprise."

"Juju, I felt you up yesterday. It can't be a surprise that I'm back for more."

She shakes her head and grins as I pass her to set the grocery bags on the kitchen counter. It's not really why I'm here, but now that I've said the words out loud, I'm getting an erection. Maybe the real surprise can wait.

"Why did you call me Juju? And how long have you been waiting?" she asks, unpacking the groceries.

Dang. She eats healthy shit. Fruit (not in a can). Veggies (also, not in a can). Things with "organic" on the label. Grass-fed. Free-range. *Shit.* I bet she hated the chicken and fries date. There's not a bag of chips or frozen pizza in sight.

"Flynn?"

"Huh?" I drag my attention back to her. "Oh. Your room-mate called you Juju." I chuckle. "And uh ... I haven't been here long," I lie.

"That's good." She buzzes around me, putting things where they belong.

I step out of the kitchen because it feels like I'm in her way.

"I had to work, and then run errands. Did you have the day off?" she asks.

"Yeah. I don't work weekends."

"What did you and Callie do yesterday?" June folds the paper bags and slides them between the fridge and the counter as I rest my shoulder on the brick wall just beyond the kitchen threshold.

"We stared into space for three hours in silence."

"Is that code for you took a nap?"

"I wish. I'm not a good napper."

She shrugs off her Billy's Bike Tours shirt, and I hold my breath for a second at the idea that she might be stripping for me. But she has a sports bra on underneath it. Still ... more skin.

"I love naps," she says. "In fact, I was going to take one after my errands. But you have a surprise for me, so it can wait." She pulls her hair tie free and unbraids her hair.

She's so gorgeous.

"So what is it? My surprise?"

I forget about the surprise when she steps into my space, tipping her chin up as if she's asking to be kissed.

"You could nap, and I could watch you." The second the words leave my mouth, I regret them.

"Sounds ... creepy." Her forehead wrinkles, but she keeps smiling.

"Sorry." I slide my hands to her ass and squeeze it. "That was a really bad way of suggesting we hang out in your bed this afternoon." Ducking my head, I kiss her neck.

Her fingers thread into my hair. "Just *hang out* in bed, huh?"

"Yep," I mumble before teasing her ear with my teeth.

Her shoulder jerks upward. "That tickles."

I turn to adjust myself as conspicuously as possible. "Come on. The surprise is waiting."

"I like surprises," she says with a giddiness that makes me want to puff out my chest and talk in a deeper voice.

"Good." I playfully smack her butt as she steps into the hallway.

She turns and catches me off guard, throwing her arms around my neck and pulling me down for a kiss.

"After—" she tries to speak, but our lips crash together again—"you—" more kissing—"left yesterday—" the dimly lit space outside of her apartment fills with the sound or our lips smacking—"I touched—" we stumble to the side a bit—"myself."

All the words piece together in my head.

After you left yesterday, I touched myself.

My head rears backward as she rubs her lips together, cheeks red and breath labored.

"June, you can't say that to me." I rake my fingers through my hair. "I don't know what to do with that ... that ... *information*." I shake my head. "Cuz I just want to rip off your clothes and screw you right here at the top of these stairs. But I know that's not right. And I don't know what I'm doing, which means I'll probably mess it all up."

Her idleness slays me. How is she so calm? Nothing

more than a hint of tension along her forehead and the twitch of a grin at the corner of her mouth.

Finally, she shrugs. "It's just flirting. Making out. Playful banter with sexy undertones. It's foreplay. Stolen moments. Building tension. Longing glances. Unbearable anticipation." She giggles, shaking her head. "It's dating, Flynn. We're dating."

"Dating," I echo, slowly nodding. "It feels like torture."

She coughs a laugh. "Torture? *You* started this. The reason I touched myself after you left yesterday is because you teased me to the point of feeling like I wanted to scream."

Again, what should I do with that bit of information?

"What's the surprise?" She holds out her hand.

I stare at it way too long before taking it and leading her down to the street level. After a quick look in both directions, I pull her across the street.

"Ta-da," I say, nodding to the red MINI Cooper.

"You got a new car?"

"I bought it for you." I pull her from the front of the car to the sidewalk as cars get closer to us. "You need a car. It must get tiring having to order rideshares for everything, especially when you get groceries like today. It's a 2008, and it has almost 170,000 miles on it. And it has a salvaged title. But it's had one owner. The inside is really good. No funky odor. No rips in the leather or sticky shit on the seats. I looked over the engine myself and took it for a test-drive. They were asking three grand, but I talked them down to twenty-five hundred."

With a slack jaw and slow blinks, she ping-pongs her gaze between me and the car. "You, uh ... you bought me a car?"

"I got paid from the Rawlings, yesterday. It was more than I anticipated, so yeah, I bought you a car. Oh, and I bought caulk too, so I can finish fixing the leak."

"Flynn." She shakes her head. "I don't want you spending your money on me. Not like this."

"It's fine. Believe it or not, this car only took half of my paycheck. I still have plenty of money."

Not gonna lie. I was expecting a little more excitement from her. But maybe she's more like me than I thought. I have trouble accepting anything that feels like charity.

"Here." I pull the key out of my pocket and dangle it in front of her. "Let's take it for a spin."

"I, uh ..." June takes the key and bows her head, staring at it while fiddling with the ring. "I don't ... well, I don't have a valid driver's license."

"Oh. So what. No big deal. Just don't speed. We don't have to get on the freeway or anything. This week you can get your license updated."

She nibbles on her lower lip while squinting against the sun to inspect traffic. "Maybe I should wait until it's not so busy."

"It's not busy. This is nothing compared to rush hour."

"Yeah, but I bet it's less busy at like two in the morning."

I laugh. "Two in the morning?"

"Also, parking is extra for my apartment."

"How much? I can pay the extra for you as long as I keep my job."

With a slow exhale, she gives me a sad smile and steps closer, leaning in the last few inches until her forehead hits the top of my chest. "This is the nicest thing anyone has ever done for me."

"I have a hard time believing that. Do you have parents who love you?"

She lifts her head, looking up at me. "Yes."

"Then we both know you've had nicer things done for you."

"You waited a week for a second date because you didn't have enough money to take me to dinner. If this car cost half of your paycheck, you've essentially given me half your money. I won't have anything remotely close to half of my parents' money until they die."

"Pfft." I roll my eyes. "I bet your parents have more than five thousand dollars to their name."

She opens her mouth, but clamps it shut just as quickly, gaze landing at my mouth. "Flynn?"

"Yeah?"

"Let's go back to my apartment and hang out in my bed for the rest of the afternoon."

I slide several locks of hair away from her beautiful face. "I'm rethinking that idea."

Her expression sags.

"I don't want to take a single second with you for granted." I brush my knuckles along her cheek. "And I like to imagine you have a really protective father somewhere who expects any man who touches his daughter to be worthy of her. I didn't buy you a car to get into your pants."

"My pants know that," she says, and it brings a smile back to her face.

I mirror her expression. "It's just ..." The jumbled thoughts in my head make me feel like a word-fumbling idiot. "This feels big. And I want to get it right because I think you only get one chance at the really big moments in life."

Her brow furrows, and it almost looks like she has tears in her eyes, but that makes little sense. Unless ... she feels rejected.

Shit.

I'm not rejecting her. Just the opposite.

"You think I'm a big moment in your life?" she whispers.

I laugh it off. Is she serious?

"Get in." I release her and open the passenger door.

Despite the confusion on her face, she slides into her car. After I get in the other side, I grin while fastening my seat belt. "Yeah, *Juju.*" I start the car and check the mirrors before pulling out into traffic. "Nothing and no one even comes close to you."

Chapter FOURTEEN

June

"WHAT WAS YOUR FIRST CAR?" Flynn asks, driving us around town.

I can't stop looking at him, hoping he'll take me home so I can kiss him goodbye, and then call my mom to tell her I found *him*.

The man who will break my heart—for the rest of my life.

She used to tell me not to give my energy and love to a man who breaks my heart once. That means he's not a fixer. She said I should find the man who will break my heart for the rest of my life because that means he knows how to put it back together.

Love isn't easy, baby girl. If you do it correctly, it will destroy you in the best and worst ways possible. It will make you feel alive one day and want to die the next. Don't live an emotionless life. That's not living. That's merely existing. And we didn't give you this life merely to exist.

"June?"

"Huh?"

Flynn squeezes my leg, and I jump because it tickles. "I asked what your first car was?"

"Oh, I don't remember. It was blue."

He chuckles. "How can you not remember what kind of car it was?"

I shrug. "I wasn't focused on cars."

"What were you focused on? Boys?"

"No." I squeeze his leg, but he doesn't flinch. "I spent a lot of time riding horses with my dad and nurturing my love of music. I had a music obsession from an early age."

"Really? That's cool. What did you play? The piano?"

"I play a lot of things. Yes, piano is one of them."

He slows at the stoplight and glances over at me. I like the wonder in his eyes. "What was your favorite instrument?"

"Cello."

Flynn wrinkles his nose. "Cello? Isn't that like a really big violin?"

"In theory, but not in practice."

"Why did you like the cello?" The light turns green and he makes a left onto my street.

"It's a sizable piece of wood between my legs that vibrates."

"Jesus ..." he rubs his temple like he's hiding his blush.

I giggle. "The cello has such a fun personality and wide range, and I think it has the most beautiful, lush sound. You can play it with the bow or pizzicato which is plucking the strings. You can play two notes really fast. That's called trills.

Or spiccato or ricochet, which is bouncing the bow on the string. And ...” I take a breath and realize we're parked, the engine is off, and Flynn is watching me with a huge grin.

“Anyway”—I clear my throat and feel embarrassment over geeking out—“I'm obviously a big fan of the cello. Highly recommend.”

“I only played one instrument,” he says.

“Which one?”

“Can't remember what it was called.”

“What? How can you not remember the name of the instrument?”

He opens his door. “Probably the same way you can't remember what kind of car you drove.”

Good point.

Just as I start to open my door, he's around the car, doing it for me.

“Thank you,” I murmur, stepping onto the sidewalk. “Was it a brass? A string? Percussion?”

He grabs the caulk from the back seat. “I don't know what any of that means,” he says, guiding me by my hand across the street.

“Trumpet? Trombone? Drums? Saxophone?”

“I blew into it.”

“Did it have a reed?”

“A what?” He stops at the lower door, and I pull out my key.

“A reed. It vibrates as air moves across it. Like a saxophone.” I unlock the door, and he pulls it open.

“I don't know. I just blew into it and it made a weird noise. I think I'd recognize the name of it if I heard it. It has a funny name.” He follows me up the stairs.

“Piccolo? Flute? Oboe? Trombone? Bassoon? Clarinet?”

"June, it doesn't matter." He laughs. "I wasn't that good."

I deflate. "Fine."

"But"—he cradles my cheek in his hand, and I think it's the best feeling in the world—"you can talk to me about the cello as much as you want to."

"You like listening to me talk about the cello?" I don't believe him because I'm pretty sure the only people who like talking about the cello are those who play it.

"I like *you*." He kisses me. "I think that means I'm interested in anything you say or do. Here." He hands me the car key.

"You keep it. I can't even drive it yet. Besides, how are you getting home?"

He holds up his hand, refusing to take it back. "Nope. I bought it for you. And I'll get a ride, take the bus. Whatever."

A long string of words line up on my tongue, all the reasons he should not have bought me a car. But they feel disrespectful and ungrateful. So I smile. "Thank you for the car. For your generosity."

My gratitude seems to add an extra inch to his height, an infusion of confidence. It looks good on him. So sexy.

"Are you working tomorrow?" he asks.

"No. It's my day off."

"Great." Flynn gives me another kiss, but it's quick, too quick. "I'm going to fix your sink then head home." He nods for me to open my door.

"You know," I say, "we're adults. I have my own room. You could stay the whole night, and no one would get in trouble." I try to sound fun and flirty, not desperate like: *Have sex with me!*

"I know." Again he nods toward the door.

I deflate and open it.

"Hey," Ally says.

"Hi," Flynn replies. "I'm just going to quickly caulk the sink." He heads straight into the kitchen.

Ally gives me a big grin. "That's really nice of you, Flynn."

"No problem," he says.

I give her a tight grin, eyes wide.

"What?" She mouths.

I slowly shake my head, and she squints.

It only takes Flynn a few seconds to caulk around the drain. "You should be good," he says. "See you tomorrow." He kisses my cheek, and I nod, lips still pulled into a tight grin.

"Byeee," Ally says.

When the door clicks behind him, I groan like a wounded animal.

"Hey, what's going—" she starts.

"I threw my vagina at him!" I dramatically collapse onto the floor like Flynn shot me dead.

"What?" Ally giggles.

"Flynn. I think I love him. But I can't tell him. It's too early. And when he kisses me ... ugh! My insides melt, and I get so ..."

"Horny?"

I stare at the ceiling and sigh. "Yes. And he bought me a car."

"What?" Ally closes her laptop. "He bought you a car?"

"Uh-huh. It was so unexpected. But really sweet." I sit up, crisscrossing my legs. "It's an old car. High miles. Twenty-five hundred dollars. But who does that? Who buys a girl a car after knowing her for such a short amount of time?"

"You don't have a driver's license."

I nod several times. "True."

"Now you have to pay for parking for a car you can't drive."

"Yeah."

"Why are you grinning?" she asks.

"Because he's trying so hard to say and do the right things."

"And you're throwing your vagina at him?"

"I haven't had sex in five years."

"You WHAT?"

I cover my face. "Don't judge me."

"I'm not. Okay, I am a little bit. Why? I mean, you've dated. I just assumed you were sexually active."

I drop my hands from my face, resting them on my knees. "I'm not a one-night-stand person. And I've had trust issues. But Flynn is different. And I'm ready, but he's not."

"He's not the right guy then. If he likes you enough to buy you *a car*, but not to have sex with you, that's a red flag."

"He can't gift a car and get a red flag. Maybe a yellow flag. But really, I think he gets a beige flag because he wants everything just right before he sleeps with me, even if it seems quirky. He's never had a girlfriend, so definitely beige flag for lack of experience."

Ally frowns. "Your poor vagina. I feel like I should send it a condolence card attached to a vibrator."

I giggle. "The gift that keeps on giving."

Chapter FIFTEEN

Flynn

I unlock the apartment door, but it's chained on the inside. "Hey, open the door!"

"Shh..." Monroe eyes me just above the chain.

"What are you doing? Unlock the door."

"Naomi's pregnant."

"Well, it's not mine. Now open the damn door."

"Shh! She's not feeling well. I'll let you in, but we have to discuss a few things first."

"Monroe." I grit my teeth, punching my arm through the crack and grabbing his shirt. "Open. The. Fucking. Door."

"You have to move out," he hisses, peeling his shirt from my hand. "I'm sorry, man, she's pregnant, and she wants you out."

"Fine. I'll move out. Just let me in, and I'll start looking for a place tomorrow."

"No, Flynn. She wants you out *now* because she doesn't

think you'll ever leave unless we just kick you out. And she knows about the money, so she said you can stay at a hotel."

"I don't have a credit card. Do you know how hard it is to find a hotel that accepts cash alone?"

"Give me the cash, and I'll book you a room with mine."

"They'll ask to see the credit card when I check in. Are you coming with me?"

He sighs. "Fine."

"Great. Now let me in."

"Promise to just get your stuff and go quietly?"

"Jeez, yes, you dumb ass."

Monroe closes the door to unlock it and then opens it again.

"Way to knock her up," I grumble, collecting my belongings. It's going to be great fun showing up to a hotel with everything I own in a dented trunk with rusty hinges.

"Dude, I love her. You don't know her like I do. She's actually pretty great when you get to know her." He follows me around the apartment like a dog that just destroyed my slippers and wants forgiveness with a pat on the head.

"She's mental. Sweet one minute, raging the next. Good luck with that."

"It's just hormones. And I want you to be my best man at our wedding."

"Whatever." I dump my toiletries into a duffel bag. "You know where to find me."

"Come on, Flynn. Just because you're not sleeping on my sofa doesn't mean our friendship has to end."

I turn and peer down at him because he's a couple inches shorter. "Get on your knees and say *please.*"

He squints for a second, then he starts to kneel on the floor.

"Get up, dipshit." I grab his shirt and pull him back to his feet. "You have nine months to grow a pair. Don't be a little pussy of a husband and father. Be the man of the house. Piss standing up. Shit wherever you damn well please. But never lay a hand on her or your kids. Got it?"

Monroe swallows hard and nods.

I release him and gather the rest of my stuff. Then I drag the trunk toward the door.

"You know I'm not a pussy. I just care about you, man. And I don't want you to hate me for choosing a chick over you."

I stop at the door and bow my head while closing my eyes. "I bought June a car today. Spent half my paycheck on it. Then I refused to have sex with her because I like her so much, and I don't know how to do the whole relationship thing. No fucking clue how to tell her about my time in prison because I'm scared of losing her. So who's the pussy now?"

Monroe grabs his keys and shoves his feet into his Jordans. "You should live with her."

"She has a roommate."

"So?"

"So, I can't buy her a car and then confess that I need a place to live."

"Why not?" He shuts the door behind us before lifting the other end of the trunk.

"I don't know," I mumble on the way down the stairs.

After he helps load the trunk into my car on the street, I playfully punch his shoulder. "Just go back upstairs. I'll figure something out."

"What?" He takes a step backward. "No. It's no big deal.

I don't want you doing anything stupid like living in your car."

"I've done it before."

He winces, shaking his head. "No. You have too much money to do that shit."

I open the car door. "I have a better idea. Don't worry about me."

"Flynn—"

"Just go back upstairs. I've got this."

He sighs, shoulders curling inward.

"Hey," I say, and he looks up. "Congratulations. Really."

Monroe grins. "Thanks. I'm scared out of my fucking mind."

"Yeah? Well, you should be," I say, getting into my car.

For a few seconds, I consider driving to June's apartment, but my ego overrules that idea. I don't want to be the male version of Naomi. Suddenly, Ally feels forced out of her home or made to feel like a third wheel. Instead, I make my way to the Rawlings' house. When I floated the idea to Callie about staying with them, she didn't respond, so I'm not sure they'll welcome me with open arms after writing me a check for five grand.

However, thanks to Callie's trust in me, I know the code for the side access door to the garage.

My phone's alarm wakes me at five thirty Sunday morning, a reminder that I will wake at the ass crack of dawn, even on the weekends, until I figure out how to get a place of my own. I climb out of the Chevelle's back seat. Then I bathe and brush my teeth in the dog wash. I stow my belongings behind neatly stacked containers labeled "Christmas garland" and head to my car before Rupert decides to play a round of real golf.

What do early risers do with themselves at this hour if not obligated to be at work?

Sleep.

I pull into the Walmart parking lot and catch another two hours of sleep. This time when my phone wakes me, it's not my stupid alarm.

"Hey," I answer June's call. "Thought you preferred texting."

"Did I wake you? You sound tired."

"Nope. I'm actually at Walmart already."

"Grocery shopping?"

I raise the back of my seat. "Uh, sure." I clear the frog from my throat.

"Sure?"

"Well, it's Walmart. You come for one thing and leave with ten. Hopefully, I make it out of here with a few groceries on my list."

"Ha. I get that. Anyway, my parents called me late last night. They're coming for a visit. I want you to meet them."

Shit.

"No pressure," she says. "It would be something simple like dinner. But if you're not ready for that—"

"No. I'm, uh ..." I fix my hair in the rearview mirror. "I'm good with meeting your parents."

"Great. How's six sound?"

"What day? I'll let Callie know I need to be off in time."

"Today. You're not working, right?"

"Today?" I roll down the window because it's hot in

here, or maybe it's the news of her parents coming today. "That's soon," I say.

"They've been in Chicago, so they thought they'd *pop up here* to visit me."

I rub the back of my neck. "Cool. Can't wait."

"They're the best. I promise you'll love them."

"Did you tell them the same thing about me?"

"Of course."

Crap. That's a lot of pressure. I get out of my car. Since I'm here, I might as well grab some snacks and something to drink.

"But I didn't get into details about us. I'm saving the really good stuff for when they get here."

"What's the really good stuff?"

"I'm going to tell them you have a fascinating job for super nice people. You put yourself between me and oncoming traffic when we're near a street. You never look at your phone when we're together. You say the most romantic things, yet I don't think you're trying to be romantic. It's just something that's effortless for you."

I laugh. "It's not effortless. It's painful because I rarely realize what I'm saying until it's too late. So as long as you know this might not end well for us tonight ..."

"They're going to love you," she says with confidence.

I wish I could see myself the way she does. What if they're the parents who do a background check on their daughter's boyfriend? This could be the beginning of the end.

Chapter SIXTEEN

June

"My girl," Mom says, hugging me the second I open the apartment door.

"Hey!" I melt into her embrace. The familiar scent of coconut oil in her long blond hair makes me feel like I'm a shy little girl again, burying my face in her hair because people are staring at me and my cleft lip.

My mom is ageless, like my grandma.

"Dad!" I throw myself into his arms when Mom releases me.

I don't have to see my mom to know she's rolling her eyes. Yeah, I've been a daddy's girl for as long as I can remember.

"How are you, baby?" he asks.

"Good. Better than good." I release him.

"Would this have anything to do with a certain man you've met?" Mom asks, kicking off her sneakers.

I blush, biting back the huge grin dying to steal across my entire face.

"Spill." Mom grabs my wrist and pulls me to sit next to her on the sofa, angling her body toward mine like she's my best friend and not my mom. She's both, really.

Dad escapes into the kitchen, opening cabinet doors until he finds a glass. He's pretending he can't hear us.

"Well, I told you his name is Flynn, and he's a muse." I wait for Mom's response.

"That's ..." Her eyes widen for a few seconds in false excitement, then she deflates. "Sorry, baby. What's a muse? I mean, I know the definition of a muse. I'm just not familiar with it in the context of a job."

"That makes two of us," Dad says, sitting in the chair next to the sofa.

So much for his ignoring our conversation.

"This guy and his wife live in a big house not too far from here. I don't know what they do, maybe they're retired. He hired Flynn to be a muse for his wife. According to Flynn, the husband, Rupert, said his wife, Callie, needs inspiration to live." I scrunch my nose. "It's disturbing. But I've met her. And she's pleasant. I'm not sure what's happened to her, but apparently her husband thinks Flynn is inspiring."

"Is he?" Mom asks with a conspiratorial grin.

When I give a little shrug, she perks up. My dad doesn't share her excitement. Mom wants me to find myself and then find love, like she did. But Dad wants me back in California chasing old dreams.

"When do we get to meet him?" Mom asks.

"I've invited him to join us for dinner tonight. *But* he

doesn't know much about my past. Not the big stuff. Well, that's not entirely true. I told him about the abduction."

My parents wince at the same time. I can't foresee a day when mentioning that time in our lives won't cause them physical pain. After several years of therapy, I called it quits. Declared myself cured. Now I mention it as if I'm talking about someone else.

"I just told him I was taken and not harmed, then they recovered me safely."

Mom curls her hair behind one ear and clears her throat. "Sweetheart, if he means enough to you for us to meet him, why have you been so selective with sharing everything about yourself?"

"You don't trust him?" Dad asks.

I shake my head. "He grew up in the system. And he wasn't treated well. In fact, I suspect he was abused pretty badly. I think he has trust issues, especially with people who he thinks have had an easier life than him. Which ..."

Mom frowns. "Which is most everyone."

I nod. "So I'm taking it slowly."

"That's best," Dad says.

Mom eyes him with surprise. Secrets nearly ended their relationship before they got married.

"Oh, in case it comes up in conversation tonight, he bought me a car." I offer a tight grin as they gawk at me. "Nothing fancy. It was only twenty-five hundred dollars. He didn't know I don't have a driver's license. It's a really, really sweet gesture. Especially for someone who doesn't have a lot of money."

Their expressions remain skeptical, so I jump into my list of swoon-worthy things about him. Starting with how he made me feel cool for having a scar on my lip.

"Oh! Here he comes," I say, pushing back in my chair at the Italian restaurant. "Just be cool," I remind my parents.

Mom chuckles behind her wine glass. "I think you're the one who needs to be cool."

Am I shaking with excitement and nerves as he worms his way toward us? Yes. Should I hug him? Kiss him? Neither? Both?

Gah!

He looks so sexy in his dark jeans and white button-down with the sleeves rolled just below his elbows.

Slicked-back hair.

A day's worth of stubble along his jaw.

"You look beautiful," he says as if my parents aren't waiting for an introduction. Then he leans in and kisses my cheek, resting his hand on my lower back. "You're giving me dirty thoughts," he whispers in my ear.

My whole body goes up in flames. Did they hear him? God, I hope not.

"Thank you," I murmur, then I clear my throat. "Flynn, I'd like you to meet my parents, Henna and Bodhi."

My dad stands and shakes Flynn's hand. "Nice to meet you. Our daughter has been singing your praises all afternoon." Dad winks at me.

"It's a pleasure to meet you, Flynn." Mom stands and hugs him.

Oh god. This is happening.

"Nice to meet you both." Flynn lowers partway to his chair before standing upright again. "After you," he says, holding the back of my chair.

Mom gives me a tiny approving nod.

When Flynn sits next to me, he rests his hand on my leg. *High* on my leg. What's happening? I've thrown myself at him, and he's given me crumbs. But now that we're in public, with my parents, he's thinking dirty thoughts and teasing me with a seductively placed hand, fingers brushing my inner thigh exposed from my short skirt?

"Did you have a good flight?" Flynn asks my parents, reaching for his glass of water.

They look at each other for a split second, nodding in sync.

"Do you like to fly?" I ask Flynn before either of my parents elaborates on their trip.

"Dunno." He shrugs before sipping his water. "Never been on a plane. Never left Minnesota, for that matter. Well, that's not entirely true. I've crossed the border into Iowa once or twice."

"How old are you?" Mom asks.

"Twenty-five."

"And you've never been on a plane?" Her eyebrows rise.

Flynn shakes his head like it's no big deal, like it's perfectly normal to be twenty-five and have no travel experience.

"I know you've been to California and here, obviously," he says to me. "Have you been to other states?"

My dad chokes on his drink.

I scowl at him while he presses his fist to his mouth. Then I smile softly at Flynn. "Yeah, I've been to a few other states. What are you going to order?"

Just as I think things are back on track—food is ordered, and Mom lists off a few places they plan to see while in Minneapolis—my dad derails the evening again. "So, Flynn," he says. "What are your intentions with my daughter?"

I wrinkle my nose at him. Could he be any more archaic? The gleam in his blue eyes negates his seriousness, but I don't know if Flynn sees it.

"Well"—Flynn finishes chewing the warm bread that he dipped in olive oil—"I have not been in her pants, if that's what you're asking."

Mom snorts, spitting a few drops of wine, instantly blushing as it splatters toward my plate.

I want to die, but there's no time for that because Flynn returns his hand to my leg and his pinky finger brushes my crotch. With a tiny gasp, I cover his hand with mine, but I don't know if I want to push him away or keep him there.

"I like you, Flynn," Dad says, tossing an approving grin in our direction. "I like you a lot."

Flynn's shoulders push back an extra inch as he takes a breath and returns his own brand of an approving smile. Does Flynn know what the word *intention* means? And why is my dad letting him get away with a ridiculous answer? Intentions are plans for the future. Flynn told my dad what had not happened in the past. That's not an intention.

I bite my lower lip when Flynn's pinky finger makes another brush between my legs. Through the corner of my eye, I catch the twitch of a smile along Flynn's lips just before he stabs his fork into his salad.

"So what do you do, Mr. Malone?" Flynn asks.

I cautiously eye my dad.

"Not enough," Mom teases.

Flynn chuckles. "Are you retired?"

Dad playfully scowls at my mom while shaking his head. "I do a little of this and that. I've worked on a horse ranch; I was a guidance counselor; I've worked for ZIP Tunes; but mostly I do whatever Henna tells me to do."

I stare at Flynn as he slowly nods. And I wait for him to ask more questions, but he doesn't. When he's not looking at her, Mom gives me a little wink.

"So how did you two meet?" Flynn asks my parents as our food is delivered to our table.

When everyone has their meal, I clear my throat. I know my parents don't enjoy sharing their story with just anyone, but I could listen to it a million times and never tire of hearing it.

Mom and Dad look at each other.

"Fine," I say. "I'll tell it."

"We met at Coachella," Mom says. "It's a music festival. And it was the spring before my senior year of high school. Then we texted throughout the summer, and Bodhi just so happened to be new at the school in the fall. We had no idea."

Dad keeps his head bowed, twirling pasta with his fork.

"That's cool," Flynn says, like it's not that exciting.

And the way my parents tell it *is not* that exciting because they leave out the best part.

"Oh shoot," I say. "I think my mom forgot to mention that my dad wasn't a student. He was her new guidance counselor."

Flynn's eyebrows jump up his forehead, jaw slack. Yeah, that's the correct response to the real story.

"She was eighteen," Dad says before swallowing his spaghetti.

"That didn't matter," I say. "It was still a scandal. But Grandpa Malone, whom I never got to meet, was sick. So Dad couldn't lose his job. But they got caught, so Mom left. They broke up. It was tragic and beautiful and ..." I sigh. "So epic."

Mom rolls her eyes, but not without grinning.

"There are more juicy details like how they messed around in his office."

"I don't think Flynn or anyone needs those details while we're eating, or ever for that matter," Dad says.

"I'll tell you later," I whisper to Flynn, loud enough for my parents to hear me.

Flynn snorts, bringing his fist to his mouth.

I want what my parents have. I want it *so* much.

Chapter
SEVENTEEN

Flynn

MONDAY MORNING, I wake up in the back of the Chevelle, bathe in the dog wash, brush my teeth, dress, and trek to the front of the house to knock on the door by six.

"Good morning," Rupert says, eyeing me with a funny look.

"What?" I say, stepping inside and kicking off my shoes.

"Nothing. I just said good morning."

"What's with the look?" I narrow my eyes at him.

"What look?" He closes the door.

"Never mind. Good morning." I tuck my hands into my back pockets. "Is Mrs. Rawlings awake? Should I get her tea?"

"She's awake. Pilates is in an hour. I'm not sure if she wants tea now or after Pilates."

"Pilates?"

"It's an exercise class."

"I've heard of Pilates. Is this something new?"

"Yes." He heads toward the kitchen. "She signed up for the class yesterday, but she used to take it before everything went to shit."

What does that mean?

"Am I driving her?" I follow him.

He chuckles. "Yes. You're driving her. And you're taking the class with her. She had me pick you up proper clothing yesterday. You're welcome."

"Dude, I don't do Pilates."

He refills his coffee mug. "*Dude*, I wrote a check for five grand. You definitely do Pilates. Yoga. Ballroom dancing ..."

I bite my tongue while he sits at the counter, wearing a smirk that acknowledges just how hard I'm biting it.

"Did you have a nice weekend?" he asks.

"It was okay. I bought June a car."

He pauses his mug at his mouth. "Wow. Things must be serious."

"Things are ..." I shake my head. "I think. I don't know. They're what they are. But she needed a car."

"Is that what she said?"

"No, but ride-sharing every day has to be expensive."

"Was she complaining about it?"

I shake my head.

"Did she say she needed a car?"

Again, I shake my head.

"Well, Flynn. In theory, a car sounds like a great gift. But it's like encouraging someone to get a cat."

I frown.

"If it requires maintenance that you're not providing, then mind your own business."

"Don't listen to him," Callie interrupts us, padding into

the kitchen in pink workout attire, hair pulled into a small ponytail. "Flowers require maintenance or they will die. Jewelry requires cleaning. Clothes must be laundered." She sets Loki down, and he weaves between my legs.

"Callie, he bought June a car."

"Oh?" she says, filling a sports bottle with filtered water from the fridge. "Was she excited?"

"Yeah."

I think.

"Then good for you."

Rupert shakes his head.

"I met her parents last night," I say.

Her eyes widen as she screws on the lid. "How did that go?"

"Great. I think they like me."

"Well of course they do," she says.

"Interesting." Rupert scratches his chin. "How much did you share about yourself?"

"Rupert," Callie scolds.

"What? Honesty matters if things have progressed to the point of meeting her parents."

"Listen"—I hold up my hand in surrender—"I have it on good authority that oversharing early in a relationship is not such a good idea."

The Rawlings study me for a second before looking at each other. They've both cautioned me about telling her too early, but also about telling her too late. How the hell am I supposed to know the definition of *early* and *late* on this matter?

"That's true *sometimes*," she says, picking up Loki and cradling him in one arm. "However, it's one thing to wait to tell her you don't like her cooking. It's another to mention, on your honeymoon, how you did time."

"That's a terrible example." Rupert scoffs. "You were fine with my legal indiscretions. But I know if I were to say one bad thing about your cooking, I'd be on the street."

"You are so full of it, Rupert Seaman Rawlings." She flicks her wrist at him. "Flynn, we're going to Pilates. Your clothes are on the vanity in the hall bathroom off the entryway. I'll meet you in the car in ten minutes."

When she's out of the kitchen, I give Mr. Rawlings my full attention, crossing my arms over my chest.

He avoids eye contact, rinsing out his coffee mug at the sink.

"Your middle name is Semen?"

"S.E.A.M.A.N," he says. "Like a sailor. Man of the sea."

"Wow." I roll my lips between my teeth to keep from grinning when he turns toward me, daring me to say another word. "I mean ... you don't *come* across that name very often."

"Go put on your unitard so you don't make my wife late for class."

I laugh at his attempt to get even, but when I stop into the bathroom and discover the black unitard, I close my eyes and tap my fists against my forehead. "Fuck."

Before I open the bathroom door to head to the garage in the world's most embarrassing getup, my phone chimes with a text.

June: What are you doing? Working?

Flynn: Mowing the lawn with my shirt off

Flynn: Chopping down trees with a big ax

I peek out the door and run toward the stairs.

"Have a good class," Rupert calls.

I don't give him the satisfaction of turning around so he can see the outline of my junk. Instead, I wave goodbye with my middle finger.

Fire me. Please. Do it!

He snickers. "Back at ya, bud."

When I open the driver's door to the Tesla, Callie smacks her hand over her mouth, eyes bugging out.

"You didn't pick this out?" I ask, sliding into the seat.

She slowly shakes her head, snorting despite her best efforts.

I grumble, pulling out of the garage.

She clears her throat to compose herself while entering the address onto the screen. "He likes you."

"Ya. For sure. This is the exact workout wear you buy for someone you like."

"It's all just a game to him. If I like you, he thinks I'll fall back in love with him. You're him thirty-five years ago. You look like him. You act like him—"

"Am I going to find out he's my long-lost daddy? You got pregnant at the wrong time. To avoid a scandal, you gave me up for adoption, but now you're trying to make things right with me?"

When she doesn't answer, I glance at her. Sadness lines her face.

"Shit. I'm joking. But am I right?" For a moment, anger boils up from the pit of my stomach to my throat, cutting off my next breath. For years I've imagined what I'd say to my biological parents if I ever met them. Did she used to have long, black hair?

"No." She shakes her head. "I don't mean it in a literal sense. Sorry."

"Sorry?" I refocus on the road. "What do you have to apologize for?"

"I'm sure it's a sensitive subject. And I didn't mean to bring up your past in that way. We're not your parents. We would never do that to a child."

"I've got June," I say.

"Yes," she says slowly.

I shrug. "I've got June. That's all that matters. Had my parents not abandoned me, had I not gone through all that I did, I wouldn't have gotten this job. And this job led me to June."

She leans her head back and closes her eyes. "Flynn?"

"Yeah?"

"You're a good man. *June* is the lucky one. Don't ever forget that."

What. The. Fuck?

Pilates is nothing more than women gathering to stretch on wonky machines while listening to Chappell Roan, Sabrina Carpenter, and Taylor Swift. They compliment each other on their "cute" workout wear and go for foo-foo coffee drinks afterward.

"Are you coming tomorrow?" one of the women asks me after class as they all gather around me in a circle. It's worth mentioning this class is only older women. They look great, but they're all old enough to be my mother. However, they love my unitard.

"He'll absolutely be here," Callie says. "And we'll get you something a little less revealing to wear. Something less distracting."

"Callie?" The instructor stops us. She squeezes Callie's hand. "I'm so glad you're back. We've missed you."

She returns a half smile. "Thank you, Tracey."

"If you ever want to talk—" Tracey says.

"I'm good, but thank you." Callie continues toward the exit.

I don't say anything on the drive home until we're halfway to the house. "Why do you need a muse?"

"I don't."

"Why does Mr. Rawlings think you need one?"

"I told you. He thinks I need to fall back in love with him, but that's not the problem. Marriages go through many seasons. Ours is in winter. It's been a long winter."

"So you haven't been to Pilates because your marriage is in winter?"

"Sort of." She keeps her gaze out the window.

"I don't understand," I say.

"It's complicated."

"Are you saying I can't handle complicated? My whole life has been complicated." I slow down to let ducks cross the road toward the lake.

"You're a muse. Not a therapist."

"Do you have a therapist?"

"I used to."

"Do you want to kill yourself?" The words come out like a breath I've been holding too long—the thing everyone is thinking, but no one wants to say.

And now I know why.

Saying it makes it feel like a real possibility. There's no more deniability. If she does it, no one can say, "I had no idea."

Fuck.

What have I done?

"What are you going to do if I say yes?" she asks with no emotion in her words.

I slam on the brakes just before pulling into the garage, racking my brain for what possible reason she would have to kill herself.

"You're depressed," I say, and I'm not sure if I'm asking her a question or stating the only possible reason she might have.

"Have you ever been depressed?" she asks.

"I don't really know what that means. Sad? Are you asking if I've been sad? Because my life has been a constant string of awful things. Is that sad? Probably. Do I want to kill myself? No."

"Do you feel sad every day?"

I shake my head, feeling irritated. Discussing emotions has never been my thing. But I can't complain because I started this conversation. "I get angry and pissed off. Annoyed by others. Sadness just feels like a worthless emotion. What's the point of it unless someone dies—" I close my eyes and slowly shake my head as a light goes on. "Someone died," I whisper.

Silence.

I'm afraid to look at her, so I open my eyes and stare into the garage. Rupert's cars. The far wall where I have my belongings hidden. I look at anything but her.

"Thank you for going with me to class," she says. "See if

there's anything Rupert wants you to do. You've inspired me enough today." She doesn't wait for me to open her door. And I don't feel like she's being honest about me inspiring her today.

When she's in the house, I call June.

"Hey!" she answers with a cheery voice.

I immediately relax. "What are you doing?"

"Shopping with my mom before I have to work this afternoon. What are you doing?"

"I'm in a unitard, sitting in Callie's Tesla, talking to you instead of checking in with Rupert, which is what I'm supposed to be doing."

"Wait." She laughs. "Back up. You're in a unitard?"

"Yeah. I look like a wrestler."

"Is there a reason you're wearing it?"

"I've been enrolled in Pilates with Callie."

June snorts. "And you wore a unitard to class? Why?"

"Because Rupert is a dick."

"I'm going to need a picture."

"Hell no," I say.

"I'll send you a picture of me."

"In a unitard?"

"In the bikini I'm trying on right now in the dressing room."

I've never snapped a selfie so fast in my life. "Sent," I say.

"Oh, just got it, let me look. Wait, it's only the top half of your body."

"That's all you get. Now send me a pic."

"I'm only sending the top half of my body."

"That's fine." I laugh.

"Ugh. No. I'll send the bottom half."

"That works too."

"Flynn. This isn't fair. No picture for you. If you want to see my bikini, you'll have to come to my apartment later, and I'll show you."

"When are your parents leaving?"

"They haven't decided yet. But I'm sure after dinner tonight, they'll go back to their hotel, and I'll be at my apartment. You should come to dinner with us again."

"I'm sure they're here to see you, not me."

"Stop. I want you to come."

"I know you do, but we're talking about dinner with your parents right now."

"Oh my god, Flynn. You're all talk. No action."

"There's a name for what I am," I say. "But I don't actually know what word I'm looking for because I've never used it. If someone said it, I'd recognize it."

"That's helpful," she says.

"It makes me think of being cold, but it's not *shiver*."

"Chivalrous?"

"That's it!"

June laughs. "You think not having sex with me is chivalrous?"

"I think your dad would think it is."

"My dad took my mom's virginity while she was in high school. He's not an expert on chivalry. Did you call me just to say that you went to Pilates in a unitard? I'm fine with it. Just curious."

"Nah, I'm just …"

"Just? Is something wrong?"

I sigh, leaning my head back. "This job. It's so weird. And I'm kinda tired of not knowing what the deal is with Callie. So today, I flat-out asked her if she's depressed and wants to kill herself."

"Whoa ... seriously?"

"Yeah. And I couldn't take it back."

"How did she react? What did she say?"

"She said, 'What are you going to do if I say yes?' So I said she must be depressed. She never answered me. But I threw out the possibility someone died, and I just got the feeling that was it. I'm still sitting in her car, but she's inside. I'm supposed to check with Rupert to see if he needs me to do anything for him. I suck at this job."

"Why did you apply for it?"

"It's ... uh ... a long story. I'd better get inside before they wonder where I'm at."

"I like long stories."

"Noted. Later. K?"

"Later," she says.

Chapter
EIGHTEEN

Flynn

"How was Pilates?" Rupert asks when I poke my head into his office after changing out of my unitard.

"What exactly do you do?" I step inside and collapse onto his sofa. "I mean, you put on a suit every day. But why?"

"Sorry. I wasn't aware there was a performance review today," he says, leaning back in his desk chair while adjusting his loose tie.

"I think I fucked up," I say.

"Of course, you did." He smirks. "But you'll have to be more specific."

I flop onto my back, and stare at the ceiling with my hands folded on my chest. "Who died?"

Crickets.

I turn my head to look at him.

He steeples his fingers under his chin. "Why do you ask?"

"I hate that question," I grumble, returning my focus to the ceiling. "It's such a stupid question. Obviously if someone asks a question, they do it because they want to know the answer."

"Let me rephrase. What makes you think someone died?"

"I was trying to figure out why your wife would want to kill herself—"

"I never said she wanted to kill herself."

"Dude"—I sit up—"you said I needed to inspire her to live. I know I'm not the smartest person in the world, but I'm not the dumbest either."

He leans forward, resting his arms on his desk. "Some people just exist. They wake, go through the same boring routine, sleep, and do it all over again the next day. And the day after, and the day after. They *exist*. And they do it with no inclination not to exist. But that's not living."

"So Mrs. Rawlings is boring, and you want me to inspire her to be more exciting?"

He studies me for several seconds before shaking his head.

"I hate being kept in the dark. That's how I fuck up. And this morning I asked Mrs. Rawlings if she wanted to kill herself."

He winces.

"It's not my fault. You blackmailed me into taking this position, as if a muse is an everyday job. Then you made me think she's suicidal, but no other explanation. You're a shitty communicator."

He squints at me.

I clear my throat. "Respectfully."

"Well"—he frowns like he's mocking me—"if you say

respectfully after insulting someone, it makes everything okay."

"Is it your son?"

"My son?"

"Did your son die? Thinking back, I had a conversation with Mrs. Rawlings about him. It wasn't a long one. But when I asked where he lived, she said, 'Wherever he wants.' And that seemed a little weird. But now that I think about it, maybe she meant his spirit. Like a ghost or something."

Mr. Rawlings twists his lips to the side for a second. "I can see how you might think that."

"So *did* he die? God, I'm not trying to be insensitive. If he died, that's tragic. But tragedy is part of life. You wouldn't be the first people to have lost a child. But when you keep everything a secret, it makes it impossible for everyone around you not to fuck up and say the wrong thing."

His forehead wrinkles, and I think that's my answer. Now I feel like an asshole for a second time. If he cries, I'm outta here.

"A week after my eleventh birthday," I say, "I was placed in a new foster home. The couple had lost their only two children in a school bus accident like a year or two earlier. I'm not sure why they thought fostering a child was a good idea. The wife got tears in her eyes every time she looked at me. And her husband told me to just mind my own business and stay out of the way unless I could do something other than make her cry. Sometimes I see that same sadness in Mrs. Rawlings' eyes."

"How long were you with that couple?" he asks.

"A few weeks. I made the mistake of going into their son's bedroom and playing with his toys."

"Then what happened?"

I pull down the neck of my shirt and point to a surgical scar. "Broken clavicle. Fell down the stairs."

His gaze stays on my chest even after I let go of my shirt. "She pushed you down the stairs?"

"No. I tripped and fell while making a mad dash because I was afraid of what they might do. Experience taught me to assume the worst."

His eyes shift, meeting my gaze and blinking slowly. "Our son's name is Seth. He's alive, but we haven't heard from him in seven years."

"Why?"

"Because"—he clears his throat and turns in his chair, so he's staring out the window instead of at me—"his two-year-old son died on our watch."

Jesus ...

I run my fingers through my hair and lace them behind my head. Then I open my mouth to respond, but I have nothing. Less than nothing. What's the response to that? It's okay? No. The kid is dead. It's not okay.

"Some things feel unforgivable," he mumbles just above a whisper. "This is one of them. It's not a misunderstanding or petty fight. He lost everything. And now we have too."

I slowly shake my head and stand. "Mr. Rawlings, I-I can't make this better for her or you or anyone. Whatever you think I can do, I can't. I'm not your son. I can't bring your grandson back. There is nothing special about me. You know this. I'm a fuck-up just trying to keep my head above water. And everything that comes out of my mouth is stupid, and probably hurtful even if I don't mean for it to be. So this isn't going to work. I can't be—"

"Flynn," he says, turning toward me. "Have you ever heard the phrase, *throw anything at the wall until it sticks?*"

I nod.

"Well, that's what I'm doing because I've lost my grandson, daughter-in-law, and my son. I can't lose my wife too. But that's what's been happening. Every day, she continues to disengage from our life together. Every smile feels forced. But for you, she'll get out of bed. She'll go to Pilates and matinees. And for your new female friend, she'll make tea and wear her best smile. A real smile. I'm not asking you to replace anyone we've lost." He sighs slowly, shaking his head. "I'm just asking you to give her a new focus. And I don't care if you don't know what you're doing. Just keep ... doing it."

Screw the money. I don't want this. My whole life has been doom and gloom. One tragedy after another. What if I give him back what's left of the money and ask to call it even?

"If you think I'm doing a good job, then why the stupid Pilates getup? Why give me shit about the cat?"

He offers a sad smile. "Maybe you're my muse too."

I wrinkle my nose. "How's that?"

Shrugging, he opens his laptop. "When I look at you, I see how far I've come."

"Uh, thanks. I guess. I'm not sure it's a compliment."

"It's not." He smirks, tapping the keys. "But I wish my dad would have joked around with me."

"I don't need a dad," I say.

"Maybe I'm not doing this for you."

I sigh. What do I say to that? "Mrs. Rawlings told me to ask you if you want me to do anything else today. I think I've depressed her enough that she's done with me."

"Bring the girl back over. That'll cheer her up."

"Now? Her parents are in town. She's bikini shopping with her mom."

Rupert eyes me over his keyboard. "Lucky you."

I roll my eyes.

"Whenever she's free is fine."

I nod and turn, but then I make the stupid decision to face him again to ask for his advice when deep down I know he will not offer me anything helpful. "How long did you wait to have sex with Mrs. Rawlings when you met her? If, uh ... ya don't mind me asking."

"Why do you ask?"

"Jesus, we just went over this."

He chuckles, closing his laptop again. "I waited until our third date."

"So like ... a couple weeks or so?"

"No. When we met, she flat-out told me she wouldn't even consider having sex with a guy until at least the third date. So I asked her to breakfast before she had class. Then I waited outside of her apartment with a bag of fried chicken for lunch—date number two. And that night, I took her for pizza and roller skating—date three."

"Three dates in one day?"

His grin oozes pride as he nods.

"So you had sex with her that night?"

"Bingo." He winks and makes a clicking noise with his tongue. "When you know, you know."

"What happened to taking it slow so a girl knows you're interested in more than just her body?" I ask.

"Nothing *happened* to it. Some of us don't have to work as hard as others. Does your friend have you waiting longer than you want? All in the name of *taking it slow*? If so, you should respect that about her. But also ... that's probably not a good sign for you. Some other guy's going to shove you aside and do all the things right that you're doing wrong."

Again, I roll my eyes. "You don't know what you're talking about." I turn and leave his office. But just in case he does know, I head straight to June's apartment to stick my dick in her, like a flag on a new frontier.

When I get to her place, I press the buzzer.

"Hello?" she answers.

"It's me, Juju."

She giggles. "Don't call me that. It sounds weird coming from you. Come on up."

By the time I reach the top of the stairs, she's waiting for me with the door open. "Hey—"

I cut her off with a kiss, sealing my mouth firmly to hers. Tongue sliding past her lips. She grips my arms to steady herself as I back her into the apartment and kick the door shut behind us.

A deep noise, another man clearing his throat, pulls me away from her. She gasps for a breath, brown eyes wide with surprise. Behind her, Henna and Bodhi eye us from the sofa.

Fuck my life.

"Still staying out of my daughter's pants?" her dad asks.

June bites her lips together as if she's dying to smile but showing restraint. Henna winks at her daughter when June stands in front of me, facing them.

"I, uh ..." I rub my eyes. "I'll come back."

"No." June faces me, nose wrinkled.

"Baby, let's take a walk," Henna says to Bodhi.

As they pass us, I pinch the bridge of my nose and close my eyes, not opening them until I hear the door click shut.

"What a pleasant surprise," June says with a little giggle.

I open my eyes. "This is not my day."

"Did things not go well with the Rawlings after your overly candid conversation with Callie this morning?"

"No. Yes. I mean ..." I grumble a few words that make little sense as I park my hands on my hips and gaze at the ceiling for a breath. "I want in your pants."

When I look at June, her lips part into an O. This is not me. I'm cooler than this. If I could just think of June as a one-night stand, I'd have way more confidence. My dick knows what to do. It's never lacking confidence. But this girl is in my head, and I want her to like me beyond my dick. But the rest of me isn't as impressive.

As her surprise settles into a big smile and even bigger blush, she starts to unbutton her white blouse.

"Whoa! No." I grab her hands to stop her. "No. Not now. Your parents just took a walk."

"They know how long it takes to have sex. I'm sure they'll give us plenty of time."

"What?" I shake my head and chuckle while stepping back to keep a safe distance. "No. I'm not having sex with you and then just pretending like nothing happened while they were sightseeing. No way."

"Take your clothes off," she says, resuming her unbuttoning.

"Stop." I continue shaking my head.

"Ally won't be home for another hour." She wets her lips.

My gaze sticks to the cleavage above the cups of her light pink bra.

"The Rawlings had a two-year-old grandson who died on their watch."

June pauses her hands on the last button as she sucks in a sharp breath. Lines of anguish spread across her forehead. "Oh my god," she whispers.

The guy Rupert was talking about? The one who will shove me aside and give June what she wants? He won't care if her parents are just walking around the block. And he definitely won't bring up the tragic death of a child just as June is ready to shrug off her top.

I have an incurable case of dipshitness. And I don't know if it's contagious, but I'm pretty sure it's terminal.

As she buttons her shirt, I slowly mourn the loss of what could have been and grieve the man I once was.

"What happened?" she asks.

"I don't know," I mumble. "I had the best intentions. A screw-it moment. *Chivalry* no longer mattered. I just wanted—"

"Flynn, I'm talking about their grandson."

My gaze shoots to hers. "Oh." I shake my head. "I don't know. He didn't say, and I couldn't ask."

"That's why Callie is so sad," June says, combing her fingers through her hair.

It should be my fingers in her hair.

"How heartbreaking." She sits on the end of the sofa with a sad expression.

"Well, uh ... that's it. I just stopped by to kiss you really hard in front of your parents and let you know about their grandson." I gesture toward the door. "Enjoy your dinner."

"What?" She chuckles while pushing off the sofa toward me. "You're leaving?"

"I think it's for the best. Might be a good idea for me to spend some time alone, contemplating all the stupid things I've done and said since we met."

"Flynn," she says with a grin, shaking her head as if she's not sure what to say next.

"Don't say my name like that."

Her head slants to the side. "Like what?"

"Like you *like* me."

"Like you?" She stares at her feet as she steps closer to me. "That might be the biggest understatement anyone has ever made." Her beautiful eyes find me. "If only I just liked you, I might sleep better. My head would be clearer. This embarrassing and unfamiliar feeling of being boy crazed wouldn't consume me."

Well, shit. I'm going to do something I've never done: love someone—this girl—so much it will destroy me.

"You lose sleep over me?" I ask, curling her hair behind her ears before cupping her face in my hands. "And here I thought I was the only one losing sleep over ... *this*." I trace her scar, and her eyes close in a heavy blink. When she opens them, her hands grasp my wrists, and she opens her mouth so her tongue and teeth tease my thumb. It makes me feel ... privileged.

"You're the most beautiful"—I kiss her cheek—"sexy"—I kiss her nose—"smart"—I kiss her other cheek—"woman I have ever met. And I want"—my lips brush hers—"all of you in every way." We kiss, and the weight of her body falls against mine like she can't get close enough to me.

"You're a good man. June is the lucky one. Don't ever forget that." Callie's words echo in my head.

I've already forgotten.

Girls like June don't give guys like me a second look. If I can make her love me, it will feel like the greatest heist in history.

I want to steal all the kisses from her lips.

Claim every inch of her body.

And if I can take her heart ... well, there are no words for that.

She turns her head, ending the kiss, but grinning as she tries to catch her breath. "Now we don't have time."

"Sorry," I say, enjoying her disappointment. It means she wants me as much as I want her.

June sighs, blowing her hair away from her face, just as her phone chimes behind her on the coffee table. She grabs it and holds up the screen for me to see the text.

Mom: Text me when UR done

I roll my eyes. "Tell them to come back here. And make sure they know nothing has happened."

June frowns. "That's no fun."

"What's *no fun* is looking your dad in the eye when I know he thinks I was inside his daughter minutes before looking him in the eye."

"Fine." She sticks out her bottom lip while replying to her mom. *"There's nothing to finish. Just talking. Come back anytime."* Sliding her phone back onto the coffee table, she collapses onto the sofa. "Why did you take the job with the Rawlings?"

"Huh?" I squint, tucking my hands into my back pockets.

"You seem irritated with your job. Sometimes a little angry and frustrated. I'm curious why you took the job?" June laces her fingers over her knee and pulls it toward her chest, hooking her heel on the edge of the worn, saddle-brown leather sofa.

This conversation is inevitable. But I'm not sure the best time to have it is mere minutes from her parents returning. Imagine her Dad eyeing me with distrust *while* I'm in the middle of explaining how I chose my current position over going to jail—again.

"I worked for a mobile detail shop, and Rupert scheduled his car to be detailed. That's how we met. The rest is history." I shrug.

"So he met you and knew you'd be a good muse for Callie?"

"Yeah. I guess I remind him of himself at my age. Back when his wife found him more ..." I wave my hand in the air. "Appealing."

"Charming?"

I adjust an imaginary tie and tip up my chin. "You think I'm charming?" I back up, leaning against the door.

"I was suggesting Callie found Rupert quite charming when they were younger." She gives me a toothy grin before laughter bubbles up her throat. "Come here." She crooks a finger at me.

I slide the coffee table away from the sofa an extra foot and kneel in front of her, grabbing her legs to pull her closer so that I'm wedged between them. Her hands slide around my neck. They're warm and soft.

"I think you're charming too," she says, brushing her nose against mine.

I close my eyes and inhale her sweet floral scent. Everything about her is delicate and soft. Seductive. A dream, really. I swear to God it feels like I'm hallucinating, on the verge of waking up in the back seat of my car with nothing but my shitty belongings and a life of loneliness.

"I'm scared," she whispers.

I kiss her neck. "Why?"

Her fingers in my hair send waves of chills along my skin. "Because you're right. This feels big. Like I'm sitting on the edge of a plane in a harness, and the person strapped to the back of me with a parachute is telling me to just keep breathing because when we jump, the fall might steal my breath."

"June," I whisper before kissing her neck a little harder. An insatiable need flooding my veins. My fingers inch up the back of her shirt and unhook her bra.

"Flynn, my parents ..." she says in a breathy voice.

I steal her lips, kissing her with an open mouth, our tongues meeting in the middle.

June moans as I cup her breasts beneath her loose bra. I pull away. Her pupils are dilated, breaths heavy past her parted lips.

I guide her back, lifting her shirt to kiss her hard nipples. Her back arches, eyes heavily blinking.

"My parents," she murmurs with wavering conviction as I kiss my way down her body.

"I locked the door." I grin, kissing her inner thigh, one hand squeezing her breast while my other hooks the crotch of her cotton shorts and panties, exposing her flesh.

A sharp breath fills her lungs when my mouth makes contact. She claims a handful of my hair and squirms, chest rising and falling in quickening breaths, pelvis rocking in a slow rhythm. I could watch her all day like this and never tire. Her face twists, mouth open, and her breaths are not just fast; they're explosive. I squeeze her breast and pinch her nipple, giving it a little tug. She moans, screwing her eyes shut. Then she stops breathing for a second before exhaling slowly with a shudder.

I kiss her inner thigh again and fix her shorts and underwear. June opens her eyes and gives me a shy grin. She's so stunning with her cheeks pink, a few locks of hair teasing her long eyelashes.

"Flynn," she whispers.

I adjust myself. "You're welcome."

She giggles, sitting up straight and hooking her bra. "We should—" There's a knock on the door.

I quickly return the coffee table to its spot while June fixes her hair and adjusts her clothes on the way to the door. Just before she opens it, she eyes me over her shoulder. I wipe my mouth with the back of my hand. Her eyes flare as she bites her lips together.

With a silent chuckle, I shake my head.

Her smile escapes. "This is so big," she mouths before turning to open the door for her parents.

"Done talking?" Henna asks, stepping into the apartment first and pressing her hands to June's cheeks as if she's trying to erase the redness.

"Yep." June pushes her mom's hands away, and they exchange a look—tiny scowls but knowing grins.

Bodhi steps past the ladies and inspects me for a second.

"Sir," I say.

His brow furrows.

I clear my throat. "Mr. Malone."

He remains unmoving.

"Call him Bodhi," June says, taking my hand and interlacing our fingers as she lobs an irresistible grin at her father.

"Sir is fine," he says.

"Sir works for me." I shrug.

June and her mom synchronize their eye rolling.

"Let's go to dinner," June says.

"It's only three thirty." Bodhi looks at his watch.

"Flynn has to get up early for his job, so he needs to get to bed at a decent time," June chirps without missing a beat.

"Works for us." Henna fixes June's hair.

Again, June bats her mom's hand away.

"Maybe we should take my new car," June suggests.

Four in a MINI Cooper? Sounds like torture.

From the confusion on Bodhi's face, I can tell he's thinking the same thing.

"Mom and I will sit in back," June says, grabbing her phone and bag. Then she hands me the key.

I relinquish a nod and tight smile, waiting for her parents to go out the door first. As they head down the stairs, I turn toward June. "Do you know how tiny your car is?" I ask as she locks her apartment door.

"Sure do," she says, facing me after it's locked. "So tiny my dad will insist he and my mom grab their own ride back to the hotel after dinner." She winks.

"Genius," I say.

"I know." She flips her hair over her shoulder and saunters down the stairs.

I could drop to my knees again. This woman is a goddess. All I want to do is worship her until she loves me so much that minor little details like prison and *borrowing* cars that aren't mine won't matter to her.

Chapter
NINETEEN

June

MY DAD and Flynn find a common interest over dinner. Basketball. Dad is a Lakers fan, and Flynn is a Timberwolves fan.

"You've been to actual games?" Flynn asks.

Dad looks at me for a second before returning a subtle nod to Flynn.

"I've thought about splurging on tickets to a Timberwolves game, but it never feels like the right time to spend that kind of money. Ya know?"

"That means you're smart," Mom says. "A lot of people your age get themselves into financial trouble all in the name of fun."

"You should have bought tickets to a game instead of buying me a car." I nudge his leg.

Flynn nudges me back and grins over his bite of steak. "No way," he mumbles.

Mom gives me a look. It says she approves of him. It also says I could lose him if I don't tell him everything. I'm going to. I just want to know that he won't resent me for waiting so long.

"Speaking of tickets," Mom says. "We bought you two tickets to the Minnesota Orchestra—this week. Think you can talk Flynn into going with you?"

Flynn wipes his mouth. "Oh yeah. She mentioned she liked the cello."

Dad raises an eyebrow and slowly chuckles. "Well, she used to."

I ignore his little jab.

"Yeah, I'd love to go with you," Flynn says. "I know nothing about the orchestra, but there's really nothing I can imagine doing that wouldn't be amazing if it's with June."

Mom presses a hand to her heart.

I'm ready for the check. To-go containers. Whatever. Just get me out of here so I can be alone with Flynn.

It takes another twenty minutes of chitchat for that to happen, but when it does, I start to feel nervous. I like him so much; it's hard to breathe sometimes.

"We're flying out early in the morning, but we'll be back. And you should come back to L.A. for a visit soon too," Mom says, pulling me in for a long hug outside of the restaurant while Dad orders a ride (as predicted).

"I will," I say. "Love you."

"You too," she says.

"Don't just say you'll come back to L.A.," Dad warns, attempting to give me a serious expression before I hug him. "Actually do it." He hugs me so tightly I nearly cry.

My dad has championed everything in my life, making my dreams his.

"I promise." I kiss his cheek.

"It was wonderful meeting you, Flynn. You should come to L.A. too." Mom hugs him.

He doesn't reply with more than a smile. I'm not sure what that means.

"Young man, take care of my daughter. Got it?" Dad says in his most manly voice.

"Absolutely, sir," Flynn says. Then he takes my hand and guides me to the car as I look back and blow my parents one last kiss.

"Is your roommate home tonight?" I ask.

"Uh, yeah. Why?"

"So is Ally. No biggie. I just wanted to be alone with you." I wrap my arms around his neck when we get to the car parked on the street.

"Thought you had your own room," he says, teasing his fingers under my shirt an inch or so.

"I do. But I don't like the thought of someone listening."

"Listening to what?" He presses his lips together, eyes wide.

"Stop." I playfully nudge his leg.

"Are you a screamer?"

"Stop." I giggle. "Don't you have your own room?"

"It's a one-bedroom. So I sleep on the sofa, for a break in rent of course."

"You sleep on the sofa?"

He nods.

"What do you do with your clothes?"

"I have a big trunk."

Why does this make me sad? But at the same time, Flynn's contentment with living the opposite of a glamorous life also makes him more interesting. I love this about him.

"How do you feel about getting a hotel room for the night?" I ask.

"It's …" He twists his lips for a second before releasing me and stepping backward with a long sigh. "I don't have a credit card."

"I'll pay for it."

"No." He scoffs. "I'm not having you pay for it. I'm pretty sure my paycheck is more than yours, and"—he holds up his hands in surrender—"I don't mean that as an insult. I have no clue why I'm being paid so much to do absofucking-lutely nothing. But I am."

"It's no big deal." I step toward him, reaching for his hand.

"Well, it is to me." He pulls away.

Our evening is spiraling—again. So I steer it in a new direction. "I love that about you. What if you give me the cash, but I put it on my card?"

"What if we just go back to your apartment and not give a shit what your roommate thinks?"

"Fine." I return a tight grin.

"Good answer." He kisses my forehead.

On the way to the apartment, I steal Flynn's attention at every stoplight, loosening my seat belt to lean over and kiss his neck.

His hand works its way up my leg, stopping short of touching me where his mouth had been earlier. When we park near my apartment and unbuckle, our mouths crash, the anticipation reaching a fever pitch. My heart might explode.

"Inside," he mumbles.

I nod, panting more than I do on the bike tours, but we don't move. He snakes his hand up my shirt, and I rub him on the outside of his jeans. I pull away and blow my hair away from my face, relinquishing a naughty grin. "Let's go."

We make it to the door and kiss again. He hikes my legs around his waist and carries me upstairs, stopping several times to kiss me without falling backward. My back *thunks* against the door, his lips demanding, hands palming my ass.

"I think I'm going to love you," I whisper when Flynn kisses my neck below my ear. "So, just be prepared."

He lifts his head, eyeing me with an unreadable expression.

My heart sinks.

Shit. Shit. Shit!

Say something. What is he thinking?

"Why wait?" he says.

I might cry because I haven't been in love like this. I haven't allowed myself to feel this deeply since the day I was taken on my twenty-first birthday. Routine has made every day simple, a steady wave of emotions. Nothing too high. Nothing too low. Years of self-medicating with monotony and a numbingly boring social life.

"I mean," he begins, saving me from my drowning thoughts, "I'm not waiting."

I lean the back of my head against the door and close my eyes, quickly wiping my tears.

"Or we can wait."

"No." I laugh, opening my eyes and grabbing his face to kiss him again.

We jolt, beginning to fall backward, and he grabs the doorframe to keep us upright when Ally opens it.

"Whoa. What's going on? I was just leaving to—"

"Go," I mumble over his lips as he walks us toward the bedrooms.

Ally laughs. "Have fun."

"This one," I say, breaking our kiss before he passes my room on the left.

He kicks the door shut behind us.

"Love you," he whispers, framing my face, thumb touching my scar. He does it every time he cups my face.

And every time I melt, feeling beautiful in his eyes.

Can I let him love me when he doesn't know everything about me? My brain says, no. Stop. Slow down. My heart is nothing more than a wild horse with the wind at its back. Maybe it doesn't matter who I was, if I'm no longer that person. This can be my life.

I close my eyes and move my head a fraction to kiss his thumb, a silent thank-you for accepting all of me. "I love you," I whisper.

My body aches to be as close to his as possible, but my heart doesn't want to rush a single second. And the way he slowly unbuttons my blouse leads me to believe that he doesn't want to rush this either.

"I need a better vocabulary," he murmurs, our gazes meeting after he slides my blouse off my shoulders and removes my shorts, leaving me in my bra and underwear.

Goosebumps erupt across my skin. "Why do you say that?"

His gaze drops to my breasts and lower, taking in all of me while wetting his lips. "Because I just keep thinking that you're the most beautiful creature I've ever seen, but"—he shakes his head—"that word doesn't feel *big* enough for what I really see when I look at you."

A new round of tears threatens to escape as I remove my bra. With my jaw cradled in his hands and his lips moving with mine, I hear Bach, "Cello Suite in G Major Prelude."

It's beautiful and haunting, the way I've always imagined it would feel to fall in love. The highs and lows. Thrumming the strings that attach my soul to my earthly body.

Love is passion. Desire with purpose. Life well-lived.

My mom said those words to me when I hit a low point, certain I could live forever without this kind of love.

Flynn removes his shirt and unbuttons his jeans. Then he steps behind me, gathering my hair and gently placing it over one shoulder so he can pepper kisses along my back, easing my underwear down my legs. It's slow, almost agonizing, as he shows control while my chest feels like it could rip open from my heart thrashing around in its cage.

My jaw unhinges with a gasp when he playfully bites the flesh along the curve of my butt. He chuckles softly as I rest my chin on my shoulder, angling my gaze down at his mischievous grin.

The impatience to feel more, feel it faster, more intensely, wins over my desire for the moment to last, so I turn in his arms and kiss him, sliding my hand down the front of his briefs.

"Jesus," he whispers, dropping his gaze between us, mesmerized by my touch. We stumble the last few steps to my bed, discarding the rest of his clothes, save for a condom from his pocket. He sets it next to my head as I lie on the bed. The music in the back of my mind is almost deafening as our naked bodies intertwine, moving together like a bow across the strings.

"Flynn ..." My fingers curl into his hair as he kisses my inner thigh.

When he crawls up my body, I peel my eyes open for a few blinks, admiring the lines of his body, taking a few extra seconds to feather my fingertips along the mottling of scars, each one squeezing my heart like I can take away some of the pain that they once caused him. What kind of monster does that to another human, let alone a child?

"Hey," he says, standing on his knees to roll on the condom. I lift my gaze, and he smiles. "It was a long time ago."

I return a sad smile. "Are you reading my mind?"

He settles between my legs, slowly pushing into me while I fall a little deeper into the depths of his dark eyes.

He drags his lips to my ear and he whispers, "God, I hope so."

We move like the ebb and flow of chords. A natural progression of tension and release. I push him onto his back, again, feeling his scars beneath my fingers as he looks up at me, reaching for my breasts and grinning. I've lost the fight with my composure, blushing while bending forward, hiding us in a cascade of dark hair.

"I love how you feel inside me," I say, kissing his top lip.

He grips my hips, playfully nipping back at my lips. "Maybe I should just stay here forever."

"I think I'd like that," I say through my shaky breaths as I approach my release.

When I succumb to the waves of pleasure, he rolls us over, and the padded headboard taps the wall like a mallet against a bass drum.

"June ..." he moans while releasing. His body a deadweight on mine like a security blanket.

I hug him with my arms and legs, our bodies hot and sweaty like we've melded together.

"We need a shower," I say with a giggle. "But I don't want to let you go yet, so ..." I nibble his earlobe.

"Then just hold on," he says.

"What are you doing?" I squeal as he climbs off the bed with me hugged to him.

He opens the door and walks across the hall to the bathroom.

"Nooo! Ew ... I'm eating my takeout," Ally says.

I give her a wrinkle-nosed grin over Flynn's shoulder as he offers her an unobstructed view of his naked backside for several seconds before shutting the bathroom door behind us.

This is what it feels like when all the notes just ... hit.

When the music isn't being played. It's playing you.

The water envelops us like a rare, late summer rain shower on a warm beach in Southern California.

My giggles.

His grin.

The long glances and even longer kisses.

We wrap up in white fluffy towels, and he lifts me onto the vanity.

And ...

He. Combs. My. Hair.

Flynn hasn't dated. I haven't had a serious boyfriend. But I have friends, and I know this isn't normal. Does he? I'm not telling him.

"Have you ever hoped for something great to happen just to make sense of all the bad stuff?" I ask. "Not to make up for it, just to *make sense* of it?"

Flynn gently works the comb through my hair, using his free hand to take the tension off my scalp while freeing it from any tangles. He's a natural.

"Hoped? No. But here I am, exactly where I never knew I wanted to be." He pauses his hands and looks at me. "And regretting anything in my past is no longer an option."

"I don't know if regret is the right word."

"No?" He continues combing my hair.

"Regret implies you had control over it. Don't you feel like the bad things that happened to you were out of your control?"

His brow tightens. "Some of it. But I've done things I should not have."

"But don't you feel like you did them because you were trying to protect yourself or someone else?"

"We're here." He sets the comb aside. "That's all that matters to me."

My smile wavers, but I try to hide it by tipping my chin. "Yeah."

"Not to sound dramatic," Ally says, knocking on the door. "But I really need to pee."

Flynn smirks, sliding me from the vanity so I'm hugged to him like we were on the way into the bathroom. When he opens the door and steps past Ally, his towel falls from his waist.

"Nooo ... not again," she says.

I giggle as he carries me to the bed. We settle under the covers, and I fall asleep in his arms within minutes.

The next morning, Flynn is gone by the time I peel open my eyes and squint at my alarm clock, three minutes after seven. I hop out of bed and retrieve my phone from my bag on the floor, among my discarded clothes. Each one is a memory of him slowly undressing me. Just the thought brings a blushing smile to my face.

My phone is dead, so I plug it in next to my bed, run to the bathroom, and make a cup of green tea. By the time I return to my room, there's just enough of a charge to turn on my phone.

A text from Flynn pops up. He sent it at five forty-five this morning.

> Flynn: Morning! What time do u work? Mr. R thinks u should stop by again since Mrs. R likes u

I'm flattered, so I text back:

> June: Hi! I have a 1:00 tour. I can grab breakfast and head that way

> Flynn: Perfect!

Chapter TWENTY

Flynn

I MAKE Mrs. Rawlings her morning tea.

We go to Pilates.

Back home for breakfast.

Then she retreats to her room with Loki without giving me any more instructions.

She's been friendly, but distant today. Did I make things awkward between us by asking her such personal questions yesterday? Probably.

While I wait for June to get here, I clean the litter box and detail out the Tesla. Just as I look out the front window, a black SUV pulls into the circle drive, and June hops out of the back seat.

We need to get her driver's license renewed.

She slowly walks toward the front door in her ripped jeans and floral sleeveless top while pulling her hair into a ponytail. I'm unfamiliar with the feeling I get from watching her. It's something between excitement and an urgent need to press my mouth against hers.

Before her finger reaches the doorbell, I open the door.

"Hi," she bites her bottom lip, but that's now my job, so I pull her into my body, and do just that.

June giggles when I don't let go. "I"—she pulls her lip free—"don't think we're supposed to be making out while you're on the clock. Where are Rupert and Callie?"

I close the door behind us as she slips off her Birkenstocks. "I don't know where Rupert is, but Callie is in her bedroom, so there's no one to see us making out. And how do you always get a black SUV as a ride?" I grab her waist and pull her to me, sliding my hands to her ass.

"Good question." She shrugs, wrapping her arms around my neck and kissing me.

I walk her backwards toward the kitchen, keeping our mouths fused despite her weak attempt to look behind her to see where we're going. Just outside the kitchen, there's a half-bath under the stairs. I pull her into it and slide the pocket door shut.

"What are we doing?" she whispers.

In the soft glow of the nightlight to the right of the sink, I pull my wallet out and grab the newly stocked condom. Then I kiss her again.

"Flynn," she rears her head back. "No. We'll get caught."

"Doubt it," I say, unbuttoning her jeans and leaning in for another kiss.

She takes a few seconds. I can feel her stiff hesitation, but then she works the button and zipper to my jeans, and I can't stop grinning as she kisses me back a little harder.

Whose life is this?

A beautiful, smart, funny, talented, mesmerizing woman

wants me as much as I want her. If this is love, then I've been an idiot for years, running from all chances to experience this.

It's quick and dirty, like bar bathroom sex, yet totally different because it's June. I release one leg from her jeans, and she pushes mine halfway down my thighs, like we've done this dance a million times. We haven't, but we should.

June rests one hand behind her, gripping the faucet, the other clenches my shirt. I hold her legs on either side of my hips. Our mouths seal in a passionate kiss with tiny moans. I've never felt so wanted.

Not as a child.

Not as a friend.

Not as a man.

Until her.

She breaks our kiss, lips sliding to my ear so all I hear are her tiny little gasps in rhythm with my thrusting into her.

If this is what Monroe feels with Naomi, I owe him an apology.

As we pull our jeans back on, June leans forward onto her toes and brushes her nose along my earlobe. "God, I love you."

I don't know if there's enough light for her to see my shit-eating grin, but it's beginning to feel like a permanent expression.

Sliding open the door, I listen for anyone, then I poke my head around the corner. The coast is clear, so I take her hand and pull her into the kitchen, jolting to a halt with June doing the same thing right behind me.

"Mr. Rawlings," I say before clearing my throat.

He doesn't look at us. He's too busy stacking vanilla sandwich cookies in a big glass cookie jar. Just a guy in a suit, perched on a barstool, stacking cookies like blocks. He's peculiar as fuck.

"Did you kids get your sexual tension worked out?"

"Oh, my god," June whispers, hiding behind me.

Rupert chuckles, but he still doesn't look at us. "It's fine. Good for you. I remember mid-afternoon quickies. It feels like a lifetime ago."

"Do you think Mrs. Rawlings would like to see June now?" I ask, ignoring everything he's said.

"Probably. Send her up." He finally looks at me while separating a cookie and licking the middle several times.

"Just her?"

He nods.

I turn toward June. "Top of the stairs. Go right. Her room is the one at the end of the hallway. I'll be up soon."

June nods half a dozen times, her face still red from either our quickie in the bathroom or the embarrassment of Rupert hearing us.

After she turns and exits the kitchen, I face him and steal a cookie from the carton. Then I open it and lick it like he's doing.

"It's good practice, isn't it?" he says, winking at me.

I pause my licking, trying to figure out what he means that's not perverted.

"How long can you go before you want the whole cookie?" He pops the rest of it into his mouth and grins while chewing.

"I'm sure I can go longer than you," I say, rolling my eyes.

"June wasn't here for more than a minute before you got into the cookie jar."

"Respectfully, fuck you." I eat the rest of the cookie because I don't like how he's watching me lick the frosting.

It's like he's watching me have sex, ready to critique my skills. "When are you going to tell me what you do for a living?"

"Nothing. My wife is rich. I highly recommend marrying a woman who comes from a wealthy family. Then you can get a job, but you don't have to make a living."

"Then what's your job?"

"That's such a good question," he says, continuing to stack the cookies. They're halfway up the jar. "I'm still trying to figure that out."

"Why do you wear a suit every day?"

"Because I look good in a suit. Don't you agree?" He glances up at me.

"I'm not an expert on suits. So I don't know if that suit looks good on you." I point to my neck. "You never wear your tie tight."

"Callie likes it loose. Well, she used to anyway."

"I'm going to the orchestra with June. You ever been?" I ask, leaning my backside against the fridge.

"Of course."

"What did you wear?"

"A tux."

"You have to wear a tux to the orchestra?"

"No."

"Then what should I wear?"

"What's June wearing?"

"I don't know."

He chuckles. "Well, find out. You decide what you're wearing based on what she's wearing. Is her outfit formal or semi-formal?"

"What if it's formal?"

"Then wear a tux."

"I don't have one."

"Then rent one or buy one."

I mumble an expletive under my breath.

"Don't grumble at me. You asked."

"What if it's semi-formal?"

"Then wear a suit. But I'm guessing you don't have one of those either." He places the lid on the cookie jar. "I'd let you borrow one of mine, but it wouldn't fit you."

"Where's the best place to get a suit or tux?"

"I don't know. Look it up."

I frown. "Where do you get yours?"

"Lorenzo comes to the house with swatches. Then he returns with my suit after he's made it."

"Who's Lorenzo?"

"My tailor."

"Can you give me his number?"

"I could, but despite your endless 'respectfully, fuck you' comments, I like you. And I don't want you to embarrass yourself by calling my tailor, who will charge you north of ten grand for a suit. And he won't have it ready in time for you to take June to the orchestra, unless the orchestra is in the fall. So, I think we'll get you something off the rack. Or you can rent a tux."

Monroe's math might have me rich in six months, but I'm not there now. I'm still poor ... and clueless.

Chapter
TWENTY-ONE

June

CALLIE'S ASLEEP when I look in on her, so I slip into her room and let my eyes adjust. There's just enough light filtering through her sheer curtains to reveal the photos on her wall, including the little blond boy with a wide, unguarded smile, the kind that punches right through your chest. I swallow hard, blinking back tears. I can't imagine what must have happened.

Behind her armchair sits a turntable with records neatly slotted beside it. I flip through them.

"Do you like music?" Callie's raspy voice startles me.

I spin around. "Sorry. I wasn't trying to snoop. Or wake you."

Callie sits up, sliding her legs over the edge of the bed. "It's nice to see you, again. Have you been here long?" She combs her fingers through her hair before standing and smoothing the soft pink cotton dress that hits just below her knees. A nightshirt, perhaps.

"Only a few minutes," I say, resting my hands on the back of the chair. "And yeah." I glance back at the records. "I love music."

"What do you like to listen to?" she asks, padding closer as Loki jumps off the bed.

"Everything. But I have a soft spot for the cello."

Her pale blue eyes widen. "So do I." She slides past me and thumbs through the records. "I took cello lessons years ago, but I gave it up after we had our son. It's brutal on your fingers."

I stare at my left hand and the soft finger pads where calluses used to live.

She places a record on the turntable. "This is one of my favorites. It's a unique mashup of classics from Bach and Beethoven with undertones of heavy metal. Metallica, mostly."

I close my eyes when the first song plays, but I open them again as she taps my arm with the album cover.

"Have you heard them?"

The cover is black with a galaxy of stars split by four comets with tails of music notes, all colliding at the center into broken instruments: a cello, bass, piano, and violin. The band is called A World Away.

"I actually have this album," I say.

"So good, right?" Her face brightens. "Rupert and I saw them in concert years ago."

Three knocks sound at the door. "Can I come in?" Flynn asks, already pushing it open.

I quickly turn.

"What are you looking at?" he asks, nodding toward the turntable before picking up Loki.

"June and I were just discussing our shared love of music," Callie says. "Specifically, the cello."

"Oh, yeah. She played it," he says.

"June, you didn't mention that." Callie elbows me lightly before sitting in her chair and tucking one leg underneath her.

"I was about to," I say, offering Flynn a tight smile.

He looks at me, confused.

"Do you know how to tune one?" Callie asks.

"Yeah," I murmur, my gaze drifting back to the photos.

"If I buy an electric tuner, would you tune mine?"

Flynn perks up. "Wait. Are you feeling *inspired* to play your cello?"

I smirk without looking at him. He sounds far too pleased with himself.

"Perhaps," Callie says.

"June, let's go get a tuner ... or whatever she's talking about," Flynn says.

I shake my head slowly, gaze snagging on a photograph of a man steering a fishing boat. He has Callie's smile and Rupert's jaw. He must be their son.

"June?" Flynn says my name again.

"Huh?"

"Let's go get the tuner thing."

I study Callie, tracing the resemblance, wondering what other features she passed along to her son and grandson.

"You don't have to tune it," she says.

I shake my head. "No. Uh, I can. Where is it?"

"Top shelf of my closet," she says. "But I said I don't have a tuner yet."

"That's ... fine. I don't need one."

Her eyebrows lift. "You don't. Then how do you know it's in tune?"

"By ear."

After a few seconds of studying me with an indecipherable expression, the corner of her mouth twitches. "Very well. Flynn, will you carefully retrieve it from the top of my closet? Left side."

"K," he says, setting the cat down.

I look away, wringing my hands. Her suspicious smirk makes my pulse jump.

"Here," she says when Flynn returns with the cello. "Take my seat."

I sit and open the case. It's a beautiful *and expensive* cello. A Paolo Vettori. Easily seventy thousand dollars. I lift the cello and bow from the case, unprepared for the rush of emotion that hits me. Bowing my head, I breathe through it, waiting for the tears to pass before they notice.

It feels like home.

The weight against my chest and thighs.

The way my posture settles, grounding me.

"Do you need some kind of external reference if you're not using a tuner?" Callie asks.

I shake my head, eyes closed, bow hovering. It's like taking a breath, a really deep one. The kind that makes you realize it's the first real breath you've taken in years. It's a relaxing flow of energy. A calmness that brings mental clarity. The sound so rich and deep it resonates through the wood and into me, waking something that never truly went dormant.

Perfect fifths. A to D. D to G. G to C. I adjust the lower

string sharper or the upper string flatter until the vibration is pure. Then, I just play.

Four beautiful notes.

Long and short bows.

Play with joy, my dear. Or don't play at all.

Practice is a means to an end. Don't practice. Play. With. Joy.

Time disappears. It always has. My dad once found me slumped over my cello, bow loose in my hand. I'd played myself to sleep. One more note. One more chord. Always just *one more*.

When the final resonance fades and I open my eyes, the silence steals my breath for a moment. Callie's mouth hangs agape, tears shining in her eyes. Flynn mirrors her expression.

I nervously smile. "It's, uh ... tuned."

More silence.

I swallow hard, returning the cello to its case. "Of course, you can check it with a tuner, but I think it's close. It's a magnificent cello." I lock the case and swing my gaze to Callie. "Where did you get it?"

After a slow blink, she murmurs, "Florence."

"Isn't that in Italy?" Flynn asks.

"Yes," I say. "The Vettori family crafts them in Florence, Italy. Dario Vettori's sons, and now his grandchildren, continue the tradition he started in the 1930s in a mountain town between Florence and Bologna."

Callie's smile swells. "That's right. Have you been there?"

"*Have* you?" Flynn asks, visibly rattled like a "yes" answer will disappoint him.

"I don't have all day," Rupert grumbles, barging into the bedroom.

Flynn jumps. "Sorry. I got distracted."

"Where are you going?" Callie tilts her head to the side.

"To get Flynn clothes for the orchestra," he says. "Did you ask what she's wearing?" Rupert nods to me.

"Oh, yeah. I forgot to ask," Flynn says. "What are you wearing to the orchestra? Do I need a suit or tux?"

"What?" I chuckle. "Flynn, you don't need either. A nice shirt and jeans are fine." He shouldn't spend another dime on me. Definitely not for a suit or tux that he'll likely never wear again.

"You two are going to the orchestra?" Callie perks up.

Rupert smiles. It's sincere and endearing. Memories of less tragic times, perhaps?

"Yes, but it's no big deal," I insist.

"Have you been to the orchestra?" she asks Flynn.

"What do you think?" he deadpans.

"Then it's a big deal. Let's go shopping. Give me twenty minutes," she says, practically skipping to the bathroom.

When she closes the door behind her, Rupert frowns at Flynn. "Boy, I told you to *quickly* ask what she's wearing. Now you have my wife involved, and a forty-five-minute errand is going to turn into hours of finding the 'perfect' everything." With a heavy sigh, he turns and exits the bedroom.

I step between Flynn's spread legs. "It's *really* no big deal."

He rests his hands on my hips, gazing at me. "How the hell did you play like that?"

"I told you the cello is my favorite." I shrug.

"Your favorite? June, my favorite sport is basketball, but I'm not Michael Jordan."

"Well," I dip my head and kiss him, playfully nipping at his lower lip, "that feels like a *you* problem. Maybe you don't love basketball as much as I love the cello. And I think I'll wear a cute skirt and blouse with sandals to the orchestra. You can wear those dark jeans you wore to dinner the first night with my parents and the button-down too."

"I can hear you," Callie yells. "No jeans. No cute skirts."

Flynn raises his eyebrows like we're in trouble. I bite my lips together and snort.

"Let's just skip the orchestra and get naked," I whisper.

His calloused hands slide along my neck and into my hair, turning my head so he can whisper in my ear. "I'm taking my cello girl to the orchestra because the look on your face when you play is the same look you get when you orgasm. I think the orchestra is your porn."

"Stop," I giggle, stepping back.

"I'm right." He smirks. "You're blushing."

Truth? I want to see Flynn in my world, even if it scares me. What if he doesn't love the orchestra? Will it feel like he can never truly love me?

"Shit!" I look at my watch. "I forgot I have a one o'clock tour. Gotta go." I kiss his cheek and run down the stairs.

"Where are you—" Rupert starts to speak as I pass him at the bottom of the stairs.

"I'm late for work!"

On the way to the bike shop, Flynn texts me:

Flynn: U should get a car

June: haha! U should not be so distracting.
Mr. R heard us in the bathroom!!!!

Flynn: Exactly. I was on the clock and u
were distracting me. If I get fired I hope u
can live with that on your conscience

I stare out the window for a second and grin.

June: After the orchestra we need to talk

Flynn: Are u breaking up with me?

June: I hope not

Flynn: K. Thx for having sex with me

I giggle as my driver eyes me in the rearview mirror.

Chapter
TWENTY-TWO

Flynn

"Suspenders?" I snap the black straps, staring in the mirror.

"They're classy," Rupert says, reclined on a cream leather sofa, drinking scotch beside Callie.

The store clerk holds out the suit coat for me to slide my arms into.

"June will love them." Callie smiles, fiddling with her necklace and sipping red wine.

I look ridiculous. "Black dress shoes with no socks?" My face sours.

"It's perfect for summer." Donny, the suit expert, adjusts my tie.

It's tight. Now I know why Rupert wears his loose, except today it's proper.

"How much is all this?" I ask.

Donny looks at Rupert.

"How much do you think everything costs?" Rupert asks.

"I don't know. A grand?"

"Do you think it's worth a grand?" He studies me.

I look to Callie for help, but she sets her wineglass on the table and picks at lint on her white pants, offering me nothing.

After one last look in the mirror, I nod. "I suppose."

"So you would pay a grand for it?" Rupert asks.

"No. June said I can wear my jeans and button-down shirt. Mrs. Rawlings already bought me loafers that don't need socks. This would be a waste of my money. I can buy gas for June's car or help her buy groceries. I think she has to pay for parking at her apartment. I bet a grand would cover that for about a year."

"June is a lucky girl," Callie says.

I remove the jacket. "I don't know about that. But I've never been able to take care of anyone, and I don't know how long this job will last. So I'm not wasting money on myself when I can do things for her." I hand Donny the jacket and step behind the curtain to take off the clothes.

Rupert and Callie don't say anything to me on the way back to their house. They don't say anything to each other, either.

"You can have the rest of the day off," Callie says when we get out of the car in the garage. "And we have a commitment tonight, so if you two want to hang out here and use the theater room or just get away from roommates, please feel free to do so."

I look at Rupert, half expecting him to shake his head, overriding her offer. But he doesn't.

"And I hope you at least take her somewhere nice to dinner before the orchestra," Callie adds.

I nod. *Good tip.*

"Night." She smiles and heads into the house.

"Would you like me to call and get you reservations at a nice place?" Rupert asks.

"Nah. But thanks." I tuck my fingers into my back pockets.

"Well, you know where the key is to my Chevelle. If you want to drive it to the orchestra tomorrow night, you can," he says. "I trust you'll return it in one piece."

"Are you serious?" I squint at him for a few seconds.

"About returning it in one piece? Yes. I'm dead serious."

I shake my head. "About driving it."

"Just be careful. She's priceless." He squeezes my shoulder.

"I'm not sure it's priceless, but—"

"I'm not talking about the car, dipshit."

June.

I nod. "Of course."

He gives me a half grin. It's a little creepy. "Very well, then. Have a good night. If you do bring June back here while we're gone, keep your bodily fluids off the furniture. Got it?"

I bite my tongue. He's being nice, so I try to do the same.

"And maybe get a haircut if you have time before the orchestra."

I nod several times. "I'll consider it."

"I'm sure you will," he says with a laugh, then disappears into the house.

～

When June gets off work, she walks toward the street, glancing up from her phone to see me at the last second as I stand in front of my car, arms casually crossed.

"Hey, what are you doing here?"

I love the way she lights up.

I nod to her bike tour shirt. "Did you go home before coming to work?"

She shakes her head. "There's a box of shirts behind the counter, so I grabbed one. I didn't love doing the tour in jeans, but ..." She shrugs before grabbing my shirt to pull me to her for a kiss.

I uncross my arms and wrap them around her.

"The Rawlings have an engagement tonight, and they said we could hang out there and watch movies or whatever. But I'm thinking pizza first."

June's smile doubles. "I love that idea. And I love that you're here to give me a ride." She teases my nape. "And I love you. Where should we get pizza from? I'm starving."

"I have a large pizza in the car."

Her whole face lights up. I make a mental note to have pizza with me at all times.

"Just to make sure you heard me," she says as I open her door, "I love you. I love you. I love you."

I chuckle, picking up the pizza box so she can slide into the seat. Then I hand her the box to hold. By the time I reach the driver's side, she has the box open and a slice in her hand.

"You don't want to wait until we get to their house?" I ask, closing my door.

June takes a bite and shakes her head, closing her eyes like it's the best thing she's ever tasted. I had a foster parent smack my face for stealing a french fry out of a to-go bag on the way home from a drive-thru.

"Besides," she mumbles over her bite of pizza. "It's better when it's hot." She looks over at me, with a funny grin just before taking another bite. "What?"

I shake my head. "Nothing. Are you sharing?"

"Maybe." She laughs, opening the pizza box.

We eat the entire pizza, parked along the street in front of the bike shop before driving to the Rawlings' house.

"Hey," I say, stopping in front of their house. "Whatever that was back there, don't ever stop."

June looks behind her. "Back where? What are you talking about?"

"Eating pizza in the car."

It takes a few seconds for her wrinkled brow to relax before she laughs. "I love this." She opens her door before I get the chance to do it for her.

By the time I get out, she's at the front of the car, reaching for my hand.

"What is the *this* that you love?" I ask as we make our way to the front door.

"Everything with you feels easy. Life is simple, the way it should be. Eating pizza in the car is a fantastic day. Being alone for a few hours feels like winning the lottery."

"The lottery?" Before I open the door, I pull her into me. Then I slide my thumb along the scar on her lip. "Well, at least the lottery is real. I'm pretty sure you're a dream."

"Kiss me," she whispers.

I grin, loving how fucking alive I feel when she whispers those two words.

"Soon," I say, reaching past her to unlock the door.

"You're such a tease, Flynn Morley."

We take off our shoes in the entry.

"I know you want to find a guest room and immediately get naked," I say.

She rolls her eyes, but her grin tells the truth.

"But I want you to do something for me first," I say, guiding her up the stairs.

"It's not sex? But is it sexual?" she asks.

"It is to me."

"Now I'm intrigued. Wait." She pulls on my hand to stop me from going into Callie's bedroom. "No. We're not doing anything kinky in her room. In fact, I don't think we should be in her room if she's not here."

"Fine, then you stay here."

"Flynn!" She protests, but I release her hand and disappear around the corner.

"What are you doing?" she asks, poking her head around the door, whispering like the Rawlings can hear us.

I pull the cello from the top shelf in the closet. "I want you to play this for me," I say, meeting her at the door. "Naked."

Her gaze snaps from the cello to me. Eyes wide.

I chuckle, nodding for her to head back down the hallway. "Kidding."

"Why do you want me to play for you? I doubt cello music has ever been your favorite." She leads the way down the stairs.

"You're my favorite person, June. So everything you do becomes my favorite thing."

She turns at the bottom of the stairs, lips pressed together, eyes narrowed. "That's the nicest thing anyone has ever said to me."

"Really?"

She nods several times.

"Huh. That's crazy." I lead her to the formal living room that overlooks the back of the house and the lake. The uplights at the base of their trees make everything look like a magical garden.

June looks around the room, then pulls a gold and white upholstered chair toward the middle. I hand her the cello case before sitting on the love seat by the window.

"What shall I play for you?" she asks, tossing me a flirty grin.

"Something that makes you think of us."

June hums, positioning the cello between her legs. She slides the bow along the strings several times. I don't know if it's a song or a warm-up, but as she continues, the melody sounds a little familiar. Her left hand shakes while pressing the strings. She's so graceful.

I lower to the floor next to the cello, gazing up at her past the long lines of the strings. She grins.

Sometimes she closes her eyes, and I want to crawl inside of her and feel everything she's feeling, hear the music the way she hears it. I don't have big dreams, but if I did, I'd want to live life through June's eyes.

When the song ends, she rests her bow hand beside her.

"What was that song?" I ask, interlacing my fingers behind my head.

"'Moon River.'"

"Why does it make you think of us?"

"The lyrics make me think of adventure, yearning, love, and dreams. It's what I see and how I feel when I'm with you. Possibilities. The unknown." She shrugs. "Following your heart, no matter the outcome. Dream maker. Heart breaker."

I roll onto my side, propping my head up on my arm

while reaching for her bare foot. She pulls it away like it tickles, but I reach for it again, rubbing my thumb along the arch. I had one good foster home growing up. The wife was pregnant, and I went to another foster home after her baby was stillborn. But while she was pregnant, her husband would sit on the sofa and rub her feet, focusing on the arch. She'd close her eyes and softly moan.

"Do you think I'm a dream maker or a heart breaker?" I ask.

June relaxes the more I rub her foot. "Maybe a bit of both."

She smirks and starts playing another song.

After she's thoroughly convinced me the cello is the best instrument, she returns it to its case. "You've seen my passion. What is yours?" she asks.

I sit up, leaning my back against the loveseat. "You."

"Good answer." She slides off the chair and crawls toward me.

I stretch out my legs, and she straddles my lap.

"But before you met me, did you have a passion for something? Goals? Dreams?"

"I like cars. Working on them. Rebuilding them. Really, I like anything that requires the use of tools. When I'm not busy thinking about you, I watch endless streams of how-to videos." I shrug. "So I guess my dream would be to own my own garage to restore old cars."

June's grin has never been so big. "I love that."

"Me thinking about you?"

"Not that." She giggles. "I love your love for putting things back together. Especially old cars."

"You do? I didn't think you were into cars, since the only thing you remember about your first car is its color."

"Flynn"—she pecks at my lips and grins—"I love hearing about your passion and seeing the sparkle in your eyes when you talk about it. Passion is sexy."

"It's pretty dim in this room. You're not seeing any sparkling."

Her cheek brushes mine, and she whispers at my ear, "I see *you.*"

I close my eyes as her hair tickles my face, and I inhale her scent. "I have something I need to tell you."

"What?" She kisses the shell of my ear.

I lace my hands behind her back. If she goes to run, I can hold her. Beg her to stay and listen to me.

She picks something off my shoulder. "Cat hair," she murmurs. "Where is Loki? Not to interrupt you. But he wasn't in the bedroom, was he? Should we be worried?"

I can't think about the cat when I'm on the verge of telling her something that could end everything. But maybe I should find him, then she can hold him while I tell her. Who can get upset while holding a purring kitten?

"I'll check on him," I say.

June stands and holds out her hand to me.

"I'll pull you down."

"I'm stronger than you think," she says.

God, I hope so.

I pretend to let her help me up.

We check in Callie's bedroom. He's not there. So we peek our heads in the other bedrooms, including Rupert's, while calling, "Here, kitty, kitty."

"I'll check Rupert's office," I say. "You check the kitchen."

"Okay," June says at the bottom of the stairs.

I don't reach Rupert's office door before June calls my name. Spinning around, I head to the kitchen.

"Oh, dang ..." I say, staring at multiple piles of vomit which look tinged with blood.

June is squatted by the fridge where Loki's on his side.

"His breathing feels a little labored. You need to call Callie and Rupert."

"Yeah," I slowly nod, counting the areas of vomit while pulling my phone from my pocket. "I'll text her first. In case she can't answer her phone."

> Flynn: We found Loki in the kitchen. He's vomited in multiple places and there's blood in the vomit

My phone immediately buzzes with a call from Callie.

"Hey," I answer.

"Where is he? How's his breathing? How much vomit? Is there a little blood or a lot of blood? Are you sure it's vomit and not diarrhea?"

"Uh ... it looks like bile and stomach stuff more than poop, so I'm guessing it's vomit. It's not a lot in any one spot, just like five or six areas. Not a lot of blood, just like streaks. He's on the floor by the fridge, and June thinks his breathing seems a little labored."

"Okay. I haven't taken him to our vet, but we have one from when we had Sally. He's actually our neighbor's son. I'll call him right now and text you the address. Can you take him for us? We're at a dedication, and I have to speak in a little bit. I'm so sorry to ask this of you."

"It's fine," I say. "Just let me know what you find out."

"Thank you *so* much. I really owe you."

The couple who could send me to jail *owe* me? Hardly.

"No problem." I slide my phone back into my pocket and pick up Loki. He gives me a weak "meow."

June grabs the roll of paper towels and a bottle of cleaning spray.

"June. No. No. No. Leave it. Get up. I'll clean it," I say.

She lowers to her hands and knees. "It's fine, Flynn."

"Here, hold Loki. I'll do it. Callie's calling her vet. But I might need to take him somewhere to get checked out. Callie is getting ready to speak at their function, dedication, whatever. So she can't come home right now. Here." I hold out Loki.

She blows her hair out of her face as she stands and frowns. "You fixed my sink. I'm capable of cleaning cat vomit." She takes Loki from me.

"I invited you to spend the evening with me. Not this. I'll take you home."

"I'm going to the vet with you."

I glance up while wiping the vomit.

She kisses Loki's head. "I want to be with you; I don't care if it's here or at the vet. And moral support is good. Have you taken a sick pet to the vet?"

I slowly shake my head, but I'm not thinking about sick pets. June wants to be with me, and she makes it sound so simple. Moral support. It's all so new to me. I'm going to lose her, and it will feel like losing everything.

I sit back on my heels. "I haven't taken a pet to the vet."

"Well, I have. And help is good. One of us will soothe Loki, the other will keep a clear head to ask the vet the right questions."

Nodding several times, I murmur, "We need to talk."

She frowns. "You don't think you need help. I'm not suggesting you're not capable."

I shake my head. "No. Not about the cat. I told you earlier. I have something I need to tell you because ..." I sigh, shoulders slumping. My feelings for June are *big*. The thought of losing her scares the hell out of me. But losing her to a lie feels more tragic than losing her to the truth. "I just have to tell you something, but I don't know how."

She squints. "Something bad?"

I nod then quickly shake my head. "I don't know." My phone vibrates, so I grab it. "Hey," I say to Callie.

"How's he doing?"

"Okay. He hasn't vomited anymore."

"That's good. I called Lenny, our vet. He said he'll meet you at his office. I'm texting you the address now. He'll bill me, so no need to worry about anything beyond getting him there. And you can take one of our cars if you need to. Also, his crate is in the garage. I *really* appreciate this. We'll pay you extra."

"It's fine," I say. "Really, I'm happy to do it. You kinda have him because of me anyway."

"Don't say that. He's mine. My decision. But, really, thank you, Flynn. Text after Lenny sees him. We'll head straight home after my speech."

"K."

"Bye."

"Bye." I end the call and look at the text for the vet's contact information. Dr. Leonard Schreiber.

"It can wait," June says.

I glance up from my phone, eyes narrowed.

"Whatever you have to tell me. It can wait. The other

day, I told you we needed to talk after the orchestra. I have something I need to tell you, too. So let's focus on Loki and talk later. Okay?"

Has she been to prison too? Seems unlikely.

Chapter
TWENTY-THREE

Flynn

JUST AS WE park at the vet's office, my phone chimes with a text from Rupert.

> Callie forgot to mention Lenny is an asshole. Great vet. Fantastic with animals. Terrible with humans. Don't take anything personally.

I chuckle, showing June the text.

She giggles. "Good to know."

I grab Loki's crate from the back seat of my car, and we head into the tiny brown building that looks like an old, single-story brick house.

"Hello?" I call. There's no one at the desk.

We sit in the two chairs by the fish tank. June grins. It's a tight, goofy grin, like we're not allowed to talk. Just us and the bubbling of the fish tank.

"You're here," a man says.

We turn toward him as he steps into the waiting room. He looks to be in his early thirties with brown hair in a preppy (floppy) style. Boring khaki pants, and a red and white plaid shirt.

"Yeah," I say, standing.

"Well, you should have said something. I came in just for you."

Yep, he's an asshole.

"I did say something." We step toward him.

"Well, you must not have said it very loudly."

"Probably the white noise from the fish tank," June says with a hint of sarcasm.

God, I love her.

"How do you know the Rawlings? Mrs. Rawlings called you *a friend*. You seem a little young to be her friends."

We follow Mr. Personality to the exam room. Seems a little ageist of him to suggest she can't have young friends.

"I'm her muse," I say.

He holds open the door as we step past him. "What does that entail?"

I set the crate on the exam table while June sits in the chair beside it. "I have an inspirational gift. It's hard for average people to understand."

"His giftedness is rare and highly sought after," June adds with a sharp nod.

I stare at her for a second, fighting my smirk.

"His great uncle is a shaman," she continues. "A muse is a spiritual healer who deals solely with spiritual connections of the living."

Dr. Schreiber eyes us for a few seconds before opening the crate. "Hello, little kitty. What's your name?"

"Loki," I say. "And I'm Flynn. This is June."

Thanks for asking, Mr. Personality.

He frowns at me before smiling at the cat. Oh, was he actually asking Loki to speak? Or are our names irrelevant?

"What's been going on?" he asks.

June and I look at each other.

Dr. Schreiber eyes us. "Well?"

I guess Loki can't tell him that. Just his name.

"He vomited five or six times, and it looked like it had some blood in it. And his breathing seemed a little labored. Not as much now," I say.

"It looked like it had blood? Or it *did* have blood in it?"

This is Rupert and Callie's neighbor, so I bite my tongue and the painful urge to be a dick to this asshole. After all, people who don't know cars might assume all dark colored leaks are oil, but it could be transmission fluid, power steering fluid ...

"It was red. That's all I know," I say.

He starts checking Loki with a stethoscope, then looks into his ears and mouth, and presses around on his belly. "Did you get a sample?"

June wrinkles her nose.

"No," I say.

Dr. Schreiber doesn't look at us. "Did you take a picture?"

June's eyes widen while curling her lips between her teeth.

He puts on a glove and squirts lubricant on the finger. Then he slides the tip of it ...

Nooo ...

I didn't need to see the butthole exam.

"No," I say to his question.

Dr. Schreiber looks up at me. It's the are-you-fucking-kidding-me look, but he doesn't say those words. He doesn't say anything.

Rupert was right. This guy smiles at Loki. Pets him. Scratches behind his ears. But I think he wants to murder June and me. Or at least me.

"What did the blood look like?" he asks.

Don't say it!

"Blood," I say, unable to stop myself. Now I'm just fucking with him.

He looks at me with a familiar expression, like I'm the dumbest person in the world.

June hides her snort with a fake cough.

"Was it bright red or dark like coffee grounds?"

"Neither. More like medium to light red," I say, earning myself a deeper frown.

"When did it start?"

"Dunno. We were at the house for a while before June noticed we hadn't seen Loki yet."

"Well, how long had it been since someone saw him?"

"Dunno. I picked up June. We ate pizza in the car. The Rawlings said we could hang out at their house. June plays the cello. She's pretty fucking amazing." I add that bit just to mess with him. "I don't know what time they left, or when they last saw Loki."

"How often was he vomiting?"

This dude can't read between the lines. We found the cat. We found vomit. The end. That's all we know.

"Dunno. Didn't see it happen."

"Was there blood in all the vomit or just some of it? Suggesting there was blood at first but then no blood or vice versa."

I refuse to answer, and he stops short of an actual eye roll.

"Do you know if he might have eaten anything unusual like a foreign object, a toy, plants, human food?"

I bite my tongue and shake my head.

"Did you happen to see any bottles like he got into someone's medication? Cleaning supplies? Anything like that?"

Again, I shake my head.

Loki lies on his side and starts to purr. Great. He's probably fine, and this guy thinks we're wasting his time.

"Did the Rawlings mention if he's had any recent change in diet?"

"I've seen her give him the same food since she adopted him. Some food that says 'human grade' on the outside. He seems to enjoy it. So if she changed his food, she did so since his first meal today. I can text her to ask."

Dr. Schreiber slowly shakes his head, focusing on Loki. "I'll draw some blood just to rule out anything serious. Then he can have water, but no food for twelve hours. Have Mrs. Rawlings call me with an update or if there are any changes. When she starts him back on food, make sure it's something bland like small amounts of boiled chicken. If anything changes, he'll need to come back in for imaging to check for obstructions or tumors. But after examining him, I don't see any cause for concern. So let's monitor him." He continues to pet Loki. "And make sure he doesn't get into anything. Okay?"

Okay? He's not my cat. Does this guy really think I'm going to sternly warn Callie about keeping a close eye on him?

"Thank you," June says while I have a stare-off with the doctor.

He won't even look at June. If this guy doesn't give *her* attention, not so much as a smile or nod of acknowledgment, then he's whacked. That's all there is to it.

Thirty minutes later, we leave with a purring cat. Normal blood work. And the look on Dr. Schreiber's face is less than friendly, like we made everything up.

"Entitled son of a bitch," I mumble, when we get into the car, and I text Callie.

> Flynn: On our way back to the house. Loki is fine

"I'm sure he wasn't happy about an after-hours call," June says, fastening her seat belt. "That doesn't necessarily make him entitled."

"All rich people feel entitled."

Callie replies with a thumbs-up before I back out of the parking spot.

"That's a little harsh. I think Callie and Rupert are very nice people."

"I'm not saying entitled people can't be nice. But they hired me as *a muse*. That's a big, fucking privilege money buys you."

As I pull onto the street, I feel June's gaze on me, so I give her a quick glance. Then I sigh. "Tell me I'm wrong. Name one person you know who has money, but you'd never know they had money? They live like us. Drive an old beater. I mean, I got my first paycheck from the Rawlings, and my head spun with possibilities. It was like a drug. Do you know what I mean?"

She twists her lips and nods several times. "Yeah," she murmurs. "I do. I just don't want you to ever feel like Callie and Rupert aren't good people. We're all human. We're all flawed. Everyone deals with temptation at some point. Focusing on the things we have in common more than our differences just feels like a better, more peaceful, way to live."

I squeeze her hand. "I like them. I just don't want to be them."

"I love you, Flynn," she says, in a sad tone, looking out her window.

When we arrive at the house, Callie comes out the front door before I even get the crate from the back seat. She's barefoot in a fancy silver sequin dress.

"Someone's a little anxious," I say to June.

She closes the door after I have the crate, then she rests her hand on my back. "Don't forget why you were hired. She's still grieving the loss of her grandson. I'm sure the idea of her kitten dying is unsettling."

As we reach the end of the driveway, Callie opens the crate and takes Loki out. "Hey, buddy." She kisses his head. "Thank you. I owe you two so much," she says, leading the way back to the house. Her hair is pulled back, and she's wearing makeup. I've never seen Callie in makeup.

"You don't owe us anything," I say.

June hugs my arm, looking up at me with an approving smile. She must be like Callie, or maybe all women love manners. I've always thought they were overrated. Acting a part. Not always genuine. Yet, I've come to like the little smiles both of these women give me when I do something polite.

"Kids," Rupert says slowly, sauntering into the foyer from the kitchen, a drink in one hand, a sandwich cookie in his other. He's in a tux with the bowtie undone. "Oh, thank goodness," he says to Callie. "I'm so glad that cat didn't die."

She rolls her eyes at him before focusing on us while sitting on the stairs with Loki hugged to her chest. "I called Lenny to thank him for meeting you there. He got me up to speed on everything."

"What did you think of *Dr. Schreiber?*" Rupert asks.

I pause for a second, distracted by June sliding her arm across my back and slipping her hand into my back pocket. "Uh," I clear my throat, "he was nice to Loki."

Rupert chuckles. "And you?"

"Rupert," Callie says, shaking her head at him like a silent scolding. "He did us a favor. Let's not be mean."

"I'm not being mean. But the guy is strange. Just ask Hubert and Carolyn. They say he's a recluse."

"Don't listen to him," Callie says. "Lenny is shy when it comes to people. His parents love him just the same. He just needs a girl like June to bring him out of his shell and make him more of a people person."

I pull June a little closer to me. Dr. Lenny Schreiber needs something, but not June or probably anyone like her. Girls like June need guys with actual personalities.

"Are you two excited for the orchestra tomorrow?" Callie asks.

"Yes," June says so quickly it makes Callie and Rupert laugh. Then she looks up at me with an irresistible smile and pink in her cheeks.

"We'll get out of here, so you can get to bed," I say.

"Thank you, again. And why don't you take the whole day off tomorrow since you have a fun night planned."

I'm living in their garage. Taking the day off isn't the gift she thinks it is. But what am I supposed to say? "Thanks," I murmur.

"Good night," June says, removing her hand from my pocket.

"Night, kids," Rupert says as we step out the door.

"Well, this evening didn't go as planned," I say as we walk hand-in-hand to my car parked on the street.

"I'm just glad Loki is okay. It was still a fun evening," June says because she always looks at the bright side.

It might be what I love most about her. She's light to my darkness. Everything comes to life, and I feel a different kind of hope with her.

"Because you got to play the cello?" I ask, opening her door.

She slips into the seat. "Because I was with you, silly."

I pause before shutting her door, and she looks up at me while pulling her hair over one shoulder.

"What?" she says.

"I love you."

Her shoulders, face, everything relaxes. I want to tell her a million times that I love her because I like how the words feel leaving my mouth when she's looking at me. It's as if each time, they're pulling a little piece of something from my chest. Something physical. Something real.

"I mean it," I say.

Her forehead tightens, and I close the door before I vomit everything all at once. As we pull onto the street, I turn on the radio to fill the silence. She loves whatever music I play, and I like watching her drum her fingers on her legs to the beat of the song or mouth the lyrics.

"We should run by your place so you can grab some clothes," she suggests.

"What for?"

"I don't know. Maybe I'm hoping you want to stay the night with me since you don't have work tomorrow."

"We've passed my place. Do I need actual pajamas?"

She giggles. "No. I just figured you'd want clean clothes for the morning."

"I'll run home in the morning. Don't you have to work?"

She nods.

I practice the speech in my head.

June, I'm living in the Rawlings' garage, but they don't know it. I stole Rupert's car, and that's why I'm working for him. I've been to prison—twice. But I'm afraid of losing you to the truth, which is ironic because you're the first thing in my life that has ever really felt true.

Just as I open my mouth to see if the words will come out, because waiting another day feels too painful, June says, "The Rawlings adore you."

"What?" I heard her, but I wasn't expecting her to say that. And I think "adore" is too strong of a word.

"I think they've suffered and felt a lot of hopeless moments since losing their grandson and as result, their son too. It's easy to feel like you'll never find your way out of the darkness when something so permanent steals your light. But I see it when they look at you. It's hope. A glimmer of light. Like reading an inspiring book or watching a movie. Even if it's not your life, you feel other people's joy. It radiates, and no one is immune to it. I think they love seeing you discover parts of yourself you never knew existed."

"What parts are those?" I ask.

She grins, resting her hand on my leg. "Your innocence."

I grunt. "I'm not innocent."

"Everyone possesses innocence. Sometimes we see it as inexperience, which can have a negative connotation. But it's innocence. Vulnerability. Something we all have in common, even if we don't want to share it. Getting a glimpse of it feels pretty great, especially when you get to be with someone as they experience something for the first time. Like I'll get to do with you tomorrow night."

I give her a reluctant smile. "And what do you think the Rawlings have seen me experience for the first time?" I ask, parking along the street in front of her building.

She unfastens her seat belt and opens her door. "Kindness," she says. "I imagine."

I grab my door handle and check the road to make sure no one is coming, but I also take a few seconds to digest her words.

When we step into her apartment, Ally yells from the bedroom. "Help!"

June gives me a funny look. Ally sounds more upset than desperate. I hang back a few feet as she heads toward Ally's bedroom.

"I think I stripped the screw. It won't budge."

"What is it?" June asks.

I step closer, craning my head to see what they're talking about.

"Maybe Flynn can help," June says, waving me into the room.

"Hey, Flynn," Ally says, frowning in the middle of the room, on the floor with pieces of wood and various screws in ripped open plastic bags.

"What do we have here?" I ask, lifting the box to see the picture of the IKEA desk.

"It said *easy assembly*. But I disagree. Something is wrong with the screws or this stupid little tool or ..." She sighs, dropping her head into her hands. "Me. Something is wrong with me. How can I pass the bar exam if I can't put together a desk?"

"Grab a drink. Chill on the sofa for a few minutes. Whatever," I say. "I've got this."

Ally lights up. "Seriously?"

I pick up a few of the pieces, inspecting them. "Yeah. Seriously. Shouldn't be too hard."

"Oh, I love you!" She jumps to her feet and hugs me.

"Down girl. He's mine." June laughs.

Ally releases me and steps back. "Sorry. But I'm just saying, if Juju doesn't marry you, I will. There's nothing sexier than a guy with skills and tools in his car."

"Oh my gosh, stop!" June laughs, pulling Ally out of the room.

I shake my head and chuckle.

In less than ten minutes, I have the desk assembled.

"No luck?" Ally asks, when I join them in the living room as they share a bag of microwave popcorn.

"Luck? I don't rely on luck. It's put together. All the trash is neatly piled by the door. I'll run it down to the dumpster in the morning."

June stands, and her big grin is all the reward I need as she steps toward me with the popcorn bag.

"Flynn, you are *the best*," Ally says, heading into the kitchen. "How can I thank you?"

"No need. I'll handle it," June says, backing me into the bedroom with the bag of popcorn between us.

I'm conflicted. The look on her face says she's offering something pretty special as a thank-you. But the popcorn smells delicious, and I love popcorn. June closes the door, eyes on me. I take the popcorn bag and sit on the end of her bed, eating it while she unbuttons her jeans.

"It was no big deal," I mumble over a mouthful of popcorn. It's butter flavored. My favorite.

"Ally easily crashes out. You saved the night. It's a huge deal." She steps out of her jeans and shrugs off her shirt.

I take another bite of popcorn.

We need to talk. But now I'm a hero in her eyes. And she's stripping. Maybe she's right. We can talk after the orchestra. At this point, what's twenty-four more hours?

"I know Ally will be a big shot lawyer, and I'm just a girl who rides a bike"—she removes her bra—"but I don't think she would suggest eating pizza in the car."

I chuckle. "Do you think I'm interested in Ally?"

She shrugs a shoulder, and I don't know if she's genuinely insecure or just messing with me. So I set the bag of popcorn on the floor, then reach for her hand, guiding her to stand between my legs. Her breasts are hidden behind her hair, but I don't touch anything but her hips as I drop my forehead, resting it over her heart.

Closing my eyes, I commit this feeling to memory.

The warmth of her soft skin. Her silky hair brushing my face. The gentle stroke of her fingers in my hair. I've never felt so human. If I focus solely on this moment, I might even allow myself to feel deserving.

"I love you," she whispers before kissing my head.

Why does she love me? What does she see that I don't? And is it real?

Chapter
TWENTY-FOUR

Flynn

"W‌HY ARE YOU HERE?" I whisper, holding June in my arms just as the sun rises.

"In bed?"

I feather my fingers up and down her arm. "In Minneapolis. Giving bike tours. Your family lives in California. Just seems odd."

"As odd as being a muse?"

I chuckle. "Not quite, but close."

"After the abduction, I needed to escape. Find a new normalcy. Search for a sense of safety again. And come to find out, I was looking for you." She kisses my chest.

"Liar."

She giggles, sliding her leg between mine. "I'm not lying. Maybe I didn't know your name or what you looked like. But I absolutely believe life is a journey, and thinking we're in control is just an illusion our ego thrives on. Tell me you think this—us—*we* were meant to be." She tries to tickle my sides.

It doesn't tickle, but I laugh at her attempt. I've never wanted anything more than to believe that June Malone is meant to be with me.

"I think I need to spray some WD-40 on your frame. It squeaks too much," I say.

"Whose fault is that?" She slides on top of me, grinning as her face hovers over mine.

"The bed frame's fault. I'll lube it, then pull it away from the wall. It's too close."

"Lube ..." she giggles.

"You and your dirty mind. It's a lubricant. It also protects against rust."

"Well, this bed is no doubt a little rusty."

"What does that mean?"

She dips her head and teases my lips. "Nothing."

"Has it been a while since you've had sex?"

She blushes. "No. I had it like ... twenty minutes ago. Am I that forgettable?"

"Well, I'm not great with words. I dropped out of school before learning all of them. But I'd say you're the opposite of forgettable. So unforgettable? Memorable?"

June grins.

"Feel free to share better words," I say.

She slowly shakes her head. "Your vocabulary is just fine. I don't need to finish your sentences or speak for you."

"You like me just how I am?"

"Yes," she whispers before kissing me.

I tell myself she will feel this way after I tell her about my time in prison, but I don't totally believe it. Everyone has their limits. If I told her I was a pedophile (I wasn't), there's no way she'd shrug and kiss me like it was no big deal.

"What time do you work?" I ask, rolling her onto her back, then kissing a trail down her body.

"One."

"Perfect." Half my body hangs off the end of the bed as I settle between her legs. "We have time for a little low-key sex before I run and grab that WD-40."

She giggles, fingers in my hair. "Low-key. Like lazy?"

"Like"—I kiss her inner thigh just to watch her squirm—"low-key as in you shouldn't be so loud this time."

"I'm not loud."

I grin even though she can't see me. "Challenge accepted."

After June goes to work, I get a haircut, then sneak into the Rawlings' garage and move at top speed to get ready, using the car's side mirror and window reflections to see how I look. My new jeans and shirt are wrinkled, and they probably need laundering. I tuck in the price tag, but I'm not sure I could return it after this many wears. Then I make dinner reservations and head to June's apartment.

"Come up," she says, answering the call when I buzz her.

The door clicks, and I throw it open, sprinting up the stairs. Before my fist hits her door, it opens.

"Jesus ..." I whisper as she punches the air from my lungs with her black dress, thin straps tied around her neck. Black high heels that make me weak in the knees. Hair braided. Lips glossed.

"You have some explaining to do," she says, stepping aside to let me in.

I'm underdressed. Even if my clothes were freshly cleaned and pressed, I'd be underdressed. "You said you were wearing a skirt and blouse. Not—"

"I was," she says, closing the door.

Heaven help me, the back of her dress exposes so much skin.

"*But*," she says, "thirty minutes ago, a woman I've never met delivered those two black garment bags. She verified my name and told me to have a lovely evening."

There's an unzipped black bag on the back of the sofa beside one that's still zipped.

"This dress was in one. The other is yours."

I shake my head. "I know nothing about this." I grab the bag and unzip it. "Shit," I whisper, staring at the suit I tried on the other day and the shoes in a smaller cloth bag at the bottom.

"Someone guessed my size correctly. Why do I think it was Callie and not you?"

I continue to shake my head. "I didn't ask them to do this."

"I don't doubt that." June chuckles. "I was only kidding when I said you had some explaining to do. Go put it on," she says with excitement in her voice.

Was I wrong? Should I have purchased the suit and thought to buy her a beautiful dress?

"Okay," I murmur, feeling too uneasy to look her in the eye.

After I put on the suit, including the suspenders, I step out of her bedroom.

She bites her lower lip for a second. "My God, you look so handsome. But you forgot to tie your tie."

"Uh," I glance down at it, tugging on both ends. "I don't know how to tie it."

"Front, back, through, pull," she says as her heels click along the wood floor toward me.

"Huh?"

She smiles, taking both ends of my tie. "It's what my dad always said. Let me."

"You smell good," I say, inhaling her floral perfume.

"Thank you." She flits her gaze to me for a brief second before refocusing on the tie. "You smell good too."

"It's Dr. Squatch soap, that I ..." *Stole from Monroe.* "Used," I grin.

"I like it." She finishes my tie, making a few little adjustments.

"Is that your stomach?" I ask.

She laughs. "Yes. I'm hungry. We should've made reservations somewhere so we're not late to the orchestra, but there's a little place down the street that might—"

"I made reservations." I tip my chin up with a little pride.

"You did?" She gets that look in her eyes like she did telling me about the clothes being delivered.

I nod.

"Love you," she whispers, gripping my jacket.

I kiss her. That little sigh she gives me is my undoing. But we have reservations, so I end the kiss and blow out a breath. "I have Rupert's Chevelle. He let me use it, but I have to get it back to his house tonight. So ..."

"That was nice of him." She turns and grabs a small

black purse from the kitchen counter before meeting me at the door.

"Yeah. He's ..." I run my hands down the front of my expensive suit. "He's full of surprises."

During dinner, June beams. I'm glad she's happy, but this isn't my life. It won't last forever. Will she be fine with chicken fingers and fries in the future? But how ridiculous of me to assume we'll have a future when she finds out about my past.

"Do you like this?" I say, nodding around the restaurant.

She swallows and blots her mouth. "Yes. The food is excellent. How's your steak?"

"No. Well," I glance down at my half-eaten steak, "the food is fine. It's good. But I mean this place. Do you like nice restaurants? Dressing up like this? The orchestra?" I shake my head. "That's not fair. Of course, you like the orchestra. But you seemed fine with us wearing more casual clothes, yet you looked pretty excited about the clothes we have on now."

June sets her fork down and reaches for her wine glass while her gaze moves around the room. "I mean, sure." She shrugs. "Who doesn't like to look nice and eat good food?"

"Don't you think about how this one meal could buy five regular meals, maybe ten? The money from these clothes could buy clothes and shoes for a lot of kids who have never owned a new piece of clothing?"

Her smile fades.

"I'm not trying to make you feel guilty. I love being here with you. And of course I want you to enjoy dinner and the orchestra, but I guess I just wonder if you dream of this kind of life." I gulp half of my water and wipe my mouth with the back of my hand.

"Flynn ..."

"It's fine. I just feel like a hypocrite being here. I hate people who can afford to live like this."

She winces.

"I mean," I shake my head, "I don't hate them in the way I hated most of my foster parents who were awful to me and other kids. I just mean I hate how rich people brag about giving to the poor. Ya know? But if you can still afford to eat like this and buy clothes like these, then maybe you're not giving enough."

"Economic equality?"

I shrug, cutting my steak. "I guess. Yeah."

"I'm not sure that's ever been fully achieved in any society. A Marxist approach. No private ownership or class divisions. It sounds good in theory. Are you really wanting to discuss the flaws in it, including human behavior and economic incentives? The risk of totalitarianism? Seems like heavy dinner conversation."

"Well, I don't know what you mean by a Marxist approach or that total ... whatever thing. I've just known many people who have worked their asses off only to eke by. And people like Rupert and Callie sit around all day and do nothing to contribute to society, but they have so much money. It feels wrong."

"I'm sure they're charitable." June sips her wine.

I grunt. "That's my point. If you live in that house, then you aren't being charitable enough."

"So who should live in that house or other big houses? Who should drive the fancy cars and wear the designer clothes?"

"No one. Their house could house several families. Designer clothes are only expensive because they can be. If rich people stopped overpaying for things just because they can, then all companies would have to charge a fair price for their products."

She slides her hand across the table and takes mine, squeezing it. "I love the world you dream of."

"So this doesn't matter to you?" Again, I look around the restaurant.

She laces her fingers with mine. "No."

"Then let's get out of here. Go to the orchestra because it's your porn. And then let's ditch these stupid clothes."

She smiles. It's soft at first, then it swells as she nods.

Chapter
TWENTY-FIVE

Flynn

THE MINNESOTA ORCHESTRA HALL is a massive glass building with a grand atrium and multiple gathering spaces outside of the main performance hall. We find our seats on the floor at the front.

"Your parents got us front-row seats?" I ask, craning my neck in all directions. This place is massive, with 3D cubes on the front wall and ceiling. Balcony seats line the back and side walls.

"Yes. There is a guest solo cellist performing tonight, so they knew I'd want to be as close as possible to see her." June sits in her chair and crosses her legs, thumbing through the program.

I continue to gawk at the impressive space while shrugging off my jacket and loosening my tie before sitting beside her. "What's up with the cubes everywhere?"

June glances up from the program, eyes pointed to the

ceiling. "They're for acoustic purposes. They disperse sound throughout the concert hall. This place is exceptional. The design and sound are remarkable."

I look at her and wonder who she is. After she played the cello in Callie's bedroom, I felt like she was an entirely different person who I didn't know. Not in a bad way. It made me realize I've fallen in love with a woman who I don't know that well. But I want to. Then in our conversation at dinner she left me in the dust, feeling stupid for not understanding any of her references.

And now, listening to her speak so intelligently about this place, it's hard not to feel stupid, like I'm way out of my league, and it's only a matter of time before she realizes there's very little depth to me.

When the concert begins, I watch June while everyone else watches the orchestra. Sometimes she reaches for my hand and squeezes it, and when the lights shift between performances, I see tears in her eyes. Am I supposed to cry too? Music has never brought me to tears. I've never even cried watching a movie.

As the guest cellist plays, June scoots to the edge of her seat, and shortly after the song begins, June's hands mimic the performer's, eyes closed. The song ends, and everyone claps. But June stands. The performer, with short, blond hair curled behind her ears, focuses on June, and she grins in a way that looks like recognition. Maybe she's June's friend.

"Have you met her?" I whisper in June's ear after the applause and June sits in her seat.

She shakes her head as she stands again, along with everyone else.

"It's over?" I ask.

"Intermission," she says.

We stretch our legs by walking the length of the common areas. There's a wall with pictures of performers. June slows to look at them. We turn around at the same time when the cellist who performed taps June on the shoulder.

"Zoya! I thought it was you," she says, a little out of breath. "I just had to find you to introduce myself. I'm Liza Stephens. I watched you perform at the Royal Albert Hall in London. You were only sixteen. I was thirteen, and I dreamed of playing like you." She shakes her head. "I *still* dream of playing like you. I've wondered where you've been. Sorry, now I'm just rambling out of control. I won't keep you. But I just wanted to say what a tremendous honor and surprise it was to perform in front of you." She finally takes a breath.

I have no breaths. My head is spinning too much to think about breathing. What's going on?

June swallows hard and glances at me for less than a second, barely lifting her gaze enough to make actual eye contact. "That's very kind of you to say, Liza. Your performance was so moving."

"Thank you." Liza presses her hand over her chest like she might faint from June's words.

Seriously. What the fuck is going on?

"Well"—Liza shoots me a quick smile before offering her hand to June—"I won't keep you. But it's been a huge pleasure meeting you in person."

June shakes her hand and gives her a wavering smile.

Liza walks away, then stops and points to a picture, glancing back at June. "It must feel surreal having your picture on the wall. I bet they'd love for you to sign it."

When she continues toward the stairs, I follow her footsteps to the picture.

"Flynn." June grabs my wrist, but I pull away.

We passed this picture five minutes earlier, and she didn't even pause at it. That's her—the young woman on the stage, front and center, sitting in a chair with a cello between her legs, one hand on the neck, her other hand holding the bow above her head like she's just finished a dramatic performance. But her long hair is partially covering her face, eyes closed. I don't know if I would have ever recognized her in this photo. But now that I really focus, it's undeniable.

The gold plaque on the frame says, "A World Away."

"What am I looking at here, June?" I ask, my jaw working back and forth. "Or ... Zoya? Is that your name?" I turn my head just enough to squint at her.

"That's what I wanted to talk to you about after the concert." Her face wrinkles as she wrings her hands together. "I played the cello professionally."

"No shit."

She frowns at my sarcasm. "I had a band called A World Away. It was an extraordinary life—a privileged life."

I look away. She will not make me feel guilty for the things I've said about people who live a *privileged* life.

"My parents adopted me from an orphanage in India when I was three. Much like Rupert Rawlings, my father married into a wealthy family. My mother's stepfather owned ZIP Tunes, one of the most successful record labels in the world, which my parents run now. My grandmother, Juniper Carlisle, was an international supermodel who had her own cable fashion DIY show. She went by 'Juni,' so I go by June instead of Zoya because too many people know Zoya Malone. And I gave up that life when I came here."

Rubbing my temples, I shake my head. "Why?"

"The reason I was taken on my twenty-first birthday was

because of my family, which made me worth a sizable ransom in the kidnapper's eyes. And despite round-the-clock security and countless hours of therapy, I couldn't relax. Walking through a crowd of people screaming my name, holding out their hands for an autograph or just to touch me felt like nothing more than people wanting to take me. I couldn't hold my cello or bow without shaking. I rushed through concerts just so I could get home and hide in bed under the covers. The one thing that brought me joy became the thing that paralyzed me with fear. I just ... fell out of love." She quickly wipes the corners of her eyes and sniffs.

Security? Crowds of screaming people? My head won't stop spinning. This was my night to tell her about my past, not her night to tell me ... this. Whatever *this* is.

All I know is I never wanted this; I just wanted her.

Everyone around us heads back into the auditorium.

"It's starting," I murmur, but I can't look at her anymore. "Let's go."

"Flynn ..." She grabs my hand, interlacing our fingers, as I head toward the auditorium, but I don't move a muscle. No curling my fingers. She's holding on, but I'm letting go.

For the second half of the show, she wipes tears from her cheeks with her gaze on the stage. After the last performance, we worm our way through the crowd. As much as I need space, I wait for her, making sure she's in front of me as a crowd of people flows through the skyway toward the parking ramp.

She turns toward me before I can open the car door for her. "This is ridiculous. I didn't lie to you. *This* is who I am, a girl who enjoys taking people on bike tours. I like my roommate and my two-bedroom apartment and taking naps." She points toward the skyway. "That's not my life any longer, even if someone recognizes me. It doesn't define me any more than the balance in my bank account. So you can't punish me for being scared to tell you. And you can't punish me for the people who adopted me."

"Just get in," I say, feeling too defeated to have this conversation. I'm not punishing her. I'm just ...

I don't fucking know.

"No. I'm not getting in until you say something. Until you tell me what you're thinking and feeling." She crosses her arms over her chest.

"June—Zoya, whatever the hell your name is, just ..." I close my eyes for a second. "Get in."

She shakes her head.

"Christ, just get in." I grab her arm, and she jerks away, stumbling backwards onto the ground. "June!" I reach for her, but not before a man in all black shoves me and helps her up.

"Hey! Get the fuck away from her," I say, lunging toward him.

He rams me into the car beside the Chevelle.

"Stop!" June pulls on his shirt as he keeps his arm against my throat.

He looks familiar—the ride-share driver.

"I've got it," June says in a calmer voice.

He releases me, and I fix my jacket.

"Who the fuck are you?" I tug on my stupid tie as he backs up, leaning against the same black SUV—the only one —she's ever ridden in. And I'm just now making the connection that's not a coincidence.

June opens the door and gets into the Chevelle.

I stare at him as he waits by his SUV with a stony expression.

"Just get in," June says, fastening her seat belt.

I close her door, eyeing him the whole way around the car.

"He's my bodyguard," she says, head bowed, hands fiddling with her handbag's zipper.

"Of course he is," I whisper, starting the car.

We don't speak on the way back to her apartment, but I'm hyperaware of the headlights in the rearview mirror the whole time.

"Is it your pride?" she asks when I park along the street in front of the gallery.

I don't respond, turning off the engine and sitting idle, staring out the window at the passing cars and people milling around the neighborhood, a line outside of the bar on the corner. Normal people. I thought she was normal too.

"You've decided you hate people with money, so now you can't be with me?"

"I don't hate people with money," I whisper.

"Then what's the big deal?" I feel her gaze on me, but I can't look at her. It hurts too much.

"I bought you a car ... and you said nothing." I grunt. "I'm sure you and your parents had a good laugh about that."

"Flynn ..."

"*One scoop* of ice cream on our first date. That's what I could afford. And I waited in misery for a whole week until I had enough money to take you to dinner." I tug on my coat. "I didn't buy this fucking suit because I wanted to save the money to pay for your parking each month, or maybe help pay for gas in your car. I brought you flowers I picked myself because they were free, and I tied them with a goddamn shoelace." I shake my head. "I'm sure you've been showered with dozens and dozens of expensive flowers, jewelry, fancy chocolates, you name it." I close my eyes. "I'm such a fucking fool."

"Flynn," she whispers, then sniffles, resting her hand on my leg. "None of that matters to me."

"Well, it matters to me! Yeah. It's my pride. Is that what you want to hear? Is that a flaw?" I force myself to look at her tear-stained cheeks and bloodshot eyes. "I have *nothing*." I jab a finger into my chest. "Except my pride, and now that's gone. I didn't walk away from a glamorous life. Do you know what a luxury that is? *Oh, fame and fortune were too stressful, maybe I'll pretend to be a common person. I'll pretend to understand what it's like to live paycheck to paycheck and slum in a two-bedroom apartment where I have my own bedroom and shop at Whole Foods.*"

She swallows hard and wipes her tears. "You're an asshole," she whispers. "Because you only see what you want to see. You did it with the Rawlings, and now you're doing it with me. And I'm—" her voice breaks. "I'm sorry that you don't feel worthy of nice things, of opportunities ... of love." She opens the door. "That's your loss."

"My loss?"

She climbs out and heads across the street between cars.

I follow her. "My loss? Are you fucking kidding me?" I run after her.

The screech of a horn cuts through the air, I look to my right, blinded by headlights, but I keep running.

"Watch out, you stupid kid!" some guy yells out his window.

June fishes her keys out of her handbag.

"You want to know what's my loss?" I shrug off my jacket and unbutton my shirt. "Pick a scar, June. Pick. A. Fucking. Scar. Let's talk about the loss of my innocence. Every broken bone. Third-degree burns. Belts to my backside. A fractured nose. Hair yanked out in chunks. Days locked in a closet." I choke on my next words. *The man who made me touch him.* I say in my head. They may never leave. I may never tell anyone. "You don't know shit about my loss," I whisper.

She frantically wipes her face through her sobs and trails of black mascara down her cheeks.

Slowly buttoning my shirt, I shrug. "I don't hate what you or the Rawlings have," I say in defeat. "I just don't want it. I never want to forget where I've been, and how many people are still there. Not for a night out in fancy clothes. Not for anything."

Chapter TWENTY-SIX

Flynn

I RETURN Rupert's Chevelle and text Monroe:

> Can u come get me? No questions asked

He picks me up twenty minutes after I send him the address. As requested, he doesn't ask questions. He drives to the empty parking lot behind the auto body shop where he works. Then he reaches into the back seat and pulls a six-pack of beer from a sack and hands it to me as we stare at the outlines of graffiti by the service entrance door.

I crack open a beer and down half of it. Monroe's phone lights up with a text from Naomi, but he turns off the screen and flips it face down on the dash. He's my only true friend, and I'm losing him to a woman and the life neither of us ever imagined. I'm happy for him. He deserves it.

"She's rich," I say. "And famous." I drink the rest of the

beer, crush the can, and toss it on the floor at my feet before opening another beer. "And I'm not pissed off that she didn't tell me. I'm pissed off that I waited too long to tell her my ..." I laugh. "My exciting news. I'm an ex-convict. That would go over well at Thanksgiving with her rich family. Right?" I lean my head back and close my eyes. "She's ... fucking brilliant, man. A cellist with a band. And they've played concerts around the world. She's talented beyond words. Smart. And for whatever reason, she liked me. But it was all a lie. We were a lie. She was hiding her greatness. I've been hiding the most regretful, embarrassing parts of my life." I lift my head and open my eyes. "Doesn't matter now. It's over."

"Because you told her and she doesn't want to be with you?"

I shake my head. "I didn't tell her. I was going to. That was the plan. Even if I lost her, I needed to tell her. But after I discovered her secret, I just ... couldn't. Man, you should have seen this person who recognized her. She went on and on like June was her idol. And I felt like a fraud standing next to her."

"I think you're too hard on yourself, Flynn."

I shake my head. "If she were my daughter, I wouldn't let her within a mile of a guy like me."

"A guy like you? Define that. A hard worker? A guy who cares less about himself than literally everyone he meets? A survivor? A loyal friend? A fucking muse?"

I laugh, shaking my head before drinking the entire contents of another can of beer. "Stupid job. That woman is either going to kill herself or she's not. And her husband will blame me no matter what. I'm not a muse. I'm a ... what's the word? Something goat?"

"Scapegoat?"

"Yeah, that." I crush a second empty can and toss it on the floor. "And I don't even care," I mumble and sigh. "Some nice person with good intentions and a tragic story of their own will pat my back and tell me it's not my fault. It's the story of my life. But I've spent a lot of time locked up for a life that *hasn't been my fault.* Ya know?"

"Maybe she's different, Flynn."

"She's not. You should have seen the look on her face when she had on the expensive dress the Rawlings sent her or the way she couldn't stop smiling while we ate dinner at that fancy restaurant. The orchestra. Just ... everything." I open another beer, feeling the start of a nice buzz. "And ya know what? I don't even blame her. Cuz it's not really her fault that she's smart, pretty, talented, and rich. But it makes it hard for her to know me. To feel me." I pound my fist against my chest. "Like *really* feel me. That's what money does. It numbs you toward the rest of the world." I slouch against the door and close my eyes.

Monroe takes the beer from me. "Where can I take you? I can't take you to my apartment. Are you staying with the Rawlings?"

"Yeah," I whisper. "Sort of." All I see is June biting her lip to hide her grin. All I feel is her fingertips on my neck. Her sweet perfume. The sound of her voice so soothing like a song. And for a few weeks, she chose me. The version I let her see.

She's right. I'm the asshole.

"What's this?" Rupert looks up from his computer when I step into his office, holding the folded suit and shoes.

Loki jumps off his lap and runs out of the office. This asshole likes the cat. I wonder if Callie knows this? I'm too tired to give it much thought. My head feels like a bowling ball crashing into ten pins. However, I'm proud of myself for thinking to charge my phone and set my alarm after waking up at three in the morning to piss.

"Thank you for the clothes, but I can't keep them." I set them on his desk. "And you can't pay me five grand a week to hang out with your wife."

Rupert leans back in his chair, hands folded on his stomach.

"I made eighteen dollars an hour at the detail shop, not counting tips. You should pay me the same amount."

He chuckles. "Are you allergic to money? Opposed to getting ahead in life?"

"It's charity. I'm not a charity case." I sit on the sofa, elbows on my legs, head bowed.

"Now feels like the right time to mention I have security cameras in my garage, but you can't see the toilet."

I lift my head.

He's seen me sleep in his car. *Fuck my life* ... he's seen me bathe in the dog wash.

"Am I fired?"

He chuckles. "Fired? I don't know, Flynn. Do you want me to fire you? I'm at a loss this morning. I don't know if, in the history of mankind, someone has ever requested a pay cut for themselves. Granted, it's probably safe to assume most people don't sleep in their employer's garage either."

"My roommate got engaged. And his girlfriend is pregnant. I was sleeping on the sofa. It's a one-bedroom apartment. After you paid me, they assumed I could find my own place. But I don't know how long this job will last, so I don't want to sign a lease. Hotels require a credit card, which I don't have. I could stay at a shelter. There's one on Hiawatha that's pretty decent. It's just been really convenient to be in your garage since I have to be here so early in the morning."

Rupert nods slowly. "Okay."

Okay? That's it?

He drums his fingers on the desk. "How was the orchestra?"

"I'm not an expert on that kind of music, but everyone seemed to know what they were doing."

He rolls his eyes.

I try to smile, but it's hard to find one today. "It was fine," I say. "Funny thing I discovered."

"An orchestra is comprised of people playing instruments?"

"Actually, yes." I give him the bird. "June has traveled the world as a cellist in a band. Her picture is on the wall at Orchestra Hall."

Rupert squints. "What?"

"Yep." I lean back, hands laced behind my head. "It would seem that I landed a rich girl too. But I don't want that life, so what a waste, huh?"

"What is her band?"

"A World Away."

"Sounds familiar. I'd have to ask Callie, but we might have seen her perform. Come to think of it, Callie thought she looked familiar. And what life don't you want?"

"This life." I roll my head, gesturing around the room.

"Flynn"—he laughs—"we've joked about my life, but I didn't marry Callie for her money. When we met, I didn't know her family was wealthy. She said her dad would hate me, but I just assumed it was because of my rough past. You don't cast someone aside because of their net worth. Is that how you want people to treat you?"

"How do you think she'll treat me if I tell her about my years in prison?"

Rupert rocks in his chair. "There's only one way to find out."

"Well, I don't actually want to know. Not anymore. I was going to tell her last night after the concert. I told her we needed to talk."

"And why don't you want to know how she'll react to your past?" He reaches for his green drink.

"Because, as unlikely as it is, I like to imagine her not caring about it. And what's the point now?"

He takes several gulps, then licks his lips. "Why imagine it? Why not just find out?"

"You're not listening. I said it's unlikely. And there's no point."

"So what?"

"So, I don't want to see that look of anguish on her face." I stare out the window at the rain clouds forming in the distance. "I've been looked down upon my whole life. I don't know if the fragmented images I have of a woman with long black hair are of my mother, but I think they are. And the look on her face is anguish. Like I'm a burden. A regret. A mistake. I like June. What we had was short, but it felt real, even if it wasn't." I return my gaze to Rupert. "Last night she looked heartbroken."

"And you want that to be the lasting image you have of her?"

"She was brokenhearted because she thought she loved me."

"Maybe she did."

I shake my head. "You can't truly love someone unless you know everything about them."

He finishes his drink and sets the empty glass on a black coaster. "I'm sorry, Flynn."

"For what?"

"For suggesting you wait to tell her about your past. From now on, you should have a twenty-four-hour rule."

"A twenty-four-hour rule?"

He nods. "As soon as you think you like someone, friend, romantic interest, whatever, tell them about your past within twenty-four hours. The ones who stay are the ones who matter. But be prepared because most won't stay. That's okay. Life isn't a popularity contest. You'll feel safer and more content if you keep your circle small."

"I bet you have a lot of friends. All rich people do."

"No." He laughs. "They don't. In fact, the wealthier you get, the smaller your circle becomes. Having more means you have more to lose, more for people to steal. Show me a really rich person, and I'll show you someone who has no *real* friends."

"You know, you're proving my point."

"Oh?" He lifts one eyebrow. "What's your point?"

"A wealthy life isn't all it's cracked up to be."

He barks a laugh. "I'll grant you that. But love is. Finding someone who is your home, your partner in this life, is pretty amazing."

I deflate. What else is there to say? He's not me, even if we've had similar experiences.

"Get Callie her tea. She'll want to hear all about the orchestra. Put a smile on your face and make her believe it was the best night of your life. Can you do that? I'll pay you eighteen dollars an hour to do that."

"Yes, sir." I stand.

"Did you just call me 'Sir'?"

"Yeah."

He slides on his reading glasses and focuses on his computer screen. "There's hope for you after all."

Chapter
TWENTY-SEVEN

Flynn

CALLIE IS on the covered balcony instead of in her room. She peeks open one eye when I set her tea on the table between the two loungers.

"It's going to rain," I say. "Not a great morning to watch the sunrise. Are we going to Pilates?"

"Yes. After you tell me about the orchestra. How did June look in her dress?"

I stretch out my legs, grateful we're going to Pilates instead of practicing three hours of silence. "She looked nice. Thank you for doing that for her. For us."

"Nice? Not beautiful? Elegant? Stunning?"

"Yes, all of those."

"Did you like the orchestra?"

"It was fine."

"Flynn, give me three better words than fine."

"I didn't graduate from high school."

"Three other words for fine," she repeats.

I sigh. "Good. Okay. And, uh … entertaining."

"Where were your seats?"

"In the front row."

She lifts her head. "Wonderful. I'm so glad you had good seats for your first time. The orchestra is such an emotional experience."

"Mr. Rawlings said you thought June looked familiar."

"How did this conversation come up?"

"Who does she remind you of?"

Callie sips her tea. "Why do you ask?"

"If you're asking me why I'm asking you, then you probably know. Did she tell you?"

I ready myself to snap at her if she tries to say, "Tell me what?" But she doesn't say that.

"There's an edge to your tone, Flynn."

"Probably because I'm feeling a little *edgy* this morning."

Callie turns, letting her socked feet touch the ground. She bows her head, mug cupped in her hands. "People who don't care, don't get edgy. They don't get angry. They don't fight."

"I never said I don't care."

"What's the worst thing that's ever happened to you?" She looks up at me.

"You don't want to know."

"If I didn't want to know, then I would not have asked."

I focus on the gray sky, stained with hints of purple and blue, rejecting the sun's attempt to break through.

"We all have stories, Flynn. Some people are an open book, others are a diary with a lock and key. Relationships take time and work. Years of patience. Love is an invitation into someone's heart. But you have to think of it like someone inviting you into their home for the first time. You wouldn't charge past them to explore every room and rummage through every drawer. Maybe the first time you visit, they don't invite you past the foyer. Perhaps you get invited into the kitchen for tea, but you pass a room along the way with a closed door. And you're curious what's behind the door, but you don't kick it down, and you don't get angry with them for not giving you access to everything all at once."

"When did you know?"

She frowns. "I suspected when we met. But I knew the day she tuned my cello. She hasn't put out new music or toured in years. Art is passion in form. If she's stopped following her passion, I have to believe she has a few closed doors."

When lightning flashes in the sky, she turns to watch it. "I know *I* have doors that I've closed, locked, and thrown away the key."

"I think Mr. Rawlings thinks I can unlock them."

She smiles. "I'm sure he does."

"I'll change for Pilates," I say while standing.

"Did you let her go?"

"If I say yes, are you going to lecture me?"

She shakes her head.

I walk toward the door. "Why?" I ask.

"Because it's not my job to open your doors."

After Pilates, Callie has me take her to the Minneapolis Institute of Art, but I suspect the trip is more for me than her. She chooses certain sculptures and paintings to stand in front of for a long time—fifteen to twenty minutes—before moving to the next piece.

"Nope," she says each time I attempt to reach for my phone.

Maybe I shouldn't have asked for a decrease in pay. This is torture.

The next day, it's not raining, so we spend the afternoon at the Walker Art Center. I've been through the Sculpture Garden next to it, but I've never seen the inside of the building.

That night, Rupert steps into the garage as I sit in his Chevelle, watching YouTube videos.

"I'll rent you a room for three hundred a month, but you have to clean it and the bathroom you choose to use."

"The car is fine." I shrug.

"I don't want you drooling on my leather seats or jerking off to porn." He nods to my phone.

"Either your cameras suck or you need glasses." I hold up my phone for him to see the screen. "They're videos of rebuilding engines."

"Well, either way, you don't need to sleep in my car. It's worth more than the bed I'm offering you. But if you want to keep sleeping in it, I'm going to charge you a grand a month."

I wrinkle my nose. "That's stupid."

He turns, heading back into the house. "Life is stupid. Get used to it."

I choose the cheaper option.

My days are spent as Minneapolis's premier muse, exploring every museum and performing tasks like reorganizing Callie's albums. I'm pretty sure she just wants me to see her collection of June's music. At night, I sleep in a king bed and stare at naked angels on the ceiling. On the weekends, I take a side gig delivering food.

It's been three weeks since I last saw June, and I fucking miss her. Instead of calling or texting, I drive past her apartment building a dozen times a day. I happen to catch a few glimpses of her roommate coming and going, but never June. The MINI Cooper is parked in a reserved lot on the north side of a building, but it's always there and in the same spot.

Why doesn't she get her license? Oh, that's right. Rich people don't need to drive. Yeah, I'm still pissed.

On a hot Saturday morning in late July, I get the nerve to buzz her apartment.

"Hello?"

"Hey, Ally. It's Flynn."

She doesn't reply.

"Hello?" I say.

"June isn't here."

"Oh, okay. Is she working?"

"She went home last week for a family emergency."

"Oh, is everything alright?"

"I'm not comfortable discussing this with you. Sorry."

"That's ... fine. Thanks anyway." I deflate, walking back to my car.

Chapter
TWENTY-EIGHT

June

IMMUNOTHERAPY.

Targeted therapy.

Surgery.

Radiation.

Chemotherapy.

Grandma Juni rolls her eyes at the oncologist while my parents and I sit with her in the conference room with a team of doctors.

"It's a mole," she says about her stage-four melanoma, which has spread to distant lymph nodes.

"Mom ..." my mom says, and she has never called Grandma Juni "Mom." It's always been "Juni" because they've been best friends more than mother and daughter.

"I'll start wearing a hat and more sunscreen," Grandma says, fiddling with the gold rings on her long fingers, including the eight-carat canary diamond she's never taken off her left ring finger since Grandpa Zach died five years ago from a heart attack.

"Juniper, that's a great idea," the oncologist says. "But that's not going to help the damage that's already been done. We need to be aggressive with treatment because you have an aggressive form of melanoma."

Grandma straightens her back, just as confident and beautiful as ever. "Did you know my granddaughter is a famous cellist? And she's going back on tour."

"Juni," Mom says.

I bow my head. Grandma is simultaneously sure she's dying and also in denial. And her "dying wish" is for me to push past my fears and "get back on the horse." A term she used to get my dad on her side. He likes me either on a horse or with a cello between my legs.

My phone vibrates, and I carefully unzip the bag on my lap beneath the table, sliding it open just enough to see the screen.

Flynn: Hi

I slip the phone back into my bag and clear my throat. "I'll play."

My parents eye me with uncertainty while Grandma pulls me in for a hug.

"Just once," I say. "Something with the LA Philharmonic. Just me. Not the band. But you agree to treatment."

Her smile fades. "I'll do a month's worth of treatment for one show."

"Jesus ..." My mom rubs her temples.

Grandma looks at my dad. "Are you really going to let

your wife guilt me after everything that happened with your father?"

Grandpa Malone died of cancer. I don't know what she's referring to as "everything," but I know he suffered. Is she afraid of suffering too?

"Dr. Hayslip," Mom says, pushing back in her chair. "Thank you for arranging this meeting. We appreciate everyone's time. But I think our family has a lot to discuss before moving forward."

Grandma is halfway to the door with her designer handbag over one shoulder, blond and silver hair over her other, before Dr. Hayslip nods, offering us a sad smile.

I chase her down the hallway. "Grandma!"

She stops, back to me. Then her shoulders curl inward, body shaking. "I'm d-dying, Z-zoya."

I hug her as tears burn my eyes. This is different. It's the first time she's cried in front of me.

"But y-you're not. So don't run f-from your destiny." She sniffles, releasing me to wipe her eyes.

My parents stop a few feet behind her, arms around each other, giving me this moment with her.

I swipe my fingers beneath my eyes and slowly nod. "One concert for every month of treatment."

After Grandpa Zach died, my parents moved in with Grandma Juni. Her twenty-five-million-dollar estate in Beverly Hills sits on two acres, a timeless design with a half-moon drive, manicured gardens, a dual staircase in the entry with a grand crystal chandelier, coffered ceilings, seven bedrooms, a pool, tennis courts, and a recording studio.

Flynn would hate it.

My bedroom has a private balcony overlooking the pool.

When I collapse onto the king bed with white cotton linens and puffy pillows in every shade of pink, Grandma's favorite color, I stare at the text from Flynn.

Hi.

That's it.

"Knock. Knock," Mom says, poking her head into the room.

"Come in."

"Whatcha doing?" she asks, plopping down beside me.

I don't hide the text from Flynn. She knows he broke my heart. But unlike her and Dad, I don't think Flynn will be able to put it back together because I'll always be Zoya Malone, only granddaughter of Juniper Carlisle and Zachary Isaac Phillips, fashion and music royalty.

"You know," Mom says, resting her head against mine, "after I fell for your dad in Coachella, he never thought he'd see me again, but we texted all summer. And I knew our time wasn't over. Our story had only just begun."

I smile. "I know. I love yours and dad's story."

She hums. "That's what I always said to my mom about her love story with my dad. And do you know what she said?"

I laugh. "Yeah, you've told me a million times."

"Well, I'm going to tell you a million more times. She said some loves are temporary, and some are forever. It's all about timing. Timing guides our lives more than love. Love is just an emotion—timing is our destiny. Missed opportunities. Serendipity. Fate ... it's all about timing, not love."

"That's why Grandma always talks about destiny."

"Yep." She steals my phone. "So explore this. See if it's your destiny." She types "hi" back to Flynn and presses send.

"Mom!" I grab the phone back. "I'm not ready."

She rolls to her side, pressing her hand to one cheek while kissing my other cheek. "My mom was my best friend, my world in many ways ... until we adopted you. I love her, but I love you more. So don't do anything that doesn't speak to your soul." She sits up and pads her bare feet to the door.

"Responding to Flynn doesn't speak to my soul."

She chuckles. "Yes, it does."

I stare at my phone and the three bubbles of his impending reply. The summer after my parents met, my mom used to text my dad:

Hi. Remember me?

And he texted back:

Hi. I'm pretty sure you're still my greatest memory.

And they'd end each conversation with a song title, something that made them think about the other one. My parents had a million obstacles that threatened their happiness, but they never gave up, and the other's net worth never factored into their love. That's why my gut tells me Flynn can't love me that way. And I don't blame him. His past is beyond anything I can imagine, and I know there's probably so much more I don't know.

Flynn: I hope everything is ok with your family

June: It's not

Flynn: Sorry

> June: Thx

Flynn: Want to talk about it?

I stare at his text for a few seconds.

> June: No

Flynn: I'm sorry

> June: U said that

Flynn: I'm sorry about the way things ended

Flynn: I'm an asshole

> June: I know

The screen flashes three bubbles, then it stops. Three bubbles again. Then nothing.

I toss my phone aside and stare at the ceiling. How did life get so messed up?

Before dinner, I swim laps in the pool and shower. With wet hair, shorts and a tee, I join my family for dinner. It's always a five to seven-course meal. Grandma has had a private chef for as long as I can remember. An entire staff to take care of the house and everyone in it.

"You play Saturday night," Grandma says with a proud smile while resting her cloth napkin on her lap. "I already called and arranged everything. They're excited and honored to have you as a special guest."

I squint, shaking my head. "I'm not ready. I need to practice."

"Well, darling, we don't have a lot of time," she says.

Mom flinches. It's a gut punch.

"We'll practice after dinner," Dad says with a reassuring nod. Always my biggest fan and most supportive cheerleader.

It's not that my mom isn't too, but she knows what it's like to feel the weight of the world bearing down on you.

My phone vibrates on the table beside my plate.

"No phones at the table," Grandma says.

"Sorry." I wrinkle my nose, removing the phone from the table, but not without taking a quick peek at the screen. It's another text from Flynn. It shouldn't make my heart skip a beat, but it does even though I don't know what it says because everyone is staring at me, so I set it face down on the chair beside me.

"Did you quit your job?" Mom asks. She has a pained expression because she knows I loved living in Minneapolis, and I loved my job.

"Everything is temporary," Dad says, staring at my mom. "That was your motto when we met."

She returns a sad smile and a nod. "Yeah."

"This is temporary," Grandma says.

We look at her while she chews slowly, blotting her mouth as she swallows. "I won't live forever. With or without cancer." She reaches for her water glass. "Promise me you'll live here even when I'm gone and eat dinner at this table. And every night you'll toast those who have moved on, say grace even if you don't worship God. Laugh at the sheer silliness of life. Celebrate the journey because every single second of it is, in fact, temporary." She raises her glass.

Mom blinks back her tears but lifts her glass. Dad follows suit and so do I.

"To this most spectacular temporary moment," Grandma says.

We clink glasses, finish eating, and I quickly excuse myself.

"Are you going to practice?" Dad asks.

"Yeah, but I'm going to dry my hair and pull it back first."

"Okay. Let me know when you're ready."

"K." I snatch my phone and run upstairs to my bedroom.

Flynn: It was a kazoo. I just thought of the word. I played a kazoo

I cover my mouth and snort.

June: I was so close to choosing the kazoo but the cello called to me just a little more

Those three dots feel like the line going up and down on an EKG monitor; their existence feels like *life* right now.

Flynn: I could play row row row your boat

I giggle.

June: My first piano song was hot cross buns. We could have done a mash-up of the two

He sends a laughing emoji.

June: I have to go

Flynn: I have to stay

Is he being funny or heartbreaking?

Chapter
TWENTY-NINE

Flynn

I DON'T WANT Zoya Malone's life, but I can't stop stalking her online. Her band has played in stadiums around the world, even at the Roman Colosseum with some dude named Andrea Bocelli ... and *Buckingham Palace*! The cello-playing girl I watch in videos doesn't feel like the tour guide I met in the gallery. June blushed and flirted. She was vulnerable and seemingly relatable. Zoya is a larger-than-life force.

Like her band's name, Zoya feels *a world away* to me.

She's polished and elegant, playing classical music one minute, but in the next video, she's playing Metallica and AC/DC songs ... on a fucking cello. It's mesmerizing as hell.

I can still feel her touch and hear her whisper *I love you.*

It's not real. The woman on stage, with tears in her eyes every time a sold-out venue gives her a standing ovation, doesn't feel like the woman I love.

And she's not.

"What are you watching?" Callie asks, setting another box on her desk.

I lay my phone face down. "Nothing."

"Looked like June," she says, opening the box.

I pull out another stack of photos to scan. Callie has so many printed photos that belonged not only to her and Rupert, but to her parents and grandparents. Some are black and white photos from the early 1900s.

"Have you talked with her?" Callie asks.

"She's gone."

"Gone?"

"She went back to California for a family emergency."

"Oh no. Did she call you?"

"I found out from her roommate." I scan another photo as Callie sorts them according to the people or groups of people in them.

"So you haven't talked to her?"

"I texted her, but she didn't say what the emergency was, and I didn't ask."

"That's good. Respecting her space and privacy for now is smart."

"I don't think she's coming back, so there's plenty of space between us."

"Well, Rupert told me you don't want to live in her world anyway." Callie holds certain photos longer than others. And some, like the one in her hands of her grandson, she holds the longest. Tears fill her eyes, then she quickly blinks them away and smiles at me before moving to the next photo.

"Sometimes I watch YouTube videos of her performing. It's a good reminder that we have nothing in common," I say.

"I look at pictures of my son and his family. They're good

reminders that I will feel emotionally gutted for the rest of my life." She shrugs while sorting the photos. "Reminders are good, huh?"

I know she's trying to make a point. But I don't need it.

"This one is ripped," I say, ignoring her comment.

"Oh, I think there's some clear tape in the bottom drawer on the left."

To get to the tape, I lift two framed certificates out of the way. One has her name under Minnesota Board of Medical Practice. The other is from the American Board of Emergency Medicine.

"What are these?" I ask, holding them up.

She gives them a quick glance. "Oh," she murmurs returning her focus to the piles of photos. "You can put those in the trash."

"MD? Are you a doctor?"

"I was."

"Are you joking? You called your degrees 'unimportant.'"

"When you're not using a degree, it is unimportant."

"You retired?"

"Sort of."

"And *why* did you marry Mr. Rawlings?"

She glances up at me and chuckles. "Don't let him fool you. He has many talents."

"Well, I know he's good at stacking cookies in that glass jar."

"Like laying bricks," she says.

"Huh?"

"Rupert was a master brick mason for twenty-five years after being trained as a carpentry and masonry specialist in the Army."

"That's ..."

"Surprising? Because he lives in a big house and drives fancy cars?" she asks.

I shake my head. "Surprising because he wears a suit every day and sits in his office on a computer."

"Mmm ... well, that's his hobby."

"Weird hobby." I scan another picture and move it to the folder with photos of her parents.

She stands, pulls a book from her shelf, and hands it to me.

"I'm dyslexic. And I hate reading," I say.

"You don't have to read anything beyond the cover."

I take the book. There's an outline of a man running toward a lake in the rain. "*Beyond the Lake*," I read the title. The author is R. Rawlings. "Rupert Rawlings?" I ask.

"Yes." She takes the book from me and returns it to the shelf. "Rupert has been writing thriller novels for over ten years. He hasn't made any bestseller lists, but he loves it. And he loves me, so he wears suits because I think he looks handsome in them."

I slowly shake my head.

"Money doesn't change everyone," Callie says. "It hasn't changed him. He could have taken a job with my family's foundation. He could have been a day trader with money he didn't make. But he chose to lay bricks while I went to medical school and practiced medicine. And he spent a lot of hours alone with our son because my job was demanding. So one day, he read a thriller novel, and another, and another. Then he opened a Word document on his computer and started writing. I knew nothing about it until it was done." She smiles, sifting through the photos. "He was so proud. So was I."

The photo I scan is of her grandson.

"When is the last time you talked to your son?"

Her joyous expression fades. "Seven years ago." She slides the stacks of photos toward the edge of the desk. "Let's call it a day."

"I'll tell you what's behind my door, if you tell me what's behind yours," I say.

Callie tilts her head to the side and gives me a sad smile. "That's kind ... and brave of you." She steps behind me and wraps her arms around my neck. She smells like flowers, but different ones than June.

I close my eyes and wonder if her son misses his mom. I never really knew mine, but I think I've missed her every day since she left me, despite hating her for doing it. It's an indescribable loneliness, a lack of belonging.

"If she's still alive," Callie whispers, "I promise she's missing you."

She.

Is "she" my mom? If so, Callie is reading my mind.

Friday night, I deliver food for two hours and grab a pizza on my way back to the Rawlings'. Nobody's in the kitchen, so I sit at the island and eat my pizza with my phone propped up against a glass of water. There's a new video of June that pops up in my feed. It's from last night. It's been two weeks since we messaged. She didn't mention performing, but if this new video of her with the LA Philharmonic is old, then someone just decided to upload it, or it's happened recently.

The title of the video is "Zoya Malone—flawless as ever!" The description says she was a special guest, and the song title is "Cello Suite No. 1 in G Major." Her hair is down in long waves, like it was in the photo at the Minnesota Orchestra Hall. High black heels, sexy and elegant. And she's wearing a strapless red dress with a wide skirt, probably to accommodate the cello between her legs. After the performance, she receives a standing ovation and takes a slow bow. The footage isn't up close, so I can't see her expression, but after the video ends, I watch it again ... and again.

When I can't sleep, because every note of the song plays on repeat in my head, I roll over and grab my phone.

> Flynn: Found out today that Mr. R writes novels. Should I revisit the kazoo as a hobby?

I don't know if it's a two- or three-hour time difference, but maybe she's already asleep. Or maybe she's in some other part of the world, playing her cello. Is the family emergency over?

My screen illuminates with a reply. It's just three blushing emojis with the hand over the mouth.

> June: Immediately searching up Rupert Rawlings on Amazon

> Flynn: He goes by R. Rawlings. Thrillers

> June: How many? Have u read any of them yet?

> Flynn: I'm dyslexic

> June: Audiobook

I roll my eyes *and* reply with the eye-roll emoji.

June: Omg! He's written 8 books. I'm
starting one tonight

Flynn: lmk what u think

June: We could buddy read/listen and
discuss every few chapters

Flynn: Or u could give me a summary and I
can act like I read it

She doesn't reply. No little dots or anything.

Flynn: were u sleeping?

Nothing.

Flynn: Cool. Good chat

Still nothing, not even to my sarcastic reply.

I set my phone aside and wait for her to reply or sleep to take me.

The next morning, I see a missed text, but she sent it at 4:00 a.m. my time.

June: Sorry. I had to get back to practicing

I type a reply: ***Nbd. What are you practicing for?***
But I erase it before sending it.
Then I type: ***I saw a YouTube video of u***
But I erase that too.
I throw off the sheets and leave my phone on the bed. Within minutes, I'm out the door, jogging across the street to the path around the lake. Zoya playing Bach's prelude with

its haunting notes spurs me to run faster and faster, like I'm chasing something. Then I see her above me, our bodies tangled in the bedsheets. Her hair tickles my face as she grins before we kiss. Fingernails digging into my back. Tiny moans vibrating between us.

My whole life flashes before me. The abandonment. The abuse. The tiny breaths of reprieve, filled with laughter and glimmers of hope. The crack of a judge's gavel after sentencing me to time in prison.

The first day of freedom after my last day served.

The first touch of a woman's hands on my body.

Freedom and no clue what to do with it.

My lungs burn, but I continue to pump my arms, passing people with reckless abandon. I just want to silence the voice in my head reminding me of all the things I've never been or will ever be.

I veer to the side and onto the grass, collapsing onto my knees, then rolling onto my back.

Breathless.

Angry.

Lost.

And then ... the music stops.

The voices quiet.

It's me and my heart beating.

Clouds swirling.

Birds soaring.

I'm no more alive than dead.

Chapter THIRTY

June

"IT'S TOO MUCH," Mom says.

My parents talk in hushed voices, but with my ear pressed to their bedroom door, I can hear everything.

"She's twenty-six. I think she's old enough to know if it's too much. We have to stop coddling her," he says.

"Bodhi, she's experienced more than most people experience in a lifetime. I don't care how old she is; it's all too much. She's still dealing with a broken heart. She's back in LA. And my mom has basically blackmailed her into performing again. Who's going to take responsibility when she cracks? It's *too* much. She didn't get to bed until nearly two in the morning."

"It was her idea," he says.

"That's not fair. You know she's all or nothing. There is no in-between with her."

"Babe," he sighs, "what do you want me to do?"

"I don't know, but I can't lose my mom *and* my daughter."

"You're not going to lose her."

"We lost her, Bodhi! She left everything, including us, and found a new life halfway across the country. That felt like losing her."

"Well, now she's back."

"She's back and going to doctor's appointments with Mom. She's back and practicing her cello for three hours in the morning and three hours after dinner. She's back and she hasn't once laid by the pool."

"She swims every day," Dad says.

"Yeah. She swims laps until she's out of breath. She does everything until she just can't do it anymore. Then she sleeps a few hours, wakes up, and does it all again."

I peel my ear away from the door. I've heard enough. My parents fighting over my well-being does nothing to help. On my way downstairs for breakfast, I pull my phone from my robe's pocket and text Flynn—my favorite escape.

> **June:** If u could live anywhere in the world, where would it be?

I sit at the dining room table where a bowl of overnight oats and fresh berries is ready for me.

> **Flynn:** Where I am

> **Flynn:** If u could live anywhere in the world where would it be?

> **June:** I'd live in a van with a full tank of gas and endless possibilities

June: My dad had an old VW van when my mom met him. She said she fell as hard for the van as she did for my dad. And she named his van Alice.

Flynn: that might be the coolest thing I've ever heard

June: If u could only eat one food for the rest of your life what would it be?

Flynn: Duh. Chicken fingers

I giggle, taking a bite of oats.

Flynn: Last song u listened to that had words

My tummy does a little flip. Are we going to talk songs like my parents did?

June: Complicated by GRAACE

June: U?

Flynn: Iris by Josh Ross

My heart fractures. I don't think I've heard that artist, but I know every lyric to "Iris," and Flynn listening to it makes everything inside hurt.

June: I have to go

Flynn: I have to stay

"There you are," Dad says, sauntering into the dining room in shorts and a T-shirt. "Let's go to the beach today. No cello. No doctor's appointments. Just a day of relaxing in the sun."

"Yeah?" I sip my green tea. "Sounds like a great idea. Just hanging out in the sun, thinking of Grandma's melanoma diagnosis. Are we taking SPF 100 and wide-brimmed hats?"

He frowns, sitting across from me. Violet, Grandma's personal chef, delivers his coffee and an omelet with a side of sourdough toast. It's like she magically knows what time everyone will arrive for breakfast.

"Jeez, Zoya, did you really have to go there?" Dad asks.

"I have a better idea." Mom's cheery tone draws our attention toward her as she approaches the table in a long, floral sundress, tying her blond hair into a messy bun. "Let's take a bike tour."

Dad eyes me, waiting for my response.

I stir my oats before taking another bite and nodding. "I don't hate that idea."

"A little piece of home. Maybe you'll pick up a few tips," Mom says.

I appreciate her calling Minneapolis my home, even if I don't see myself going back anytime soon.

"Let me know if you find something to book," I say with a toothy grin before heading out to the pool where Grandma Juni is swimming laps.

When she notices me, she stops and pulls off her swim cap. Then she rests her arms on the pool deck. It's hard to believe she has cancer spreading through her body.

"Good morning." She gives me her brightest smile.

"Hey." I sit on the end of the padded lounger and hug my knees.

"It's a beautiful day. What are you going to do to make the most of it?" She's said those exact words to me too many times to remember.

"I was just going to ask you the same thing."

She laughs, attempting to lift herself out of the pool, something she's always done with ease. When her elbows buckle, she frowns and wades to the stairs. I act like I didn't notice, averting my gaze until she wraps up in a towel and sits on the lounger beside mine.

"Your mom said there's a young man in your life."

I shake my head. "Was."

"What's his name?"

"Flynn."

"What happened?" She pulls her hair over her shoulder and wrings out the water.

"He had a difficult childhood, and it's jaded him."

"Invite him to LA. It's pretty amazing what a week in the sun can do."

I roll my eyes. "No. Inviting him here is a terrible idea. He has an aversion to ..." I wave my hand around. "This."

"What's this?"

"Excess."

She eyes me. "Excess?"

"Mansions and pools. Personal chefs. Designer clothes. And I love that about him, even if the root cause is sad. But he can't separate me from the life that was chosen for me."

"Then he's not the one, my dear. If he has a chip on his shoulder now, he'll always have one. It's not your job to make him like you. Don't make yourself small for anyone." She squeezes my hand. "Not ever. Understood?"

"Is that what you think I did by moving to Minnesota? You think I made myself small?"

She spreads her towel out and reclines on the lounger. I doubt she's wearing sunscreen. "I think you ran away. And that's okay. I've done it. Your mom did it. There's nothing wrong with taking a break. A reset. But we don't just become other people. You can downsize your life, but it doesn't change who you are."

I turn to sit on the side of the lounger, squinting against the sun. "Who am I?"

"If you don't know that by now, then your time in Minnesota was all for nothing. And don't lie to yourself." She closes her eyes. "You didn't leave the stage because you fell out of love with the music. That kind of talent and passion are inextricably woven into your soul. It's like running away from your shadow. You can't do it. It's always there unless you live in darkness. And you and your Mom can bellyache all you want, but you've been relentlessly practicing for *you*, not for me. You'd give the same flawless performance on stage with no practice. Music will always be your first love. You won't truly *live* without it. And I don't want to die until I know you're not just existing, but truly living. So think of me and this experience I'm having as your muse."

"My muse?"

"Yes, a muse is—"

"I know what a muse is," I say. "I'm going inside. Do you need anything?"

"I'm good."

When I return to the dining room, my parents look up at me. I can tell they were talking about me again. "Did either of you tell Grandma that Flynn is a muse?"

They look at each other, brows furrowed, then they look at me, shaking their heads.

"Why?" Mom asks.

"No reason," I mumble, heading toward the stairs.

Chapter
THIRTY-ONE

Flynn

"Notice anything?" Callie asks as we spend another boring afternoon in silence on her covered balcony.

"I notice everything. There's nothing to do but notice stuff. You have a wasp building a nest in that corner. The tree over there"—I point to the right—"has two bird nests. There's not a cloud in the sky beyond the jet stream. Two different hummingbirds take turns at the feeder. One is smaller than the other. When we first came out here, all I could smell was coconut, something I assume you put on your skin or hair, but now all I smell is meat smoking somewhere. There's a button missing on the red cushion over there. And the wind chime is no longer soft and relaxing. Since the wind picked up, it's harsh and, frankly, a little unnerving."

I roll my head to look at her.

She keeps her eyes closed and grins. "You don't fidget."

"Huh?"

"You used to fidget nonstop. Now you don't fidget. Practicing being present, in the moment, has helped your nervous system. You're much calmer. Do you feel calmer?"

I shrug. "I don't know."

"I'm ready," she says.

"For what?" I rack my brain. Did we have plans to go somewhere? Was there something I was supposed to do for her? Get for her?

"Let's open our doors," she says.

I take a slow breath.

"My grandson's name was Linus. He had the most infectious giggle. Blue eyes that were just like mine. Curly blond hair. Chubby cheeks. And so much energy. We always got our exercise when he was here. Up and down the hallways, chasing Sally. Up and down the stairs at a frightening pace, gripping the spindles until his knuckles turned white. And he loved to sit on the park bench by the lake and feed the ducks."

The painting from the gallery was her grandson.

"He was ..." she trails off.

I glance at her as she wipes a tear running down the side of her face.

She swallows hard. "He was everywhere. His laughter. The pitter-patter of his bare feet. The scent of peanut butter because he dipped everything in it—bananas, berries ..." She laughs. "His fingers." Her hands press to her cheeks. "He used to grab my face and say, 'fishy kissy.'" Her lips quiver as more tears go unchecked. "He developed a cough and started vomiting after they picked him up from our house. I told them to take him to his pediatrician. He was diagnosed with croup and given medication, but it got worse over the following week. So I told them to bring him into the emergency room. My colleague felt it was a bad virus or food poisoning. I requested an X-ray. And we discovered he had swallowed a button battery that had eroded his trachea and larynx."

Callie presses her lips together to suppress her emotions, but her body shakes, eyes screwed shut. I'm way out of my emotional depth, but after a few seconds of hesitation, I kneel beside her lounger and pull her into my arms.

"I knew th-the battery was m-mine." She wraps her arms around my neck and sobs. "Oh g-god ... it was a-all m-my fault ..."

I don't know what to say, so I don't say a word. There's nothing I can say to convince her otherwise. Nothing I can say that will bring her grandson back.

"A ..." she releases me, sniffling while wiping the never-ending trail of tears. "A battery fell out of a fake tea light, and I knew it was on the floor somewhere, but I never found it. And ..." she swallows and shakes her head, teeth clenched, "I thought he had something in his mouth, and when I chased him to look at it, he stuck his tongue out at me, and nothing was there. So I just thought it was"—she continues to shake her head—"nothing," she whispers.

I sit on the edge of my lounger, hands folded between my spread legs.

"So"—she shrugs, using her shirt to wipe her face—"I'm a little dead inside. And I will be for the rest of my life."

"Your son and his wife have to know it was an accident. Tragic. But still, just an accident," I say.

Callie's face fills with tension, and then it relaxes, leaving a distant, almost lifeless look in her eyes. "His wife," she whispers, "took her life a week later."

Jesus.

"I think my son is alive." A new round of tears well in her eyes. "But"—she shakes her head—"I don't know."

I stand, resting my hand on her shoulder for a few seconds, before heading into the house.

"Flynn?"

I stop.

"You have to tell me what's behind your closed door."

I slowly shake my head because it's not a competition, and even if it were, she would win. It feels like an insult to even pretend I've experienced the level of emotional pain she's feeling.

"Just ... a sick fucker who liked to touch me and make me touch him. I was with him and his wife for three months. But nobody died."

"Flynn ..."

I don't face her. I just bow my head and murmur, "I'm sorry for your loss. I'm sorry that you'll carry it with you forever. I'm sorry there is nothing I can do to inspire you."

"Flynn," she says again. "It's not a contest. And some things feel as traumatic as death. I'm so sorry that happened to you. And if you want to talk, I'm *always* here for you. Okay?"

After a beat, I nod.

Chapter
THIRTY-TWO

Flynn

June: I'm sorry

I STARE at her text while eating a sandwich in the kitchen. Rupert and Callie are at a funeral today. It's just me and Loki.

Flynn: For what?

June: For waiting so long to tell u about my life before MN

What are we doing? She's there. I'm here. She had her secrets. I still have mine. We are so far apart in every way, whatever *this* is that we're doing seems pointless. What do I say?

Yeah, you should feel sorry. I would never keep anything from you.

Flynn: I lied about my job

June: ?

I took Rupert's Chevelle for a joyride and got caught. He gave me the choice to work for him or he'd call the police. Also I was in juvie for 18 months and prison for 3 years total

Even I cringe at all that information. So I delete the last part and stick with:

Flynn: I took Rupert's Chevelle for a joyride and got caught. He gave me the choice to work for him or he'd call the police

I wait.

And wait.

No dots.

No emojis.

Wow. That's it? Thank god I didn't give her everything. Or maybe I should have. If that minor indiscretion has her speechless, what would the word *prison* do to her?

"Okay then." I laugh, swiping out of the texting screen. "Nice knowing ya, June." I keep eating my sandwich even though I'm no longer hungry, and my chest aches. I don't want it to be love. Nope. No broken heart shit for me.

My phone vibrates, and the screen lights up.

June: How long is your sentence?

My sentence? Does she mean how long do I have to work for the Rawlings?

June: I bet you're the highest paid convict
ever

Flynn: No clue. Afraid to ask

June: I bet you're the highest paid convict
ever

What happened? Was she distracted? Is that why she didn't respond right away? Maybe she's practicing her cello, but that doesn't make sense because she texted first. No. She paused, needing a moment to digest what I confessed. And she has no idea how much irony there is in her word choice.

Flynn: I asked for a pay cut

June: Who does that?

Flynn: People who want to stay focused on
what matters

Again, she doesn't respond. What's wrong with wanting to stay focused on other people's struggles? Not wanting the love of money to turn me into someone who looks the other way?

June: Can't talk. Need to stay focused on
my terminally ill grandmother

"Shit ..." I smack my phone face down on the counter and sigh.

I don't need emojis to tell me she's pissed.

I hop off the barstool and pace the room. Then I grab my phone and call Monroe.

"What's up?" he answers.

There's clinking and grinding noises in the background. Typical sounds in an auto repair shop.

"I think I should just say 'fuck it,' and be a rich asshole. I don't know if there's a heaven, but I bet a few rich people get in if there is. So what's the point, ya know? What's the point of keeping a level head if I can just pick a charity to Venmo a few thousand bucks to every month from my yacht? Where is the alternative getting me in life? I'll tell you, nowhere. I just keep sticking my foot in my mouth which makes me look and feel like an asshole, so if I'm going to be an asshole either way, why not be a rich one?"

"Well," he chuckles, "first, I'm working. Second, that's a lot to unpack. Third, it must be nice to have the option to be rich or stay poor. I would choose rich seven days a week. So judge me all you want, but I don't know why you think being poor is some ethical choice poor people are making. And if being rich is so awful, why are you still working for rich people? Go to jail. Hang out with your tribe of poor criminals. You already sound stuck-up and entitled by calling me at work to rant about your dilemma that everyone else would love to have. And I say all of this with the most love possible. Okay?"

I sigh. "June's grandma is terminally ill."

"Sorry to hear that. But everyone is going to die. If you make it to be a grandparent, I don't think anyone should feel cheated when you die. Now, if we're done here, I have to work."

"Thanks, man," I say.

He laughs. "I didn't do a damn thing, but you're welcome."

I set my phone on the counter and exhale. What is this life of mine?

"FUUUCK!"

The voices in my head return. I don't even know whose they are, perhaps a mix of every person who has ever tried to tell me anything. So I go for another run, using memories of Zoya playing Bach to propel me around the lake.

Once.

Twice.

Three times.

After six miles, I drop in the same spot, stare at the same sky, and wait for a different outcome.

When I return to the house, entering through the back door by the laundry room, I hear voices. *Loud* voices. Rupert and Callie are home, and they're arguing. I've never lived in a house where the couple didn't scream at each other. Why should this house be any different?

"It's a fucking decision, Callie," Rupert says. "Right now. Not tomorrow. Not in ten years. Not in another life. Just make the choice to let go and be happy. Otherwise, what are you even doing?"

"What's that supposed to mean? If I can't reach your perceived level of happiness, then I shouldn't be here? Do you mean with you? In this house? In this life?"

"I'm not saying that," he says.

"Sounds like it. Rupert, you can't undo what's been done. You can't erase it from my brain. It doesn't matter how many people you find to distract me. You can hire a hundred Flynns, and I'll find a soft spot in my heart for every single one of them. But I don't need a muse. I don't need inspiration. The only thing I need is for you to accept me for who I am now. Not the woman you married. Not the person I was before he died. ME! The Callie who will have good days and bad days for the rest of her life. The grandmother who will never forget what happened and who will always feel a little dead inside. If I were disabled from a car accident, unable to walk again, you wouldn't tell me to get out of my stupid wheelchair and just walk like it's a decision. This heartache—"

Her voice cracks. "This heartache is every bit as permanent and disabling as losing a physical ability. And if you weren't such a selfish man who yearns for a time that is lost and can never be again, then you'd accept me where I'm at. You'd take the good days and magnify each moment. But you'd also give me space on the days that I just want to allow my heart to feel the grief that comes in waves."

I step around the corner into the hallway to hear better as Rupert lowers his voice to a volume of defeat.

"I fix things," he says. "I build things. I create things. It's who I am. And when the woman I love more than anyone in the world has bad days, I feel incapable of doing nothing."

"You are Flynn. He is you," she says. "You're both hell-bent on seeing the world as you think is just and right, instead of how it is. Sometimes you have to let go and trust the process. There's an ancient philosophy that states by doing nothing, everything is done. Stop resisting. Let yourself flow with life around you. Welcome changes in your life and how you see life around you." She sniffles. "We buried a friend today. Of course it triggered painful memories, and I felt them because I'm alive. I get to feel. Pain. Grief. Regret. Happiness. Hope. Love. I *get* to feel all the emotions. I want to feel everything. So just ... let me."

I peek around the corner into the kitchen. When their heads are bowed like there's nothing else to say, I dash to the stairs, taking them two at a time. After a shower, I lie on my bed and type out a text to June.

If a guy from MN wanted to visit a girl in CA how would he go about doing that?

I stare at the screen for more than thirty minutes, then delete it before heading downstairs, listening for voices before descending the stairs. No one's in the kitchen, so I check Rupert's office. It's empty. Then I check downstairs, and he's hitting balls with his golf simulator.

"Do you golf?" he asks, focusing on his shot.

I open my mouth to say it's a rich man's sport, and he should know the answer. "Never had the opportunity," I say instead.

"Well, let's see whatcha got." He hands me the club and nods for me to stand by the rubber tee.

"Slide your grip back a little." He grabs another club and demonstrates.

I mirror him.

"Widen your stance an inch."

I do as he instructs.

"A little bend in your knees. That's it. When you bring it back, keep your lead arm straight like this. Rotate your torso and shoulders, but don't let your hip jut out too far. Keep your swing fluid, leading with your lower body, shifting your weight to your front foot like this." He swings slowly. "Head steady. Chest facing the target."

I take a slow swing, making little adjustments. Then I hit the ball on the tee and look at the screen.

"Not bad at all," Rupert says, giving me an approving nod.

"I talked to Callie the other day about your grandson," I say, setting another ball on the tee.

"Yes, she told me."

"Well," I hit another ball.

"Let your right elbow bend a little more," he says.

I nod. "I don't know how long I have to work here to pay for my joyriding incident. But I don't think there is anything I can do to help her. So I was wondering if you'd be okay with me flying out to California?"

"To visit June?"

I nod then hit another ball. "Figured I'd sell her car since she's not here, and I don't see her returning. And I'll use the money for a plane ticket and a hotel room when I get there."

"Are you asking for permission to quit?" He lifts his golf club over his head to stretch.

"I think so. If you'll let me, without calling the police."

"Well, calling the police would be a real dick move on my part, wouldn't it?"

I grin. "It would."

"Did June invite you to come see her?"

"No. She's not speaking to me." I swing the club and whiff.

"You're going to California by yourself to see a girl who's not talking to you?"

"So it would seem." I hit the ball this time.

"Nice." Rupert watches the screen and whistles. "Thought she was too rich for you."

"She is."

"But?"

I hand him the golf club. "I think I've been waiting for things in my life to make sense, since they never have. June made sense, or so I thought." I climb onto the barstool at his fully stocked bar.

It looks just like something from an actual pub. Draft beer. Shelves of every kind of alcohol imaginable.

"I now think waiting for something to make sense is the

biggest waste of time. When I die, I don't think I'll care about things making sense, but I know I'll remember how her hands felt on my neck or in my hair. I'll remember the way she brought me to my knees with a single look. The music she made. The look in her eyes when I touched the scar above her lip."

Rupert returns the clubs to his bag. "Well, shit, Flynn. You might just be smarter than ninety percent of all other men. But you still haven't told her about your past?"

I shake my head. "I will."

"And what will you do if she doesn't want to be with you?"

"Dunno. I'll figure it out if I have to."

He pulls a cold mug from the freezer and fills it with beer. Then he slides it to me across the polished bar.

I can't hide my grin.

"Would you like me to get your airfare arranged?" He fills a second mug with beer.

After I take a swig, I shake my head. "No. But I appreciate the offer."

He gives me an approving smile. "Well, you have my number. Don't choke on your pride or drown in misery. If you need something, call. Okay?"

I nod several times.

"At least let me make a call to help you get a credit card and a bank card if you don't have one. You'll need it for booking things."

I twist my lips.

"It's not charity. They'll be your bills to pay."

After contemplating it, I nod and murmur, "Thank you."

An awkward silence lands between us, and I glance

around the bar area. "So ... you're an author, who secretly loves cats."

Rupert frowns when I look at him.

"No." I snicker. "It's cool. Your secret is safe with me. Well, that's a lie. I already told June about your books."

"Don't pass up an opportunity to try new things," he says. "Writing stories is fun."

"I'm dyslexic," I say.

"Your brain is not broken. You could write a story if you wanted. Speech to text."

"My brain feels a little broken." I shrug. "Anyway, June's grandma is terminally ill. Any suggestions on what I should say?"

He chuckles, shaking his head. "You should ask Callie. It's been brought to my attention that I have a tendency to force my need to fix things on other people. You can't fix what's happening to her grandma. I'd probably go with KISS —keep it simple, stupid. Something like, 'This sucks. I'm sorry you're going through this. I'm here if you need anything.'"

I nod slowly. "KISS. Got it."

"I'd avoid criticizing anyone, even if you attach it to a *respectfully.*"

"Good tip." I laugh.

He sets his beer on the bar and slides his hands into his pockets. "I didn't hire you as a punishment. Callie didn't make you sit with her on the balcony for hours as a punishment."

"I know."

"I hope one day, you'll look back and think the best mistake you ever made was taking my car for a joyride."

I drink the rest of my beer and stand. "I don't have to wait for that day. I already know it was."

His smile swells. It's fatherly pride. And since I don't remember my father, I'll remember this summer with Rupert and Callie Rawlings. The summer I grew up. Fell in love. And wore leather loafers without socks.

Chapter
THIRTY-THREE

Flynn

ALLY GIVES me the key to the MINI Cooper without any resistance, and I sell it for five hundred dollars more than I paid for it. I'll be back, so I don't make a big deal over saying goodbye to Monroe. He gets a short text with which he replies with a thumbs-up emoji. Callie and Rupert insist I keep my trunk of belongings at their house until I return.

With my credit card, I fly to LAX and catch my first glimpse of the ocean on the way to my hotel.

It's been two weeks since June stopped texting me back. This might be the dumbest thing I've done, but it feels like the bravest too. I don't know where her parents live.

Where to find the best chicken fingers.

Or whether I should let housekeeping in my hotel when I'm not here.

With my feet officially in West Coast sand with endless miles of ocean in front of me, I text June.

Flynn: Hi

She doesn't respond, so I keep walking down the beach. It smells fishy as I get closer to the water. The breeze feels bigger. The sun feels hotter. Everything is grand.

Flynn: If I were to send u something what address would I use?

No reply.

I don't want to tell her I'm here. Not yet. I thought about asking Ally for her address, but I didn't trust her not to tell June. I stare at my phone, racking my brain for something that will get her attention. Maybe I'm making this too difficult.

Flynn: Falling in love with you was easy. Falling out of love with you is impossible. I know. That's a me problem

All of my messages say delivered. Is she reading them? I don't know.

After I get my fill of the beach, I find insanely good chicken at The Red Chickz. Hot chicken tenders with French toast, homemade honey butter, and syrup. I might not return to Minneapolis. I bet there are drugs in these crispy tenders. They are that good.

I take a photo and send it to June. Let's see if she reads the name of the restaurant on the wrapper and realizes there are no Red Chickz locations in Minnesota.

When she doesn't respond, I finish my meal and go back to the hotel.

The next morning, I send off another text.

> Flynn: Good morning. Are u spending the day with your grandma?

No reply.

Callie gave me a list of things to do here if I had time to waste while waiting for June to give me another chance. So I visit the Los Angeles County Museum of Art first. I channel my inner Callie and find works of art that interest me, then I stare at them for fifteen ... twenty minutes. Canting my head to the right then left like Callie does.

My phone vibrates in my pocket, and I quickly grab it. But my excitement dies when it's Rupert texting me.

> Rupert: Did you reunite with your lover?

I roll my eyes.

> Flynn: No. She won't answer my texts

> Rupert: She performs tonight at Segerstrom Concert Hall with the Pacific Symphony

> Flynn: Thanks

I look it up on my phone. It's less than an hour by train or bus.

> Rupert: Callie has a friend who can get you a ticket. Pick it up at the box office. It will be under your name

> Flynn: Tell Callie thx

> Rupert: Will do. Don't forget to grovel

I send him the eye roll emoji. But yeah, I'm not beyond groveling at this point. Since she's performing tonight, maybe that's why she hasn't responded.

Segerstrom Concert Hall is intimidating without June by my side. I feel like everyone is staring at me, even though they're not.

"Hi, I think there's a ticket here for me. Flynn Morley," I say to the lady at the box office.

"Can I see your ID?" she asks.

I dig my wallet out of the pocket of my linen pants which Callie bought me.

"Enjoy the performance," the lady says, handing me the ticket.

"Thanks." I make my way to the concert hall.

"Can I help you find your seat?" an older gentleman dressed in all black asks.

"Uh, sure." I show him my ticket.

"You're in the front row." He points toward the stage. "But on the opposite side. So you can go out this door and make your way to the other side and someone there will help you find your seat."

"Thanks."

Front row? Who's Callie's friend? Do I want to be in the front row? Will June's parents be here? What has she told them about me and what happened between us?

An usher on the opposite side escorts me to my seat as a handful of musicians warm up on stage like they did in Minneapolis. I check my phone again.

Nothing.

When the hall is filled, a violin player enters the stage. Everyone applauds, so I do too. But I don't see June. They go through some tuning thing before the conductor comes on the stage and the concert begins.

I scan the program and there's a picture of June. *Dang, she's so stunning.* All I can do is wait patiently for her performance. When the moment arrives, I take a deep breath as she steps onto the stage in a long dress that could double as a wedding gown, the color of champagne. Delicate straps of lace and pearls. Her hair is partially pulled up with locks framing her face. Earrings matching the pearls on her dress. She flows with grace, sitting in a chair center stage, poised posture as her body molds to the cello.

When the applause ends, she looks to her right and smiles. I wonder if her parents are at the opposite end, recipients of that smile. As she settles back into her stance, composing herself, her gaze slides along the front row like an afterthought, like she's not really focusing on the people in the chairs. But her eyes backtrack, landing on me. Her lips part, a tiny line forms on the bridge of her nose as she ever so slightly squints.

I don't make a big deal of the moment, keeping my smile as subtle as her expression. She closes her eyes, inhaling while bringing the bow to the strings. The song is "Serenade" (Schubert).

One song.

One performance.

A standing ovation.

She takes a bow, leaving me in awe and breathless.

After the show, I crane my neck to see her parents past the sea of people funneling toward the exits. I see Henna's long, blond hair and Bodhi behind her, but they're on the opposite side.

"Excuse me. Sorry. Pardon me." I shoulder past people in front of me, eliciting a few rude comments. By the time I make it to the exit where her parents were, they're nowhere in sight.

I step to the side, behind one of the ushers, and text June.

Flynn: I need to see u. Where are u?

She doesn't answer, so I call her, but she doesn't have a mailbox set up. I shove my phone into my pocket and stab my fingers into my hair, turning in a slow circle and scanning every inch of the crowd. Every door. Every corner. She has to be here, or she's leaving. Why would she stay?

I find the nearest exit and jog around the building's perimeter. In a loading dock, Henna climbs into a black SUV with June and Bodhi behind her.

"June!" I call, jogging toward the vehicle.

Bodhi squints, and June says something to him. He kisses her forehead and climbs in the back seat. Her bodyguard shuts the door, standing in front of it with his hands crossed.

I slow my stride as I approach her because she's not giving me a smile or any sort of vibes that she's happy to see me. She's in a simple black sundress instead of her performance gown.

"You were incredible tonight," I say.

She frowns, looking so sad. "You're here," she murmurs looking sadder by the second. "Listen, I don't know why you came all this way, but my rich parents and even richer grandma are waiting for me in this expensive SUV. We're driving back to our mansion in Beverly Hills. Back to our life where we don't have to worry about *caring for anything that matters*."

I drop my head. "June ..."

"I can't do it, Flynn. I can't magically not be wealthy, even if I tried. And I'm not complaining. I'm sure that seems like a real privileged problem to have. It's just ..." She shakes her head. "Since you found out about my life, I feel constantly judged, like I'm walking around on eggshells. If I offer to pay for something, if I enjoy eating at a nice restaurant, wearing a pretty dress ... it's all wrong in your eyes. I know love takes work, and it's not always easy, but this is too much."

"June, I'm sorry—"

She holds up a hand. "Don't be sorry. Not wanting to lose who you think you are and what matters most to you is not a flaw. I don't want you to change who you are to fit into my world, and you shouldn't want me to change to fit into yours. Our time was perfect, until it wasn't. But that's life, right? Moments that become memories. I like our memories together, and I don't want anything to ruin them. That's why I think it's best if we let go before anyone gets hurt."

"Hurt? June, I quit my job, got on a plane for the first time in my life, and came her for you *because* everything fucking hurts without you." I take a step backward as if putting space between us will keep me from losing control of my emotions. "I know I'm an idiot. A fool. A coward. And a cruel asshole with a past that's left me bitter toward a lot of people, maybe the whole world. But I just ..." I lace my fingers behind my head and stare at the night sky. "God, I'm terrible with words. I just ..."

I'm losing her, and I hate it. But maybe I deserve it.

"I love you." I let my arms fall to my sides. "I know that's not original, and it probably means nothing because I've already said it. But I've never said those words to anyone … and I mean anyone before you. Not a mother or father. No siblings. No family. Not a pet. Not even a fucking imaginary friend." I hold my fist at my head and slowly shake it. "I love you. And I don't know why you would love me because there is nothing special about me, but you said those words to me and …"

Fuck …

I pinch the bridge of my nose. No. I'm not going to cry. Not now. Not with that guy standing a few feet behind her. Not with her parents probably looking at us out the tinted window.

"No one," my voice cracks and I swallow hard, "has said those words to me." I take another step backward.

She wipes tears from her face, unbothered by anyone seeing her. That's probably normal. Sharing emotions. *Feeling* deeply. I fucking hate feeling anything. But here I am, feeling everything.

"I don't want you to fit into my world, June. I want you to *be* my world."

She chokes on a sob and shakes her head a half dozen times. "I hate you so much," she stutters with a shaky breath. Then she turns and waits for her bodyguard to open the door.

I pivot and walk away with no regret. Not knowing would have been worse than knowing. At least I can move on with the closure from having said everything I could, even if the words aren't enough. Even if I'm not enough.

I hear the vehicle pull away behind me, and I take a deep

breath. This hurts. She's it. I tried the falling-in-love thing, and I'm done. Never again.

"My dad expects you to keep a close eye on me."

I stop.

"How are you supposed to do that with your back to me?"

I turn as she waltzes toward me with a big bag over her shoulder, feet clicking in flip-flops. "Thought you were leaving," I say.

"I had to get my bag and tell my mom that you weren't done breaking my heart, so you must be the one."

"Thought you hated me."

She stops right in front of me. "I hate you so much *because* I love you despite all common sense."

I take her bag from her, and then I take the last step between us.

"Are you done breaking my heart?" She grabs my shirt with both fists.

I lower my head, brushing my lips over hers. "Probably not," I whisper.

Not even close.

She closes her eyes and whispers, "Promise to always put it back together?"

I slide my hand to cup the back of her head, fingers in her hair. "Promise."

When we kiss, I vow never to kiss another. If she leaves me, I will not kiss another woman. This is it. June is my all or nothing.

"I love you," I say between kisses. "My first, now, and always."

"Baby," she grins, kissing a line from my jaw to my neck, tightening her grip on my shirt, "don't ever say you're not good with words. You're the most poetic accidental romantic."

I chuckle because I don't know what an accidental romantic is, but as long as she calls me her "baby" and kisses my neck, she can call me anything.

"Are your parents coming back for us or at least you?"

"Nope." She hugs my arm and nudges me forward. "We're walking to the nearest hotel. You have some proper apologizing to do. And I thought it best to do it with a little privacy, since you're such a screamer."

Chapter THIRTY-FOUR

June

THERE'S a hotel across the street from Segerstrom Concert Hall, so that's where we go.

"I have a credit card now," Flynn says as we enter the lobby with me hanging from him, lips on his neck, hands snaking up the back of his shirt.

"Great," I mumble. "Give it to them before we take off our clothes."

He chuckles, trying to dig out his wallet from his pocket. "We need a room," he says to the gentleman at the front desk.

"Do you have a reservation?"

"No," Flynn says.

"Would you like a king room or two queens?"

"We probably won't make it past the elevator, but just in case, let's do a king room," Flynn says.

I giggle, nibbling at his earlobe.

"Driver's license," the guy says.

Flynn hands him his credit card and driver's license. The guy gets us keys to the room in record time, probably to get our PDA out of the lobby.

We step into the elevator, and he drops my bag at his feet and buries his fingers in my hair and tongue in my mouth, pushing me against the back wall, his leg wedged between mine.

Our needy hands don't let go.

Not down the hallway.

Not in the hotel room.

Not when we reach the bed.

I sit on the edge with him standing in front of me. He pulls off my dress and I unbutton his pants.

Shirt.

Underwear.

"Oh god ..." I arch my back as he sinks into me, pushing my hands above my head.

He dips his head, trapping my nipple between his teeth, and I moan.

"Flynn ..."

He grins before doing it to my other nipple. It sends an intense, electric sensation straight between my legs.

"Zoya," he whispers over my lips.

I press my palms to his face to stop him before he kisses me. "Say it again." I brush my thumb over his bottom lip.

Flynn grins, rocking his hips with mine. "Zoya ... Juju ... June ... Malone." He kisses me, swallowing my giggle.

This man owns my heart, all its pieces, the fragile cracks, and every single beat. Grandma Juni thinks music will always be my first love, but she's wrong.

June, I don't want you to fit into my world. I want you to be my world.

I will replay his words in my head for the rest of my life.

He rolls us over, hands sliding down my back to my ass. I sit up, and he does too. When he curls my hair behind my ears before kissing me, I get a little emotional. This love is *so big.*

~

"I love you. I love you. I love you," I repeat, kissing Flynn's face, neck, and chest, early the next morning.

He chuckles. "I don't know what's happening, but don't stop. In fact, go a little lower."

I grin, shimmying myself on top of him so our faces are hidden under my hair. "I'm making up for all the times someone should have said 'I love you' but didn't."

He gets a funny look with some tension along his brow. "What?" I ask.

"Nothing. It's just you know I'm going to mess up and break your heart again. That was established last night."

I kiss the corner of his mouth. "Yes, but can you give me a little break? Maybe wait until my grandma finishes her treatment before you mess with my heart again."

He rolls us to the side so our legs are scissored. "How is she?"

"It's hard to say. She's good at pretending things are fine even when they aren't. She's had several months of treatment that she doesn't want, and the doctors are cautiously optimistic. It's malignant melanoma that has spread to distant lymph nodes. She's doing targeted immunotherapy, a new experimental drug. She has several alternative health practitioners she sees. We're literally trying everything."

"Why doesn't she want the treatment?"

I adjust my head on his arm and tease my fingers along the stubble on his jaw. "At first, I think she was in denial because she didn't feel sick. Now she has some obvious bad days and more symptoms, but I don't know if it's from the cancer or the treatment. She was at the concert last night. Did you see her get into the vehicle?"

He shakes his head.

"Well, thankfully yesterday was a good day. Of course, her doctors don't like her in big crowds because she's immunocompromised, but she won't miss my performances. It's the reason she's doing treatment." I lean in and kiss him.

He pulls away. "What do you mean?"

"She wasn't going to do it, but she wanted me to perform again, so I agreed to one performance a month for every month she did treatment. Not my band, just me. So I've been doing guest performances, but just in California."

"I've seen them," he says.

I wrinkle my nose. "What? Last night wasn't your first?"

"I've watched YouTube videos. Last night was my first live performance." He laughs. "I haven't been here stalking you for months."

"I can't believe you're here now. Last night, I thought I was hallucinating."

"Speaking of last night, how did you get away without your bodyguard?"

"Grandma Juni told my parents it was time to let go and let me live again. Nobody argues with her. So here we are. I say we have food delivered and stay in bed all day. Go back tomorrow."

Flynn smirks, kissing his way down my body. "I have no objections to that idea."

I giggle, threading my hands through his hair as his mouth settles between my spread legs.

Chapter
THIRTY-FIVE

Flynn

IT'S NEVER the right time to tell someone about your prison record. June doesn't want her heart broken again so soon. But if I wait, she'll feel like I should have told her. That is ... if she ever speaks to me again.

As promised, we spend the next twenty-four hours in bed. Food delivery. Showers. Fluffy white robes. And so much sex I start to feel like I'm the one hallucinating. I've bought my fair share of condoms, but I've never had them delivered to a hotel room. Didn't know that was a thing. But it is.

June's literally my world right now. No job. No parents. No responsibilities.

"Where are you staying?" she asks, the following morning, freshly showered. We dress into our clothes from the other night.

"In a hotel not too far from the airport."

"Got room for one more?" she asks, giving me a flirty grin while combing her fingers through her hair.

"Can I be honest?" I ask.

"Not if you're going to break my heart."

I roll my eyes as if it's ridiculous, as if I'm not going to obliterate her heart when I vomit the rest of my past all over her fragile world. "Other than finding you and groveling, I didn't have a plan when I flew out here. I don't think living out of a hotel is an option. I need a job." I sit on the end of the bed and put on my shoes.

"Well, I can't leave." She frowns. "But if you need to go back to Minneapolis, I understand."

"I don't want to go anywhere without you."

June's frown morphs into a grin as she steps toward me, resting her hands on my shoulders. "I was hoping you'd say that. How do you feel about getting an apartment with me? You can get a job. I'll go to my parents' house to practice my cello. I can show you around L.A. What do you think?"

I lean forward, resting my forehead between her breasts. "I think I love you."

"You *think?* Flynn, I'm going to need you to do more than *think* you love me." She teases her fingers through my wet hair.

"You're pretty intimidating. On that stage the other night, I was tempted to leave and get on a plane back to Minnesota. *This girl* loves me?" I laugh. "I was like, no fucking way."

She tips my chin up. "You're my muse. Falling in love with you made me want to play again."

"What's so inspiring about me?"

"You're sexy, and confident." Her head bobs a few times. "But not overly confident. Sometimes you get nervous, and I love those tiny glimpses of your vulnerability. I love your sense of humor. Your protectiveness. You say what you feel."

"I stick my foot in my mouth."

June grins. "Sometimes. And you're giving."

"I sold your car to afford this trip."

Her smile widens. "You're frugal and scrappy. And I know Rupert hired you because he saw something special in you, and I want *that*. I want what you don't see in yourself. That's inspiring."

"Well," I turn my head and kiss the inside of her wrist, "you inspire me too."

"Yeah?"

I snake my hands up her dress and peel her underwear down her legs. "Yeah," I whisper.

She looks at the alarm clock on the nightstand. "We have to check out in fifteen minutes."

"Then you'd better stop talking."

"So ..." June rocks bath and forth on her heels after we get off the train. "I'll go back to my house, check in with my family, and pack a few things. Text me your hotel and room number. And this afternoon we'll start apartment hunting."

I pull her closer to me when a group of guys slides past us in front of Union Station. The breeze brings the stench of something not so fresh from the garbage bin behind us.

"Or," I say, "we can go to my hotel and I'll change clothes. Then we can go to your house together."

Her lips twist, nose wrinkled, but I don't think it's from the rotten smell. "It's not a good idea for you to come to the house."

"Why? Are your parents mad at me?"

She shakes her head, glancing around the area. "No. It's just however you felt about the Rawlings' house, you'll feel that times a hundred when you see their house. Technically, it's my grandma's house, but after my grandpa died, my parents moved in with her. And I lived there too until I moved to Minneapolis."

"It's a big house," I say.

She nods.

"I figured." I shrug.

She nervously cracks her knuckles. "It's the definition of wealth and excess."

"June"—I adjust her bag on my shoulder—"your grandma has cancer. Do you really think I'm going to make a big deal about her house?"

She sighs, scraping her teeth long her bottom lip. "Fine. Let's get a ride to your hotel."

I grin, looking down at my phone to order a ride. "I'm going to go with the flow."

"Are you capable of going with the flow?"

"Juju"—I take her hand and pull her closer to the street to keep an eye out for our ride—"I guess you'll just have to wait and see."

After I change into jeans and a T-shirt at my hotel, we get a ride to Beverly Hills. And June wasn't wrong. Her house is mind-blowing. It looks like a small hotel, not a single-family residence.

I swallow my reaction to the *two* staircases going to the same place. It makes no sense.

"Stop," she whispers, taking her bag from me and rolling onto her toes to kiss my jaw just below my ear.

"Stop what?" I force a toothy grin.

"We all go to the same place when we die," she says. "None of this matters." She pulls me up the stairs.

I kinda love that she said the thing I've tried to tell myself for weeks.

"Where is everyone?" I ask.

"Grandma is probably on the terrace reading or napping. My parents should be at the stables. My mom texted me this morning about it."

This is a modern contrast to the Rawlings' older home. Sharper lines. More glass and less marble. Sleek instead of ornate.

"Where are the stables?" I ask.

"In Hidden Hills where there are trails for riding the horses." She opens a door to a corner bedroom with floor-to-ceiling windows and a private balcony.

She left this life for an apartment in Minneapolis?

"Have you ever been on a horse?" she asks from her closet.

I stare at the photos on the built-in shelves. There's not a single one of her with her cello. Just photos of her with her parents. Several where she's on a horse. Another with Juni and maybe her grandpa? There are a few with groups of girls, maybe friends. It's all so normal. Not photos of people rich with wealth, just rich in life and love. I would have given anything for that life.

Family.

Friends.

Belonging.

"Flynn?" She steps out of her closet in shorts and a tank top while gathering her hair into a ponytail. "Have you ridden a horse?"

I shake my head. This is wrong. I have to tell her. She's

all smiles and making plans to get an apartment with me. She's playing concerts to motivate her grandma to keep living. This woman loves me, but I feel like a fraud. Even if I'm not the same person who went to prison, it's part of my story. How can I ask her to be part of it, too, if she doesn't know everything that made me into the man she loves?

"Babe." She presses her palms to my cheeks. "Earth to Flynn."

I wrap my hands around her wrists. "I have to tell you something."

"You sound so serious." She tries to laugh it off and pull away from me, but I keep her hands on my face.

Her smile fades. "Flynn, what is it?"

I close my eyes for a second. *She loves me. Her love is the truest thing I've ever experienced.* It's why I don't want to tell her. It's why I *have* to tell her.

"I did something stupid when I was eighteen." I open my eyes. "Because I needed money. I stole a car."

Her brow furrows. "Like when you took Rupert's car for a joyride."

I slowly shake my head. "Like I stole a car and sold it for the money. And I spent a year in prison for it."

The tension in her brow deepens. "What?" she whispers.

I can't stop. It's all or nothing.

"A year later, a man accused me of sleeping with his wife. He was drunk. And he, uh ..." I swallow hard. "He said he was going to fuck me harder than I fucked his wife, and he tried to pin me down, but I fought back. And I just kept fighting until I realized he was pretty bloody."

She draws in a sharp breath and tears fill her eyes as she slowly shakes her head.

"And who believes someone with my record? So I spent

two years in prison for assault. The wife spoke on my behalf, so I pled guilty in exchange for a lesser sentence of two years instead of five."

She eases out of my grip, and I don't stop her. "Jesus, Flynn." She presses a hand to her mouth and shakes in silent sobs.

I reach for her, but she takes a step back and shakes her head.

"I know you asked me not to break your heart again so soon, but ..." I sigh. "I've been trying to tell you this for so long. At first, I didn't want to scare you away, then I didn't want to ruin what we had because I've never had anything like this. And after the orchestra, when I found out about your past, I was angry, but it wasn't because you didn't tell me. It was because you were hiding something extraordinary about yourself, and I was hiding something fucking awful, embarrassing, and so regrettable."

She turns her back to me, staring out the window while wiping her nose with the back of her hand and sniffling.

"I was selfish. And I'm sorry. But after I told you about my time in juvie, I couldn't imagine not losing you if I told you everything."

"You should have told me everything."

"I know, I just ..."

She turns. "You just what? You were afraid of losing me to the truth? Well, this no longer feels like the truth. It feels like betrayal. How am I supposed to trust you?"

"June." I shake my head. "That's it. I'm not keeping anything else from you. And I would have told you, but how would you have reacted? Because when I told you about juvie, you walked away."

"Jesus, Flynn. I'm human. I had a human reaction. But I apologized."

"Exactly!" I blow out a slow breath. This isn't how I want to react to her. She has every right to be upset. But I can't help this feeling of desperation. "You're human," I say. "And you were abducted. I can't imagine what that was like for you, but I would expect your *human* reaction to be severe. And I don't know how to make this okay because apologizing for not telling you feels like I wish we weren't together. You would have run. And I wouldn't have blamed you. So here I am, apologizing for not telling you, but really I'm apologizing for hurting you *again* because I don't know if I can be sorry for everything that's happened between us."

Her red eyes bleed more tears as her lips quiver. "Jesus, Flynn. You should have trusted me."

"You can't say that. You didn't trust me."

"No!" She swallows hard, jaw clenched. "I can't compare my secret to yours."

"I'm not comparing secrets. I'm just saying you didn't trust me, and I didn't trust you."

"N-no..." she laughs through a little sob. "My family's wealth is not about something I did or didn't do. It wasn't a choice I made. But going to prison, *twice*, is just ..." Again, she shakes her head a half dozen times. "What happens when there's a knock at the door someday, and you're arrested for something you forgot to mention?" She balls her hands into fists. "Why didn't you get a job instead of stealing the car?"

I shake my head. "I ... I couldn't get a job. Nobody would hire me."

"That's bullshit."

I rest one hand on my hip and rub my temples with the other. "I'm not lying. I'm not saying it was right. But you don't know what it's like to live the way I did."

"Because I'm rich?"

"Because you were raised by people who loved you. And you've probably never lived on the street or out of your car."

"That doesn't make it okay to steal from people."

"I know," I whisper.

"Did you sleep with that man's wife?" She crosses her arms over her chest.

I've lost her. And she has every right to be mad. But fuck, it hurts so much. After a few seconds, I nod.

More tears well in her bloodshot eyes, and she bites her quivering lip. I hate that I'm hurting her. But it was always going to hurt, and if I would have told her before she was emotionally invested in me, when it wouldn't have hurt, she wouldn't have given me a chance. That's just a fact.

Does it make me selfish? Yes.

A liar? Yes.

But I think everything in my life has led me to her. I have to believe it.

One. Good. Thing.

I have to believe I'm deserving of *one good thing*.

"I don't know if I can do this," she whispers, wiping her nose with the back of her hand.

"Do this? What is this?" My words come out louder—more desperate—than I intend. "Talk? Be with me? Move in to an apartment together? Love me?"

"I ... I don't know," she says, as if something inside of her has died.

Drawing in a sharp breath, I prepare to make another

plea. But after holding it for a few seconds, I exhale in silence. It's over.

Bowing my head, I step past her toward the bedroom door.

She reaches for my wrist. Her fingers wrapping around it feels like slow motion. It's how my heart feels, stumbling over its next beat, looking for a steady rhythm, looking for purpose. No one has ever been this gentle.

Fuck every single tear that breaks free. I use my other hand to wipe them away. Her body shakes with more silent sobs. When she's ready, I'll walk away. But I won't until she lets go. It can't be me. I tried letting her go, but my heart is not capable of that.

"This stops now," she says softly. "I bet you don't know what it feels like to trust someone."

"Don't do this," I say as emotions strangle my words.

"For someone to trust you." She turns to face me.

But I can't turn toward her. Not yet.

"I trust you," she says. "And you can trust me."

I pinch the bridge of my nose and hold my breath as the lump in my throat thickens.

"I trust that you love me." She touches her palm to my cheek.

I grab it, holding it tightly as a sob rips from my chest.

"And you can trust me when I say you don't have to cut yourself open and bleed for me. I will love your scars the way you have loved mine."

My knees buckle, and I fall to them, hugging her waist while I cry more than I have ever cried in my life. Tears for the three-year-old boy whose mom abandoned him and every single moment that left one of those scars.

"Oh god ..." I sob, my entire body shaking because I've never felt emotion like this—bone-deep.

I didn't find June, Rupert, or Callie. Through them, I've found myself.

321

Chapter THIRTY-SIX

Flynn

"There she is." June slides open a glass door that's a whole wall. I've never seen anything like it. We step onto a covered terrace filled with furniture and an outdoor fireplace. A swimming pool with fountains and a diving board lie just beyond the terrace.

A blond and silver-haired woman in a white bikini and a long, sheer black cover-up eyes us from a round chair that's the size of a small bed. "Zoya," she says with a smirk.

"Grandma, I'd like you to meet Flynn."

She sits up, sliding her legs off the side of the white cushion and offers her hand. "I'm Juni, it's nice to meet you. I've heard so much about you." She winks at June.

I shake her hand. It's a little cold. "Nice to meet you. June has said a lot of nice things about you."

"June?"

June clears her throat, pulling me to sit beside her on the sectional. "When I moved to Minneapolis, I chose a different first name."

Juni narrows her blue eyes. "Zoya is a beautiful name."

June nods. "It is, but it's not common, and I wasn't looking for recognition. So I thought about my favorite grandma and chose a variation of her name."

Juni eats up every word, clearly taken with her granddaughter. "I'm flattered. But you're home now, so Flynn should call you Zoya." Juni stands.

"What do you need," *Zoya* asks, standing too.

"The restroom, dear. I think I can do it on my own."

Zoya looks at me, and I return a tight grin like we're in trouble. She sits back down, leaning into me as I put my arm around her, kissing the top of her head.

"I love you *so* much," I murmur.

She reaches for my hand wrapped over her shoulder, interlacing our fingers. "I don't know what's going to happen to my grandma or how I'm going to handle the ups and downs. But I need you with me. And when the time comes, you'll wonder things like ... should I ask this woman to marry me. And the answer is yes. Okay?"

When I don't answer, she shifts her body, sliding her leg over my lap to face me.

"You want to marry me?" I probably look as confused as I sound.

"Eventually." She leans forward, resting her forehead against mine. "Do you want to marry me ... eventually? A house with a big garage for cars that you'll work on. A room on the second floor with a balcony where I'll play my cello. And kids. We'll have two kids. Maybe three. And you'll teach them to play the kazoo."

I laugh and so does she. Everything inside still feels raw.

I don't know what to do with this new kind of vulnerability. So I lean into it. I trust her.

"I mean," she shrugs, brushing her nose against mine, "if I'm your whole world, it would be weird for you to marry someone else. Right?"

I frame her face and kiss her.

A wife?

House?

Kids?

And a kazoo?

"I would have thought you two would have gotten your fill after the concert," Juni says.

Zoya grins, sliding off my lap and rubbing her lips together.

"Ahh ... young love," Juni says, sitting in her mammoth chair. "I remember when I met Zach. We couldn't get enough of each other. Every touch and every look was foreplay. A slow dance to the closest place to rip off our clothes and go at it like rabbits."

"Grandma!" Zoya giggles, cheeks stained red.

"So how long are you staying, Flynn?"

I look at Zoya. She squeezes my hand.

"As long as Zoya will be here."

"So until I kick the bucket?"

Zoya stiffens.

"Well, if I find a good job, we might continue living here after you kick it."

"Flynn!" Zoya smacks a hand over her mouth, eyes wide, flitting between me and her grandma.

Juni throws her head back in a belly laugh. "I like this one, Zoya."

"Ya know," I say, "I'm kind of an expert at keeping people alive. I'm a professional muse."

"Stop." Zoya giggles.

Juni's eyebrows lift. "Tell me more."

"How do you feel about cats?" I ask.

"What kind of cat?"

I shrug. "Dunno until we check out the shelter. In my expert experience, you don't choose the cat; the cat chooses you."

Zoya twists her body, caressing one cheek before kissing the other. Her eyes sparkle when she looks at me and grins. "This is so big," she whispers.

The next morning, I sneak out of Zoya's room, as if her parents don't know I checked out of the hotel yesterday, and I'm sleeping in her bed until we find a place.

"You're a jogger too. Good to know," Bodhi says, catching me just as I open the front door. He's in shorts and tennis shoes too as he comes down the stairs. "We can chat," he says resting his hand on my shoulder for a second.

I don't know if I should trust his smile or not.

"This way." He nods to the right and starts jogging.

I follow him.

"I understand you don't want to live this lifestyle. And I respect that," he says. "I didn't want it either."

We veer to the right on a dirt trail that goes up into the hills.

"But then we got Zoya, and that girl has loved music her whole life. So I joined the family business to take this journey with my daughter. I don't know what will happen between the two of you, but we are team Zoya. If she wants to live in Minneapolis and ride around the city on a bike, we support that. If she wants to travel the world, playing sold-out concerts, we support that. If she wants to fall in love with you and have a family—"

"You support that," I say, not trying to interrupt him. But, dude, I get the point.

He chuckles, looking over at me. "Yes. The question is, do you?"

"Of—"

"And before you answer," he interrupts me. "Just know that it's okay if you have aspirations that don't align with Zoya's. Henna and I spent time apart because our needs and desires didn't align. Holding on because you're afraid of losing someone, isn't good. Giving up your dreams for someone else's, also isn't good. But I can promise you, Zoya needs music like she needs air."

We jog around another corner. It's a winding trail.

"Can I be honest with you?"

He laughs. "I expect nothing less."

"I have no idea what I'm doing."

"And?"

"Nope. No *and.*" I shake my head. "That's it."

Bodhi slows to a stop, a little out of breath as he steps to the side to stretch his quads and hamstrings.

I do the same. "Here's what I know," I say. "I know I love your daughter. I know there's nothing I wouldn't do for her or to protect her. Beyond that, I don't know what comes next. I'm terrified of fuck—" I clear my throat. "*Messing* up. What if something happens to Juni? What if Zoya does want to play music with her band again? Can I find a job? I don't know what she's told you about my past, but I don't have a clean record, so getting a job could be a challenge."

"We know about your past. Zoya doesn't keep secrets from us."

I stare at the ground, still not used to this level of vulnerability—of accountability.

"We can be on your side too. If you're willing to swallow your pride and allow us to help you. We can help you get a job, but you'll have to do it well to keep it. And as far as what to expect with Juni's health or Zoya's career decisions, none of that is certain. We're just taking it a day at a time."

I rest my hand on my hip and nod several times. "Okay."

"Okay?"

"Yeah," I say, looking him in the eye. "I can take it a day at a time too. And I'd appreciate you putting in a good word for me if I find a job I'm qualified for. That's basically a mechanic position. I'm out of the muse business."

Bodhi grins. "Fair enough." He nods toward the trail, and we keep jogging up it.

I've never spent time contemplating my life or my pride, probably because I've never had a reason to. Zoya's a pretty damn good reason to rethink literally everything in my life.

Chapter
THIRTY-SEVEN

June

"Has anyone seen my boyfriend?" I ask with a huge yawn while shuffling my bare feet along the limestone floor to the dining room table.

Mom and Grandma look up from their plates filled with fruit and some sort of vegetable hash.

"I heard your dad talking to him. I think they went for a jog," Mom says, smirking behind her coffee mug.

"What's that look for?" I ask, sitting in a chair, hugging one leg to my chest under my nightshirt.

"I love how a few days ago, we didn't dare mention Flynn's name, and now you're casually asking the whereabouts of your *boyfriend*."

I bite into my high protein bagel with blueberry cashew cream cheese. "He's so good at breaking my heart," I mumble before swallowing, "and putting it back together. How could he be anything but my boyfriend?"

"Well, I hope you're using condoms. When I went to Coachella the spring I met your dad, Juni sent so many condoms with me, and she texted *condoms!* So I'll mention it now, and text you later. CONDOMS!"

"I'm twenty-six. Almost twenty-seven. You were eighteen when you met Dad. I think I'm mature enough to handle birth control. But thanks."

"Yes, but sometimes you just need to bang one out," Grandma says. "And you don't want to mess with the logistics of birth control. You just can't wait for him to be inside of you. Grinding and groaning."

"Juni ..." Mom nearly snorts her coffee out her nose.

Grandma casually lifts a shoulder. "I heard you and Bodhi in the shower this morning. Don't act so innocent."

"Ew ... nope. Not doing this," I say, taking my bagel and a napkin to the bedroom as Mom and Grandma laugh.

While I'm finishing my breakfast on my balcony, the door behind me opens.

"Good morning, beautiful."

I wrinkle my nose when Flynn kisses my neck. "You're sweaty."

"Sorry," he says, leaning forward to take a bite of my bagel. "Your dad likes running hills."

"How was jogging with my dad?" I turn my chair to face him. "What did you talk about?"

He leans his hip against the railing, wiping his sweaty face with his shirt. "What I discuss with your dad is confidential." He drops his shirt and smirks.

I shrug. "That's fine."

He lifts an eyebrow. "It is?"

I lick my fingers before hugging my knees to my chest.

"Yes. My dad loves me, and if he loves you too, that's pretty much all I could ever ask for."

"Well"—Flynn chuckles—"he didn't declare his love to me yet."

I twist my lips. "But you're working on it. Right?"

He kneels in front of me, pulling my legs away from my chest.

"I said you're sweaty."

He shrugs off his shirt.

"Stop ..." I giggle.

Flynn takes my hands and presses them to his cheeks, and I instinctively brush my thumb over his lip where he brushes mine.

"Your dad is concerned that I might have dreams that don't align with yours."

My smile fades.

Leaning in, his lips stop short of touching mine. "I didn't tell him I only dream of you," he whispers.

His words resurrect my grin. "Let's go dirty up my sheets," I say before biting his lower lip.

He grins, pulling away. "They're already dirty, but yes, I'll let you lick my naked, sweaty body in a minute."

I roll my eyes.

"I need to go back to Minneapolis next week, just for a few days. Monroe is getting married. It's just a small ceremony in a park, but I'm the best man. And I need to get the rest of my belongings from the Rawlings' house. And I want to say goodbye to my old boss."

I nod slowly. "You have some loose ends to tie up."

"Yeah."

"Is that it?" I rub my lips together.

"Uh, yep. Pretty much."

"Okay," I say, squeezing past him to stand and head back into the bedroom.

"Where you going?" he asks.

"I'm going to swim laps."

"Thought we were getting back in bed."

"I changed my mind." I grab my swimsuit from the closet.

Flynn stands in the doorway. "What am I missing?"

"Nothing," I brush past him toward the bathroom.

He grabs my wrist to stop me. "No. We're not doing this. At least not now. Not until I get better at it."

I give him a dead stare. "Better at what?"

"Games. I used to watch Monroe and Naomi play these ..." He bobs his head as though he's searching for the right words. "Head games. She'd get upset with him and act like you're acting."

"How am I acting?"

"Cold. Like you're waiting for me to figure out what I did wrong. This is new to me. So I'm going to lose every time because I don't know the game or the rules. Do I stink? Is it about Minneapolis? You think your grandma will take a turn for the worse while I'm gone?"

I close my eyes on a long sigh. "Don't you get a plus-one?"

"Huh?"

Oh, Flynn ...

"You're right. No games. I want you to ask me to attend Monroe's wedding with you. Can you do that?"

Flynn's lips twitch before slowly curling into a huge grin. "You want to be my wedding date?"

"No." I fight to keep a straight face. "I want to be your world."

He grabs my face. "Zoya June Juju Malone, will you be my wedding date?"

"I'll think about it."

"Dear god, what have I gotten myself into?"

Before I can answer, he kisses me, backing me into the bathroom and kicking the door shut behind us.

"I hate it," Flynn says, staring out the window of Grandma Juni's private jet on our way to Minneapolis.

Grandma convinced us (him) to take the jet since we have so much to bring back from there.

"I know you do," I say, sitting opposite him and keeping my gaze on the pages of my novel.

"The reason I hate it," he continues.

I bite back my grin.

"Is because I like it. And I don't want to like it. This lifestyle is a drug."

"Mm-hmm," I hum, trying to acknowledge his concerns without feeding his flames. It's a thin line.

"I bet your parents found it pretty funny that I asked about their flight when we had dinner with them. Of course, they had a good flight. Who doesn't have a good flight when you have your own jet?"

I look at my watch. "You have a minute left," I say.

Flynn has a lurking grin when I look at him. We agreed he could have five minutes a day to complain about wealth disparity. That's it. No more. End of conversation.

"Are there snacks?" he asks with maximum grumpiness.

I nod.

"I bet they're free, huh?"

My head bobs. "Depends on your definition of free. But for all intents and purposes, yes, they're free. So if you're hungry, I'll get you a snack." I nod to the bag on the table across from us. "But there's chicken and fries in that bag."

His right eyebrow lifts. "Don't play with me. Are you serious?"

I can't help but chuckle. "Yes. I'm serious. How did you not smell them before now?"

He unbuckles and snatches the bag, poking his face in it when he sits back down. "I love you so much."

I return my attention to my book. "I know you do. And your time is up. So eat. Smile. Watch your YouTube videos. Tell me I'm pretty. Whatever."

Like flipping a switch, Flynn's grin reaches his ears just as he pops a fry into his mouth. "You're fucking gorgeous."

I tell myself his change of mood has nothing to do with his time expiring, and everything to do with me, but it's the chicken and fries. As he indulges, I set my book on the table and fold my hands in my lap, staring out the widow as we ride the sea of clouds.

"I'm scared," I say.

"Scared?"

I nod.

"Of what?"

"Everything." I flit my gaze to him for a second.

He slows his chewing, tension building in his brow.

"Scared to dream. Scared not to. Scared of death. Scared of life." I lean my head back and sigh. "I'm deliriously happy, but utterly lost."

Flynn wipes his fingers across his lips as he swallows.

"My grandma's going to be okay," I say with as much conviction as possible. "And when she is, I want to find a place on the map that feels like our own. Some place like Magnolia Springs, Alabama, or Harpers Ferry, West Virginia. A little one-bedroom apartment. Maybe a tiny house. You'll get a job at family-owned garage where they have a hound dog that hangs out by the door. His name will be Dewey or Ruckus."

Flynn grins, eyes alight with as much hope as I'm feeling.

"I'll work at a yarn store and take up knitting. We'll have the weekends to make pancakes with syrup and local berries that we pick in the wild. Of course, we'll have a convertible like Rupert's Chevelle. And you'll drive us along windy roads with my hair tangled in the wind, sun on our faces. And we'll—I don't know. Just find ourselves. Fall deeper in love."

His eyes remain captivated as he hums.

"What do you think?" I ask.

His smile fades a bit. "I think it's missing something."

"A cat?"

Flynn shakes his head. "A stage. A beautiful dress. A cello from Italy. And an auditorium of adoring fans." He sets the bag aside and leans forward, reaching for my hand. "Me in the front row. Sitting between your parents, of course."

I lace my fingers with his. "Lise will live with us. I'll even put on a dress. But my adoring audience will be you, you, and you."

"Lise?"

I nod. "Lise Cristiani, my cello. Lise was the first female concert cellist. A Parisian virtuoso."

He sits back. "You should be touring with your band. It's your passion."

"I'm pretty sure you've been the recipient of my passion most recently." I smirk. "Flynn, I don't want everything all at once. I just want you."

"Well"—he focuses on his bag, pulling out a chicken strip—"I think I'm available. Can I get back to you?" He holds out the chicken strip.

I shake my head.

"Take it. It's all I have to offer."

"Stop it." I giggle. "You had your five minutes of playing your violin."

"It's a kazoo."

I take the chicken and toss it over my shoulder.

His jaw drops, then he grabs his phone, thumbs tapping the screen.

"What are you doing?" I reach for his phone, but he pulls away. So I dive across the table and onto his lap, stealing his phone while straddling his legs.

He has a long list of grievances in his Notes app.

Wastes food

My gaze shifts to him, and he shrugs. "When I get five minutes again tomorrow, I don't want to forget anything." He can't even say the words without grinning.

"Ridiculous." I set his phone aside and grab his face. "I'm the sole heiress to the Juniper Carlisle and Zachary Phillips fortune. So you'd better get extra storage on your Notes app."

"And you're going to give it all away," he says, tipping his chin up.

We have a stare-off.

I loosen my grip while brushing my lips over his. "Yeah," I whisper. "I probably will."

Life is nuanced. Not all secrets are lies. Good people do bad things.

On our first date, had Flynn told me about his time in prison, it would have been our last date.

Honesty requires vulnerability.

Vulnerability needs trust.

And love ...

Well, it's all about timing.

Epilogue

Flynn

Two years later ...

RUPERT WAS RIGHT. Rich people have very few true friends.

Juniper Carlisle is being laid to rest next to her beloved husband Zachary. It's the first funeral I've attended. Like with everything else, I don't know what I'm supposed to do as Henna and Zoya cling to each other.

A warm breeze.

Sun peeking through the canopy of trees.

The tent filled with Juni's small circle.

I tune out her pastor's final words while standing behind Zoya's chair. Maybe a life without love is better. It's like she and Henna are dying too. And there's nothing I can do.

After five months of therapy and Zoya playing concerts, Juni went into remission, so we moved. But nothing lasts forever. We returned to L.A. two months ago when Juni's cancer returned, having spread to her brain. Juni refused more treatment.

Henna and Zoya couldn't sway her. Not with begging. Not with the promise of playing concerts again.

I miss our little rental house in Petoskey, Michigan. My job at the auto repair shop (minus the hound dog). And our simple life.

But my virtuoso girlfriend has been unsettled over the past six months. Jumping from job to job, yet claiming she *loved* each one. But I've seen the look in her eyes when she truly loves something, and working at a pet store isn't that kind of love. Zoya needs music.

Bodhi rests his hand on my shoulder when the pastor finishes speaking. "Let's give them a few minutes."

Henna and Zoya kneel next to the casket as everyone else exits the tent. I look at him and his eyes are red. It's the first time I've seen him cry.

"Yeah," I murmur with a nod.

As he turns, Bodhi leans down, resting one hand on Henna's back and one on Zoya's. He says something to them, but I can't hear it. So I continue out the tent. My gaze snags on two familiar faces.

"What are you doing here?" I ask, knowing it's a stupid question the second it leaves my mouth.

Rupert and Callie walk toward me, stepping past another headstone.

"We thought maybe you saw us at the funeral," Rupert says, holding out his hand.

When I take it, he pulls me in for a hug.

"I might have looked at you, but I'm not seeing straight today," I say as he releases me.

"That's understandable," Callie says, hugging me. "Sorry for your loss."

"Thanks." I step back, sliding my hands into my suit pockets, the same suit they bought me. "It's really kind of you to travel all this way."

"Well," Rupert says. "We couldn't talk you and Zoya into coming back to Minneapolis to visit us, so this felt like a good reason to visit. Although Michigan is closer."

I frown. "Yeah. I don't think we're going anywhere anytime soon. She's restless. I think she needs to play again. I think the world deserves her music."

"Well, I'm sure this is a big change in her family's life. Give it time," Callie says, tucking her hair behind her ear. "Let her decide when she's ready."

"Yeah. You're probably right." I reach into my pocket. "Also, a couple weeks ago, Juni gave me this ring and told me to give it to Zoya when the time comes." I hold up the ring with the big yellow stone. "We got interrupted before I could clarify the actual time. But I wonder if today is the day. If she wanted her to have it before she died, I assume she would have given it to her herself. Right?"

Callie's lips part, eyes wide. But Rupert shakes his head, pinching the bridge of his nose.

"What?" I ask.

"Put the ring back in your pocket," Rupert says.

I slip it back into my pocket. "I should wait?"

"Are you going to marry her?" Rupert glances over my shoulder, and I follow his gaze to Zoya and Henna by Juni's casket.

"I hope so," I say.

"I think you should. And when you propose, give her that ring," he says.

Callie bites her lips together.

You'll know when the time is right. When you're ready. That's what Juni said. I'm an idiot.

"It's not a diamond ring, so I didn't think—"

"Flynn, I can assure you that's a diamond. A canary diamond. I'd say a good eight to ten carats. And worth a lot of money. But more than that, it's sentimental, so don't lose it," Callie says.

"I'm an idiot."

Callie says *no* as Rupert says *yes*. Then she elbows him.

"I'd hold off," Callie suggests. "I don't think proposing while she's grieving is the best time."

I nod. "Right. Of course."

"We miss you," she says. "And we'll be in L.A. for a week or two. We're going to head north and check out a few wineries. We'd love to take you to dinner. And if Zoya's feeling up to it, we'd love her to come too. But if she needs time, I understand."

"Thanks. Uh ..." Again, I glance back at her. Juni wants me to propose. And I was going to casually hand her the ring. "I'll check with her." Just as I say those words, she stands, pulling a white rose from the arrangement on the casket.

Then she looks around and spies us. Her smile is sad. But she gives it her best effort while making her way to us.

"Sweetheart, I'm so very sorry for your loss," Callie says, hugging Zoya.

They hug for what feelings like an eternity, drawing a few tears from Callie.

"Thank you so much for coming," Zoya says, releasing Callie to hug Rupert.

"Of course," Rupert says.

The ring feels like a hundred-pound weight in my pocket as I hold my hand over it.

"I told Flynn we'll be here for a while. If there's anything we can do, please let us know." Callie squeezes my arm.

"Thank you." Zoya hands me a few unused tissues, and I slide them into my pocket for her as she puts her arm around my waist and holds the white rose to her chest.

Before we can say more, a couple I've never met pulls Zoya's attention away, giving their condolences.

"We'll check in with you later," Rupert murmurs.

I give him a nod. "Thank you."

Zoya, having well-practiced manners, introduces me to everyone who approaches her. Then we join Henna and Bodhi by the casket after most everyone else has left the cemetery. Two guys with the funeral home maneuver a lever and straps to lower the casket into the vault.

Henna sobs, falling into Bodhi's arms.

I stand behind Zoya, holding her tightly.

She sniffles. "I need a new tissue."

"Oh, here," I say, digging the tissues out of my pocket. *Shit!*

The ring comes out with them, and it falls to the ground.

"What's ..." She bends down at the same time I do.

I grab it and make a fist.

"Is that ..." her brow tightens.

Only this level of fuckery would happen to me. *Yes, it's Juni's ring. No, I didn't steal it. Just focus on the casket.* But I don't say any of that. Instead, I avert my gaze as if a bird has caught my attention.

"Flynn." Zoya peels open my hand.

Now she's drawn the attention of her parents.

"We'll talk about it later," I mumble, closing my hand again and sliding the ring into my pocket.

Henna wipes her tears, and Bodhi squints. Did they see it?

"Why do you have my grandma's ring?" Zoya asks.

I feel a sliver of redemption after Rupert and Callie made me feel stupid. Clearly, Zoya doesn't know why I have it. So it's not obvious to everyone. But now I wish it were because it looks like I stole it. But I'm not proposing over her grandmother's grave. That's not the story I want her sharing.

"I'll meet you at the car," I say before turning and heading down the hill.

"Don't walk away. Why do you have her ring?"

I stop and drop my head. "Dammit," I whisper.

"Sweetheart," Henna says. "Juni gave it to him."

I open my eyes. Juni told Henna?

"Why did she—" Zoya's realization happens in real time.

"Are you proposing?" Zoya asks. "Look at me." She sounds a little angry.

I rub my hands over my face before dropping them to my sides and I turn. Shoulders slumped on a long sigh.

"We've been together for two years, and you chose today to do this?" She wipes her nose.

Henna and Bodhi are no help. They don't look mad, but they're not exactly jumping in to help me anymore.

I slowly walk back up the hill. "First. I'm sorry. *So* sorry. You're grieving, and I'm a distraction." My gaze points to Henna. I feel like I owe her the biggest apology.

Sorry for messing up the burial.

Sorry for getting your daughter worked up.

Sorry for being an idiot.

"Yes, Juni gave me her ring to give you. I just, uh ..." I

scratch my jaw. "I was a little confused. I didn't know diamonds came in yellow. And well, I thought when she asked me to give it to you, when the time was right, I thought she just wanted you to have it. After she died. Like ..." I feel my face cringing. "Like I was supposed to just give it to you. To have. Not like give it to you for, uh ..."

Henna cups a hand over her mouth, tears still shining in her red eyes. But she snorts. Bodhi rests his hand on his hip and bows his head. I feel every ounce of his disappointment or secondhand embarrassment.

Zoya blinks. Nothing but an unreadable expression.

"So I stuck it in my pocket, thinking it might make you feel better, like having a piece of her with you after the funeral. Then I showed it to Rupert and Callie, and ..." I shrug, leaving my shoulders at my ears a little longer than necessary.

"So ... you're not proposing?" Zoya asks, blotting her eyes.

I look at her parents.

Nothing.

Not the hint of a nod or headshake.

They shift their gazes to Zoya.

"Not really," I say cautiously.

She turns back toward the grave. Henna does too. But Bodhi gives me a little headshake. What does that mean? Where was that when I needed guidance a few seconds ago. What does that mean?

Don't propose now?

Ever?

Don't worry about her reaction?

Don't take another step up the hill?

I wait.

After a few more minutes, Zoya and her parents walk toward me.

"Just give me the ring before you lose it," she grumbles holding out her hand.

"Give it to you? Propose?"

"Zoya, let's go home," Henna says.

Zoya snaps her fingers twice and holds out her flat hand. When I don't move, she brushes past me toward the car. Henna follows her, reaching for her arm, but Zoya pulls away.

I look at Bodhi.

"Just go big," he says loosening his black tie.

Big ...

"Really, Juju?" I call, heading down the hill.

She and Henna turn, just as they reach the black SUV.

"At a cemetery? *This* is where you want me to propose?" I hold out my arms and turn in a slow circle. "I'm not as smart as you, but I suppose there's something symbolic about it. The end of an era. The beginning of a new one?"

Henna steps away from the vehicle, as if she and Bodhi can fade into the distance, like hiding behind a curtain while their daughter takes center stage.

"I would have married you the day we met. That's exactly how long it took for me to know that I would never look at another woman the way I looked at you—the way you looked at me."

She looks away for a beat, wiping her tears.

"Love at first sight." I laugh. "That's bullshit, right?" I step closer, until there are maybe ten left to take. "Yet here we are two years later, and there isn't a day that passes where I don't replay that moment in the gallery. You looked at me, and I looked away. Then I looked at you, and you looked away. But when our gazes locked, you stripped me down in a single breath. Looking at you felt like really seeing myself for the first time. Feeling my heart beat for the first time. That moment was *so big*."

She laughs, but it comes out as a sob.

I pull the ring from my pocket. "So yeah, you can have your grandma's ring. And it doesn't have to mean anything." I walk the last ten steps between us and take her hand, sliding the ring onto her finger. "But I hope it can mean everything."

She stares at the ring, tears spilling down her face. Then she sniffles. "Ask me," she whispers.

"Will you—"

"Yes." She throws her arms around my neck, lips pressed to mine.

This will forever be so *big*.

Acknowledgments

Thank you to my readers for continuing on this journey in The Chain of Lakes Series. It's such an honor to write for you.

A big thank you to the usual suspects: Jenn, Sarah, Monique, Leslie, Georgana, Anna, Boja, my team at Valentine PR, and every influencer who shared in this release.

Last, but never least, thank you to my family for giving me inspiration to keep writing love stories.

Also By
JEWEL E. ANN

<u>Standalone Novels</u>

Idle Bloom

Undeniably You

Naked Love

Only Trick

Perfectly Adequate

Look The Part

When Life Happened

A Place Without You

Jersey Six

Scarlet Stone

Not What I Expected

For Lucy

What Lovers Do

Before Us

If This Is Love

Right Guy, Wrong Word

I Thought of You

The Chain of Lakes Series

The Homemaker

The Muse

Sunday Morning Series

Sunday Morning

The Apple Tree

A Good Book

Wildfire Series

From Air

From Nowhere

The Fisherman Series

The Naked Fisherman

The Lost Fisherman

Jack & Jill Series

End of Day

Middle of Knight

Dawn of Forever

One (*standalone*)

Out of Love (*standalone*)

Because of Her (*standalone*)

Holding You Series

Holding You

Releasing Me

About The AUTHOR

Jewel E. Ann is a *Wall Street Journal* and *USA Today* bestselling author. She's written over thirty novels, including LOOK THE PART, a contemporary romance, the JACK & JILL TRILOGY, a romantic suspense series; and BEFORE US, an emotional women's fiction story. With 10 years of flossing lectures under her belt, she took early retirement from her dental hygiene career to write mind-bending love stories. She's living her best life in Iowa with her husband, three boys, and a Goldendoodle.

Receive special offers and stay informed of new releases, sales, and exclusive stories:

www.jeweleann.com